PEARL OF CHINA

Red Azalea
Katherine
Becoming Madame Mao
Wild Ginger
Empress Orchid
The Last Empress

PEARL OF CHINA

ANCHEE MIN

BLOOMSBURY
LONDON · BERLIN · NEW YORK

First published in Great Britain 2010

Copyright © 2010 by Anchee Min

The moral right of the author has been asserted

Bloomsbury Publishing, London, Berlin and New York

36 Soho Square, London W1D 3QY

A CIP catalogue record for this book is available from the British Library

ISBN 978 1 4088 0182 6
10 9 8 7 6 5 4 3 2 1

Typeset by Hewer Text UK Ltd, Edinburgh

Printed in Great Britain by Clays Ltd, St Ives plc

Mixed Sources
Product group from well-managed
forests and other controlled sources
www.fsc.org Cert no. SGS-COC-2061
© 1996 Forest Stewardship Council
FSC

www.bloomsbury.com/ancheemin

For Pearl S. Buck

I belong to China for I have lived there from childhood to adulthood
...Happy for me that for instead of the narrow and conventional life of
the white man in Asia, I lived with the Chinese people and spoke their
tongue before I spoke my own, and their children were my first friends.

Pearl S. Buck
My Several Worlds

Behind the calm steadfast eyes of a Chinese woman, I feel a powerful
warmth. We might have been friends, she and I, unless she had decided
first that I was her enemy. She would have decided, not I. I was never
deceived by Chinese women, not even by the flower-like lovely girls.
They are the strongest women in the world. Seeming always to yield,
they never yield. Their men are weak beside them. Whence comes this
female strength? It is the strength that centuries have given them, the
strength of the unwanted.

Pearl S. Buck
Letter from Peking

Part One

CHAPTER 1

Before I was Willow, I was Weed. My grandmother, NaiNai, insisted that naming me Weed was better. She believed that the gods would have a hard time making my life go lower if I was already at the bottom. Papa disagreed. "Men want to marry flowers, not weeds." They argued and finally settled for Willow, which was considered "gentle enough to weep and tough enough to be made into farming tools." I always wondered what my mother would have thought if she had lived.

Papa lied to me about my mother's death. Both he and NaiNai told me that Mother died giving birth. But I had already learned otherwise from neighbors' gossip. Papa had "rented" his wife to the town's "Bare-sticks" in order to pay off his debts. One of the bachelors got Mother pregnant. I was four years old when it happened. To rid her of the "bastard seed," Papa bought magic root powder from an herbalist. Papa mixed the powder with tea and Mother drank it. Mother died along with the seed. It broke Papa's heart, because he had intended to kill the fetus, not his wife. He had no money to buy another wife. Papa was angry at the herbalist, but there was nothing he could do—he had been warned about the poison.

NaiNai feared that she would be punished by the gods for Mother's death. She believed that in her next life she would be a diseased bird and her son a limbless dog. NaiNai burned incense and begged the gods to reduce her sentence. When she ran out of money for incense, she stole. She took me to markets, temples, and graveyards. We would not act until

3

darkness fell. NaiNai moved like an animal on all fours. She was in and out of bamboo groves and brick hallways, behind the hills and around ponds. Under the bright moonlight, NaiNai's long neck stretched. Her head seemed to become smaller. Her cheekbones sharpened. Her slanting eyes glowed as she scanned the temples. NaiNai appeared, disappeared, and reappeared like a ghost. But one night she stopped. In fact, she collapsed. I was aware that she had been ill. Tufts of hair had been falling from her head. There was a rotten smell to her breath. "Go and look for your father," she ordered. "Tell him that my end is near."

Papa was a handsome man in his thirties. He had what a fortune-teller would describe as "the look of an ancient king" or "the matching energy of sky and earth," meaning he had a square forehead and a broad chin. He had a pair of sheep eyes, a garlic-shaped nose that sat on his face like a gentle hill, and a mouth that was always ready to smile. His hair was thick and silky black. Every morning, he combed and braided it with water to make his queue smooth and shining. He walked with his back straight and head up. Speaking Mandarin with an Imperial accent, Papa wore his voice like a costume. But when Papa lost his temper, his voice would slip. People were shocked when Mr. Yee suddenly took up a strange voice. Ignoring NaiNai's opinion that his ambitions would never be realized, Papa dreamed that one day he would work for the governor as an adviser. Papa attended teahouses where he showed off his talent in classic Chinese poems and verse. "I must keep my mind sharp and literary skills tuned," he often said to me. One would never guess from the way he presented himself that Papa was a seasonal coolie.

We lived in Chin-kiang, a small town far away from the capital, Peking, on the south side of the Yangtze River in Jiangsu province. Originally, our family was from Anhui province, a harsh region where survival depended on an endless round of crushing physical labor. For generations my family worked the region's thin and unfertile soil and struggled with famine, flood, locusts, bandits, and debt seekers. NaiNai bragged that it was she who brought "luck" to the Yee family.

4

She was purchased by my grandfather when he was forty years old. No one was allowed to mention that the purchase took place in a local sing-song house. When NaiNai was in her prime, she had a slender figure, a swanlike neck, and a pair of fox eyes with both ends tilted up. She painted her face every day and modeled her hairstyle after the Imperial empress. It was said that men's blood would boil when NaiNai smiled.

By the time the family crossed the Yangtze River and migrated to the south, NaiNai had given the Yee family three sons. Papa was the eldest and the only one sent to school. Grandfather expected a return from his investment. Papa was expected to become an accountant so that the family could fight the government's tax collectors. But things didn't turn out right—Grandfather lost his son to the education.

Papa believed that he was too good to work as a coolie. At sixteen, he developed the expensive habits and fantasies of the rich. He read books on China's political reform and chewed tea leaves to sweeten his peasant garlic breath. An ideal life, he told others, would be to "compose poems under blossoming plum trees," far away from the "greedy material world." Instead of returning home, Papa traveled the country, making his parents pay the bills. One day he received a message from his mother. The message informed him that his father and brothers were gravely ill and near death from an infectious disease that had swept through his hometown.

Papa rushed home, but the funeral was already over. Soon enough, his house was possessed by the debt seekers. NaiNai and Papa fell into poverty and became coolies. Although NaiNai vowed to regain their former prosperity, she was no longer healthy. By the time I was born, NaiNai suffered from an incurable intestinal disease.

Papa struggled to keep his "intellectual dignity." He continued to write poems. He even composed a piece titled "The Sweet Scent of Books" for my mother's funeral. Invoking a newfound spirituality, he insisted that his words would make better gifts than jewelry and diamonds to accompany his wife in her next life. Although Papa was no different from a beggar in terms of possessions, he made sure that he was lice-free. He kept his appearance by trimming his beard and never missed a chance to mention his "honorable past."

Papa's honorable past didn't mean anything to me. For the first years of my young life, food was the only thing on my mind. I would wake hungry every morning and go to sleep hungry every night. Sometimes the clawing in my stomach would keep me from sleeping. Having to constantly scavenge for scraps, I existed in a delirium. Unexpected luck or a good harvest might bring food for a while, but the hunger would always return.

By the time I was seven, in 1897, things had only gotten worse. Although NaiNai's health had continued to deteriorate, she was determined to do something to better our lot. Picking up her old profession, she began to receive men in the back of our bungalow. When I was given a fistful of roasted soybeans, I understood that it was time to disappear. I ran through the rice paddies and the cotton fields into the hills and hid in the bamboo groves. I cried because I couldn't bear the thought of losing NaiNai the same way I had lost Mother.

Around this time, Papa and I worked as seasonal farmhands. He planted rice, wheat, and cotton and carried manure. My job was to plant soybeans along the edges of the fields. Each day, Papa and I woke before dawn to go to work. As a child, I was paid less than an adult, but I was glad to be earning money. I had to compete with other children, especially boys. I always proved that I was faster than the boys when it came to planting soybeans. I used a chopstick to poke a hole and threw a soybean into each one. I kicked dirt into the hole and sealed it with my big toe.

The coolie market where we got our jobs closed after the planting season was over. Papa and I couldn't find any work. Papa spent his days walking the streets in search of a job. No one hired him, although he was received politely. I followed Papa throughout the town. When I found him wandering into the surrounding hills, I started doubting his seriousness about finding a job.

"What a glorious view!" Papa marveled as he beheld the countryside spreading below his feet. "Willow, come and admire the beauty of nature!"

I looked. The wide Yangtze flowed freely and leaped aside into small canals and streams that fed the southern land.

"Beyond the valleys are hidden old temples that have stood for hundreds of years." Papa's voice rose again. "We live in the best place under the sun!"

I shook my head and told him that the demon in my stomach had eaten away my good sense.

Papa shook his head. "What did I teach you?"

I rolled back my eyes and recited, "Virtue will sustain and prevail."

Virtue finally failed to sustain Papa. The demons in his stomach took over—he was caught stealing. Neighbors no longer wanted to be associated with him. The pity was that Papa never actually succeeded as a thief. He was too clumsy. More than once I witnessed him being beaten by the folks he stole from. He was thrown into the open sewage. He told his friends that he had "tripped over a tree stump." Laughing, they asked him, "Was it the same stump you tripped over the last time?" One day Papa came home holding his arm, which had been knocked out of its socket. "I deserved it," he said, cursing himself. "I shouldn't have stolen from an infant's mouth."

By the time I was eight years old I was already a seasoned thief. I began by stealing incense for NaiNai. Although Papa criticized me, he knew that the family would starve if I stopped. Papa would sell the goods I stole.

I snatched small items at first, such as vegetables, fruit, birds, and puppies. Then I went for farming tools. After selling what I stole, Papa would rush to a local bar for rice wine. He took his sips slowly, closing his eyes as if concentrating on the taste. When his cheeks began to redden, he would recite his favorite poem. Although his friends had long since left him, he imagined his audience.

The Grand Yangtze River runs toward the ocean,
Never to return, so went the dynasty's glorious days.
When would the time come again for heroes?
Though music continues playing, swiftly and triumphantly,
Reform miscarried, reformers beheaded,
Foreign troops plagued the country
His Majesty locked in the island of Yintai.
Where have been the gods' responses?
Weep the learned man,
Brokenhearted and in despair . . .

One day a man clapped. He was sitting in a corner. He stood up to congratulate Papa. He was tall, a giant in the eyes of the Chinese. He was the brown-haired and blue-eyed foreigner, an American missionary. He was by himself with a thick book and a cup of tea in front of him. He smiled at Papa and praised him for his fine poem.

Absalom Sydenstricker was his name. The locals called him the "plow-nosed and demon-eyed crazy foreigner." He had been a fixture in town for as long as I could remember. Not only was he ceiling tall, he also had hair growing on his forearms and the backs of his hands like weeds. All year long Absalom wore a gray Chinese gown. A queue went down his back, which everyone knew was fake. His costume made him look ridiculous, but he didn't seem to care. Absalom spent his time chasing people on the street. He tried to stop them and talk to them. He wanted to make us believe in his God. As children, we were taught to avoid him. We were not allowed to say things that would hurt his feelings, such as "Go away."

Papa was familiar with Absalom Sydenstricker since he, too, spent time wandering the streets. Papa concluded that Absalom was laying up credit for himself so that his God would offer him a ticket to heaven when he died.

"Or else why leave his own home to wander among strangers?" Papa questioned.

Papa suspected that Absalom was a criminal in his own land. Out of curiosity that day, Papa listened to what the foreigner had to say. Afterward, he invited Absalom home for "further discussion."

Thrilled, Absalom came. He didn't mind our dirty hut. He sat down and opened his book. "Would you like a story from the Bible?" he offered.

Papa was not interested in stories. He wanted to know what kind of god Jesus was. "Based on the way he was tortured, stabbed to death, nailed and tied to posts, he must be a royal criminal. In China such elaborate public torture would be given only to criminals of high status, like the former Imperial prime minister Su Shun."

Excitement filled Absalom's voice. He began to explain. But his Chinese was difficult to understand.

Papa lost his patience. When Absalom paused, Papa interrupted. "How can Jesus protect others when he couldn't even protect himself?"

Absalom waved his hands, pointed his fingers up and down, and then read from the Bible.

Papa decided that it was time to help the foreigner. "Chinese gods make better sense," he said. "They are more worshipper-friendly . . ."

"No, no, no." Absalom shook his head like a merchant's drummer. "You are not understanding me . . ."

"Listen, foreigner, my suggestions might help you. Put clothes on Jesus and give him a weapon. Look at our god of war, Guan-gong. He wears a general's robe made of heavy metal, and he carries a powerful sword."

"You are a clever man," Absalom told Papa, "but your biggest mistake is that you are knowledgeable of all gods but the true God."

I observed that Absalom's face was a big opium bed with a high nose sitting like a table in the middle. His eyebrows were two bird's nests and under them were clear blue eyes. After his talk with Papa he went back into the streets. I followed him.

"God is your best fortune!" Absalom sang to the people who paused in front of him. No one paid attention. People tied their shoelaces, wiped snot off their children's faces, and moved on. Absalom stuck his long arms out like two brooms in the air. When he saw Papa again, he smiled. Papa smiled back. It took Papa quite a while to figure out what Absalom was trying to say.

"We have shed blood unlawfully," Absalom said, waving the Bible in Papa's face. "It may be innocently, but the stain remains upon us. Mankind can only remove it by prayers and good deeds."

I discovered where Absalom lived. His house was a bungalow located in the lower part of town. His neighbors were coolies and peasants. I wondered what had made Absalom choose the place. Although Chin-kiang was the smallest town in Jiangsu province, it had been an important port since ancient times. From the water's edge, stone-paved streets led to shops and then the center of the town, where the British Embassy was located. The embassy occupied the highest point, with a broad view of the Yangtze River.

Although he was not the first American missionary to come to China, Absalom claimed he was the first to arrive in Chin-kiang during the late nineteenth century. According to old folks, soon after Absalom arrived, he purchased a piece of land behind the graveyard, where he built a church. His intention was to avoid "disturbing the living," but to the Chinese, disturbing the dead was the worst crime one could commit. The church's tall shadow stretched out over the graveyard. The locals protested. Absalom had to abandon the church. He moved down the hill and rented a shop as his new church. It was a room with a low ceiling, crooked beams, falling studs, and broken windows.

Most of the people thought Absalom a harmless fool. Children loved to follow him around. His feet were the main attraction, because they were huge. When Absalom asked the local shoemaker for a pair of Chinese shoes, it became news. People visited the shop just to see how much material it would take and if the shoemaker would double the charge.

When asked his reason for coming to China, Absalom replied that he was here to save our souls.

People laughed. "What is a soul?"

Absalom let us know that the world was coming to an end, and that we would all die if we failed to follow God.

"What evidence do you have?" Papa asked.

"That is what the Bible is for." Absalom winked an eye and smiled. "The Lord explains the one and only truth."

Papa said that he was rather disappointed by Absalom's description of the Western hell. Chinese hell was much more terrifying. Papa loved to challenge Absalom in teahouses and bars. He reveled in the gathering crowd and his growing popularity. Behind Absalom's back, Papa admitted that he followed Absalom around for the food, especially the cookies baked by Absalom's wife, Carie.

Compared to NaiNai, Carie was a big woman. She had light brown eyes and a wrinkled, soft, white round face. She wore a funny-shaped hat, which she called a "bonnet." Stuffed inside this hat was her brown curly hair. Carie wore the same dark dress all year long. It was the color of seaweed. Her skirt was so long that it swept the ground.

Carie had been warning her husband about Papa. She didn't trust Papa. But Absalom continued to treat Papa like a good friend, although Papa refused to attend his Sunday church on a regular basis.

Like a true artist, Papa fooled Absalom by pretending that he was interested. He was giving me an opportunity to steal. The day after I took the church's doormat, I heard Carie cry, "There is no need for housekeeping because everything is gone!"

CHAPTER 2

When Absalom held up his Bible-story drawings, I asked about the beard-men who had golden rings on their heads. "Why are they walking in the desert with sheets draped around them?"

Absalom didn't know that I only asked questions to distract him, so I could carry on with my stealing.

It was hard for Absalom to concentrate. He was interrupted by people's cries. "When can we have food, Master Absalom? Would you ask God to bring food for us now?"

As Absalom went on with his speech, children pulled his arms and pushed him around. "Who is Virgin? Who is Mary?"

"Who is Madonna?" I asked loudly, attaching myself to Absalom like a leech. My hands were inside his pockets.

By the time Absalom blessed me with a "Jesus loves you," I had his wallet.

Slipping the wallet into my pocket, I hurried down a side street and made my way out of town. I sensed that I was being followed and cut a jagged path. Still I felt the pair of blue eyes at my back. They belonged to a cream-skinned white girl wearing a black knitted cap. She was a little younger than me. She always sat in the corner of the church room with a black leather-bound book in her hands. Her eyes seemed to say, "I saw you."

By now I knew who she was. She was the daughter of Absalom and Carie. Her family servant had called her Pearl. She spoke to the servant in the Chin-kiang dialect. Her mother and father never seemed to need her. She was always by herself and was always reading.

To get rid of her, I ran as fast as I could toward the hills. I passed the wheat and cotton fields. After a couple of miles, I stopped. I looked around and was glad that she was no longer in sight. I took a deep breath and sat down. I was excited about my harvest.

As I began to open the wallet, I heard a noise.

Someone was approaching.

I froze and held my breath.

Slowly, I turned my head.

Behind me, in the bushes, was that pair of blue eyes.

"You stole my father's wallet!" Pearl yelled.

"No, I didn't." I imagined the food the money in the wallet could buy.

"Yes, you did."

"Prove it!"

"It's in your pocket." She put down her book and tried to reach into my pocket.

I knocked her aside with an elbow.

She fell.

I held tight to the wallet.

She rose. Anger made her pink lips quiver.

We stood face-to-face. I could see sweat beaded on her forehead. Her skin was white, as if bleached. Her nose had a pointed tip. Like her father's fake queue, her black knitted cap hid her blonde curly hair. She wore a Chinese tunic embroidered with indigo flowers.

"Last chance to give the wallet, or you'll get hurt," she threatened.

I worked up a mouthful of saliva and spit.

While her hands went up to protect her face, I ran.

She followed me through the fields and up and down a hill. By the time she caught me, I had already hidden the wallet. I raised both of my arms and said, "Come and search me."

She came and didn't find the wallet.

I smiled.

She gasped, taking off her knitted cap. Golden curls fell across her face.

From then on she followed me everywhere. I was unable to steal. I spent day and night thinking about how to get rid of her. I learned that she had one living sibling, a younger sister, Grace. The Chinese servant who took care of the girls, Wang Ah-ma, had been with the family for a long time.

"Pearl and Grace want so much to look like the Chinese girls," Wang Ah-ma chatted to her knitting friends. They sat outside the house under the sun. Wang Ah-ma was making new caps for Pearl and Grace. The caps would cover their blonde hair so that they could look like Chinese girls. Wang Ah-ma said that she had to knit fast because the girls were wearing the old ones out. "Poor Pearl, every day she begs me to find a way to help her grow black hair."

The women laughed. "What did you tell her?"

"I told her to eat black sesame seeds, and she went crazy eating them. Her mother thought that she was eating ants."

Before the spring planting season, farmers came to town to purchase their supplies for the year. While men bought manure and had tools fixed and sharpened, women inspected the livestock. Going in and out of food stalls and supply shops, I hunted for stealing opportunities. It had been weeks since I'd had a full meal.

Papa had pawned nearly every piece of furniture we owned. The table and benches and my own bed were all gone. I now slept on a straw mat on the packed-earth floor. Centipedes crawled over my face in the middle of the night. NaiNai suffered from an infection that wouldn't heal. She could barely move from the one bed we still owned. Papa spent more time with Absalom, trying to get hired.

"Absalom needs my help," Papa said every day. "Absalom doesn't know how to tell stories. He puts people to sleep. I ought to be the one to tell his Bible stories. I could turn Absalom's business around."

But Absalom was only interested in saving Papa's soul.

One night I heard Papa whisper to NaiNai, "The dowry would be handsome." It took me a while to figure out what he meant. One of his friends had made an offer to purchase me as his concubine.

"You are not selling Willow!" NaiNai hammered her chest with her fist. "She is just a child."

"It takes money to make money," Papa argued. "Besides, you need to buy medicine. The doctor said that you are getting worse . . ."

"As long as I am breathing, don't even think about it!" NaiNai broke down.

What if NaiNai died? I became scared. For the first time I looked forward to Sunday, when I could attend the church, where Absalom would talk about heaven and Carie would serve meals. Papa and NaiNai wanted to join me, but they were embarrassed to show their despair in front of foreigners.

Absalom's church was a room with benches. The walls were mud-colored. Absalom said that his God was a humble god, one who cared more about his followers than about the appearance of his temple. Absalom said that he was in the middle of raising funds to build a proper church.

I wanted to tell Absalom that people were not interested in his God or his church. Food was the reason we came. We waited for Absalom to finish preaching. We had to endure. I cried joyfully when it was time to clap our hands together and say "Ah-men."

After the meal we felt good. We sang songs to thank Absalom's God. Carie taught us Hymns and Oratorio. The first song Carie sang to us was called "Amazing Grace." Her big voice surprised everyone. It was deep like a Chinese gong. The room vibrated. The sound was like a spring waterfall pouring down from the mountains. Carie's soft round face melted into a sweet expression. She sent her notes up through the ceiling effortlessly.

I fell in love with "Amazing Grace." The song moved me in a strange way. I grew up with Chinese operas, but it was Carie's song that made me think of my own mother. Never before had I been able to imagine what my mother looked like. The song brought her to me, vivid and clear. Mother was as beautiful as a Chinese goddess. I could almost smell her fragrance. Her face was egg-shaped and her eyes gentle and bright. She was petite but had a full figure. "Come, my child," I could hear her say. "I have been longing to see you."

Tears filled my eyes. I noticed that I was not the only one who was falling in love with "Amazing Grace." NaiNai wanted me to learn the song so that I could sing it at her funeral.

Carie had a monstrous instrument she called a "piano." She often played it to accompany her singing. Her fingers danced over the keys as she sat on a stool with the bottom of her dress covering the ground. We spent many Sunday afternoons together. Word by word, Carie taught me "Amazing Grace." I went home and practiced in front of NaiNai and Papa.

> *Amazing Grace,*
> *How sweet the sound,*
> *That saved a wretch like me.*

I sang the same way I would sing a Chinese opera. My voice was charged and loud.

> *I once was lost but now am found,*
> *Was blind but now I see.*

Papa and NaiNai enjoyed the song and waited eagerly for me to go on. I had to tell them that this was all I had managed to learn so far.

Papa went quiet for a while and then said, "Although 'Amazing Grace' is a foreign song, it is about us, because we are lost, confused, and scared." NaiNai agreed. "Willow," she said, turning to me, "make sure you learn the full piece from Carie, because I could go at any time."

I asked NaiNai if she was going to heaven and if so whether she and my mother would meet. NaiNai nodded. "Your mother would love to hear you sing 'Amazing Grace.' "

I went to Carie and begged her to teach me the rest of the song. She was delighted. She sat me next to her by the piano and began.

> *The Lord has promised good to me,*
> *His word my hope secures;*
> *He will my shield and portion be,*
> *As long as life endures.*

Carie's voice changed. The tone became tender, reminding me of a gentle creek flowing through a meadow.

> *And mortal life shall cease;*
> *I shall possess within the veil,*
> *A life of joy and peace.*

From Wang Ah-ma, we learned that Carie had lost four of her children after arriving in China. "I don't know any woman who has experienced worse, four male children," Wang Ah-ma sighed, putting up her four fingers.

According to Wang Ah-ma, Carie had her dead sons' names carved on her bed board. "The Mistress speaks to their spirits every night before sleep."

People wondered what kind of food Absalom's family ate and what it tasted like.

"Cheese and butter," Wang Ah-ma said. She stuck a finger in her throat and bent over to imitate retching. "It tastes like spoiled tofu."

"What about Pearl?" I asked.

"Pearl is different. She has a Chinese stomach." Wang Ah-ma smiled with approval. "Pearl eats what I eat. She is strong as an ox."

"Do you mean she won't die like her brothers?" I asked.

Wang Ah-ma lowered her voice to a whisper. "It doesn't make sense to me that four of Carie's children had to die. It was the same disease. I mean, the boys suffered the same as the Chinese children. Why did the Chinese children survive? Pearl's body has learned to fight the disease like a Chinese. For Buddha's sake, she has been successful!"

The listeners nodded in admiration. "You did well for your mistress, Wang Ah-ma!"

Wang Ah-ma's face bloomed like a summer lotus. "Pearl eats double meals. One in the kitchen with the servants, and the other with her parents. The child has an incredible appetite. She loves soy nuts, lotus seeds, and roasted seaweed. Pearl's favorite is scallion pancakes, which I buy every week especially for her."

I should have seen it coming when Pearl caught me. My mouth was stuffed with pancake, which I had stolen from Wang Ah-ma. Pearl waited for the moment. She made sure that she had a witness. My hand was in Wang Ah-ma's basket, although Wang Ah-ma hadn't realized what was happening.

Pearl dragged me to Carie, who was sitting in front of her piano.

The town followed.

Papa and NaiNai were called.

"*A rat naturally knows how to dig a hole,*" children cheered. "What do you expect, the father sets an example?"

"I caught her in the act," Pearl announced.

Carie didn't look at her daughter. She turned to me.

"You didn't do it, did you, Willow?" Carie asked, closing the piano lid.

Fearing that Papa and NaiNai would lose face in front of the town, I boldly lied. "No, I did not do it."

Carie rose to greet Papa and NaiNai. In a gentle voice she said to them, "I'm sorry, my daughter made a mistake."

"But Mother!" Pearl interrupted. "I caught Willow in the middle of her act!" She turned to Wang Ah-ma. "Please, Ah-ma, tell Mother the truth . . ."

"Mistress," Wang Ah-ma said, stepping up. "Pearl made no mistake . . ."

Carie signaled a stop with her right hand and said, "Ah-ma, the soup on the stove is boiling."

"It is not boiling, Mistress. I have just checked."

"Go and check again," said Carie.

"Yes," Wang Ah-ma said, nodding, "I'll go now. But Mistress, Pearl was right about the pancake. Willow did steal it."

"No, Willow did not," Carie repeated without looking at anyone.

NaiNai and Papa exchanged relieved glances.

"Mother!" Pearl's tears streamed down her cheeks. "If you check Willow's breath, you will smell the scallions!"

"That's enough, Pearl." Carie waved a hand.

"I swear to God." Pearl began to weep.

"Go and help set the dinner table," Carie said. "Your father is on his way home."

"Mother, I'm not the one who lied!"

"I didn't say you lied, Pearl."

I had a hard time that afternoon. My neck felt stiff, as if pressed under a stone grinder. I went up into the hills and sat alone. I didn't move until the sun set and the boatmen returned. Mist began to spread along the riverbank. The moisture was thick in my lungs. I lost sleep that evening. I was deeply ashamed. Pearl's tearful face hovered before me all night long. I got up and admitted to Papa and NaiNai that I had taken the pancake.

They were not surprised.

CHAPTER 3

The teahouses celebrated spring by hosting parties. "Men of words" gathered around blossoming camellias and peach and plum trees and composed poems. Papa loved the parties, while I loved the blooming peach flowers that looked like pink clouds. Then came the April wet season. The southern China rain didn't come in showers. It came like a spreading thick fog. When I stuck out an arm, I could feel no drops. But once I stepped outside, wetness would wrap me. In ten minutes of walking, moisture would soak through my clothes. If I wiped my face with a hand, water would come off. Very slowly, my hair would droop. Strands of hair would paste against my skull.

In a month, the river would rise a few inches. Water and sky would become one gray color. Toads, eels, earthworms, and leeches would be found everywhere. The dirt path would become sluggish. Bamboo would thrive. By the time summer arrived, it would cover the southern slopes of the hills.

My teeth were green from chewing milkweeds. I had just turned nine. It became harder to resist the urge to steal. I had been thinking about a boy who had visited us during the past Chinese New Year. He was a distant relative and seventeen years old. His name was San-bao. He was an apprentice working for the local blacksmith. What I really had been thinking about were the soy nuts San-bao had promised me. I wondered when he would deliver his gift.

My legs carried me to San-bao's shop. I wished that I had nicer clothes. San-bao was surprised to see me. He wore a dirty apron and was bare-shouldered. He was a strong and cheerful man who had a horse's jaw. I could see wormlike thick veins under his skin. Putting down his sledgehammer, he asked what had brought me to visit.

I couldn't tell him the truth. I couldn't say that I had come for the soy nuts. I said that I was just passing by. He smiled gleefully.

"Have you eaten?" he asked after a moment.

"No." I was embarrassed for replying too quickly.

"What would you like me to get you?"

Before I could stop myself, my tongue went, "Soy nuts would be nice."

"Oh, right, soy nuts." He remembered his promise. He told me to wait and went inside the shop. When he came out, he said, "We'll take a walk, and I'll get you the soy nuts."

As soon as San-bao paid for the soy nuts, I reached for the bag.

"No, not yet." San-bao took it away. "I don't want the beggar children to jump on you. We must find a quiet place to sit."

I followed San-bao. We arrived at the back of the old churchyard where the weeds were waist-high. Black crows shot into the sky. Field mice ran through the wild berry bushes. We sat down. San-bao watched me eating the soy nuts. As soon as I finished, he put his arm around my shoulders.

"I am good to you, aren't I?" he asked.

I nodded, feeling a little awkward.

"Do me a favor," he said, pulling my hand over and placing it on top of his crotch.

I was shocked.

"You don't have to be so serious." He grinned.

"I'm going home, San-bao."

"Come on, Willow."

"No, San-bao."

"You owe me." He dropped his smile and his voice turned cold.

I was frightened. I got up and ran, but he caught me.

"You really believe that I'd let a cooked duck fly away?" He pushed me down.

I struggled to free myself.

He held my neck and twisted my head to the side. "I paid for your soy nuts."

"I'll give you the money back!"

"You have no money."

"I'll find a way."

"I want it right now!"

"I don't have it."

"Yes, you do. You have something I like. All you have to do is to let me touch it . . ." He reached inside my clothes.

"San-bao, please!"

"Willow, give me no trouble."

"Let me go!"

"Don't make me hurt you."

"No!"

"You bitch!"

"No!"

He pressed my face down to stop me from screaming.

I fought and kicked, but he was too strong.

My clothes were ripped.

I begged him to stop.

Refusing, he forced himself onto me.

Losing strength, I broke down. There was no way I could escape. I regretted my foolishness.

It was when San-bao pushed my face to the side that I saw a shadow. There was a figure hiding behind a stone tablet.

A familiar black knitted cap revealed who it was.

"Help!" I screamed.

Before San-bao could react, Pearl ran up. She struck San-bao with a big rock.

Instantly, San-bao fell over and was still.

"Oh, my God." Pearl stepped back. "Did I kill him?"

I gasped getting up.

Pearl bent down and put a finger under San-bao's nose.

"He's not dead!" Pearl said. "Should I hit him more?"

"No, no more!" San-bao pleaded, trying to raise himself.

"You deserve to die!" I yelled.

Pearl picked up the rock again.

"No!" San-bao rose and ran.

Pearl chased him until he disappeared.

Gratitude filled my chest.

Pearl came back and brushed the dirt off my clothes.

"Thank you for the rescue, my friend," I uttered.

"Who is your friend?" She turned away. "Liar!"

"Please forgive me, Pearl. I'll do anything to make it up to you."

"Do you expect me to trust you?" She looked at me, disgusted. "You took my father's wallet and spent his money; you stole Wang Ah-ma's pancakes and lied to my mother . . . You little donkey ass!"

She walked down the hill, swinging her basket.

I tried to hold back my tears.

She sang a Chinese song that I knew well. The hills echoed. The colorful wild flowers in her basket bounced under the bright sunshine.

Jasmine flower, sweet jasmine flower
Your beauty and fragrance is the best among the spring
I'd like to pick you and wear you in my hair
But I fear that you would be upset and wouldn't come back the next year

Noises filled the Sunday church. Men exchanged opinions on the weather and methods for pest control. Women knitted, mended, embroidered, and chatted. Someone shouted across the room. Children threw pine nuts at each other. Mothers nursed their infants and yelled at their elder children. Absalom was unable to quiet the crowd until Papa rang a merchant's bell.

"Folks, the Western monk needs our help," Papa said with raised voice. "In my opinion, Absalom offers not an alternative but a better deal. Look, we have fed our gods and they are fat and happy. But what have they done for us? Nothing. Now, folks, I'd like you to take a hard look at Absalom's God, Jesus Christ. Just look at his appearance. Anyone who is not blind can tell that he works harder than the Chinese gods. So listen, folks, listen to Absalom."

Absalom picked up the opportunity. "Today we shall learn about the Baptism of Christ." He pulled out his color drawing and pointed. "The two men are Lord Christ and John."

I saw two figures standing in a river performing a ceremony. John and Christ had almost oriental features, with smaller noses and slightly slanted eyes. Absalom had finally taken Papa's advice. He had smoothed the deep-set Western eyes and flattened their pointed noses. Christ now had longer earlobes, resembling Buddha's.

Papa told me that Absalom at first had insisted on presenting a fully bearded Christ. It wasn't until Papa proved to him that no Chinese would worship a god that looked like a monkey that he agreed to trim the beard.

"Buddha's face changed as he traveled from India to China." Papa pointed out to Absalom the difference between the early India Buddha and the later Chinese Buddha. Buddha's eyes grew smaller as he arrived in China, his skin lighter and smoother. The Chinese sculptors made sure that Buddha appeared well fed. With his eyes half closed, Buddha looks like he is about to nap after a satisfying meal.

When Absalom baptized Papa, it was a big day for the town. Everyone wanted to see Papa being dipped in the river like a pot sticker in soy sauce. It was the first time Pearl and I sat together. We both had been trying to help our fathers draw a crowd.

Absalom and Papa stood face-to-face in the river with water up to their waists. Absalom was in his dark gray robe, while Papa wore his washed white cotton gown. Papa was red-faced and looked nervous, while Absalom was serious and solemn.

Speaking his heavily accented Chinese, Absalom explained, "Descending into the waters implies a confession of guilt and a plea for forgiveness."

Papa repeated loudly after Absalom.

"Make a new beginning!" Absalom shouted. "Come to the light on the Cross!"

Papa tried to stand still but wasn't able to. "When should I take a breath?" he asked.

Absalom ignored him. " 'Take me and throw me into the sea,' says Jesus," he sang.

"Tell me when," Papa spoke again.

"Wait." Absalom held him.

"I am afraid of drowning," Papa said. "I really am."

"Trust in God."

Gently, Absalom pushed Papa back until his head went under the water.

The crowd held its breath.

"Lord Jesus bears all righteousness!" Absalom hailed.

The crowd cheered.

Papa looked frozen. He emerged from the water and immediately sank back again.

"Papa, what are you doing?" I shouted.

"He is accepting Christ's death," Pearl said quietly.

"For what?"

"For his sins and the sins of humanity."

Papa reemerged from the river, spilling water like a fountain. He didn't choke. I was relieved. I saw NaiNai among the crowd wiping her tears. The night before she had told us that she liked the idea that her son was getting a cleaning.

"God calls out, 'This is my beloved son!' " Absalom shouted. " 'This is the anticipation of his death on the Cross and his Resurrection!' "

Led by Absalom, Papa walked out of the river.

"I feel God and his Will!" Papa said to the crowd. "Jesus made me shake off a failed life. I am to begin a new one!"

I was sure Papa did it for Absalom to thank him.

As if touched by Papa's transformation, Absalom stuck out both of his arms toward the sky, calling out, "Praise the Lord!"

Speaking together as if singing a duet, Papa and Absalom stood side by side in the church on Sundays. Folks were curious when they heard about Papa's new luck on getting blessed by the foreign god. They came to see if they could acquire the same protection.

Papa delivered an outstanding performance for Absalom.

"We live in an underworld filled with demons," Papa began with the same enthusiasm he showed when reciting his Chinese poems. "Doomed by fate, we are captured by evil, spellbound by mean spirits. We, the incense burners, the coolies, the losers, gamblers, drunkards, thieves, and deaf-n-blinds. Be afraid no more, because Jesus is here to help. All you have to do is to make a new start by signing up with Absalom."

Papa asked the town's seventeen-year-old widow, Lilac, who was an egg seller, "Am I right to guess that Buddha hasn't answered your prayers?"

"No, he certainly has not," Lilac replied.

"Are you losing faith in him?"

"I am afraid to say yes, but yes."

"You are disappointed."

"I don't mean to offend Buddha. But yes."

"Lilac, you have been visiting the temple since birth. The incense you have burned could make a hill. Did your life change for the good? You were bought and sold twice. You were married to a sick man who was dying. You were forced to sleep with the crop in order to balance his yin and yang elements. You barely escaped from your in-laws. You came to Chin-kiang friendless and family-less and still are. Have you ever questioned the god you worship?"

Lilac shook her head and began to weep.

"Well, consider your disappointment an investment!" Papa said.

"An investment?" Lilac's big eyes widened.

Absalom frowned.

Papa's tongue had never been so slippery as his words poured. "This investment warns you not to make any more bad choices, so that you won't end up captive to evil spirits forever!"

"But I have been burning incense!" Lilac protested. "I don't deserve bad luck forever!"

"Have you ever asked yourself the reason that bad luck still follows you?" Papa asked.

Lilac shook her head.

"Why you and no one else?"

"Why?"

To drive home his point, Papa punched his right fist into his left palm. "It's the wrong god you have been worshipping!"

Lilac was stunned.

"The Christian God says, Lilac, you deserve a chance for a better life. Yes, you, Lilac!" Like an opera singer, Papa commanded the stage. "God tells me that Lilac deserves the same chance as his beloved son, the Lord Jesus Christ! Now make your wish and claim it!"

"I'd certainly make that wish," Lilac said in a small voice. "But first and most of all I wish that my eggs be given a chance to become chickens."

I admired Lilac because she never complained about her misfortune. She was always cheerful and kind. Her egg service was fully booked before winter. This year she thought that I was old enough to help her separate the good eggs from the bad. She hired me. What surprised me was that Pearl was there too. I learned that Pearl had been visiting Lilac since she had been a little girl. Lilac's egg house was her playground. Lilac adored Pearl because she was such a dependable helper. Carie told Lilac that her daughter was permitted there for the learning experience. Pearl had so much fun that she would forget to go home. Wang Ah-ma had to come and drag her back at the end of the day.

At Lilac's request, Pearl showed me the way. I learned that it would take about a month and a half for the eggs to hatch. Pearl taught me to separate eggs from the main basket. We removed the eggs that were too small or whose shells were too thin, or had a broken yolk or had been in the storage too long.

Pearl told me that what she loved to do most was shine the eggs. This was done after Lilac sealed the egg house, leaving only a small hole in the door. Pearl and I took turns holding the eggs in front of the hole where the sunlight shone through. This was called "the first look." The purpose was to see if the egg yolk carried a pearl. If there was a pearl, the hen had been visited by a rooster, which meant that the egg would turn into a chick.

After the examination, we placed the qualified eggs in warm baskets padded with cotton. Lilac would take the baskets and store them underneath her big brick bed behind her stove. We had to wait for four days to have "the second look."

The purpose of the second look was to see if the pearl had swelled. Lilac taught us to hold the egg in our palm. Back and forth we turned the egg toward the sun. We looked for a shadow, the pearl. It was not an easy task and it took an experienced eye. Afterward we removed the eggs that hadn't swelled. Again we put the qualified eggs in the cotton-padded baskets and put them under Lilac's bed.

We would repeat the procedure every four days. It was what Lilac called "the third look" and "the fourth look." When the shadow became clear to our eyes, we moved all the egg baskets from underneath Lilac's big bed and transferred them to ceramic pots. Inside the pots was a mixture of earth and straw. It looked like a hot cave. A tiny fire was built underneath the pots to keep the temperature warm. According to Lilac, this was the most crucial step. If it was too hot, the eggs would be cooked. If it wasn't warm enough, the pearl wouldn't turn into a chick.

The success or failure of Lilac's year would be determined in a few days. Lilac invited all her gods onto her walls. She lit incense and performed ceremonies begging to be blessed. This year she put up a picture of Jesus Christ.

I was tempted to take a peek into the pots. But Pearl refused to go along with me. She followed Lilac's instruction faithfully. Like a mother hen, Lilac wouldn't leave her eggs. Day and night, she guarded the pots, adding and withdrawing straw to and from the fire. She no longer spoke but whispered—she was afraid to disturb the eggs.

I watched Pearl draw pictures of Lilac, who was sleeping with her mouth wide open. Lilac had been talking about making good money hatching her eggs before she fell asleep. In the last two-week period Lilac had grown thin. She had no time to eat or sleep. She feared that the temperature would waver and destroy her harvest. Her eyes became red and her cheeks sunken. Pearl and I avoided talking to Lilac because she was irritable and nervous.

When Lilac put out the fire, we knew that the winter was over. In just a few days the air warmed. Spring came with dampness, and we had to battle excessive moisture.

The three of us took the eggs out of the giant ceramic pots to air them. We put the eggs on Lilac's brick bed with cotton pads underneath. Lilac sent Pearl and me to notify the farmers that the time to pick up their baby chicks had come.

We were thrilled when we saw the little beaks appearing. The young chickens chipped away at the shells and worked their way out. Pearl called it a grand birthday party when all the chicks finally broke through.

"What beauties!" Pearl cried to the chicks hopping on and off her hands.

Lilac was too tired to celebrate. She snored, leaning against the wall, while Pearl and I counted the chicks. We put the chicks into baskets to be picked up. Lilac laughed and cried in her sleep. Her face glowed with pleasure. "What should be done in summer, you don't do in spring!" she yelled. "Am I not right?"

"You are perfectly right, Lilac!" Pearl and I answered. We helped her to the bed, where she would sleep for days.

Chapter 4

It was early September. Hot, sweet air filled my lungs. Pearl and I ran down the hills. We passed little children playing with dirt and earthworms. We passed the town's oldest man napping in the shade of a tree. I was thrilled because Pearl had finally invited me to her home.

"My mother doesn't know that I am bringing you," Pearl said excitedly.

"Will she . . . mind?" I felt nervous. "After all, I did lie."

"Oh, she has long forgotten that."

"Has she?"

"Mother said that sometimes people can't be held responsible for what they do, because they don't know God."

I stopped. "What if she remembers? What if she tells me, 'I don't want a liar as my guest'?"

"Oh, she knows you, and she's always liked you."

"How do you know?"

"Willow, my mother was bound to adore you."

"Why?"

"Because you can sing."

I looked at her.

"Willow, my mother has been trying to organize a children's choir, but she can't find any children who can sing or are willing."

"She knows that I'm willing," I said. "But I don't know if she thinks I can sing well enough."

"Yes you can."

"My voice can't hold the highest notes. It cracks."

"Mother will teach you how to carry the high notes. Besides, the church songs are no Chinese operas. They are much easier to sing."

"Will you sing too, Pearl?"

"Yes, I love singing, although I don't really have much of a voice. But it doesn't matter. I can sing 'Jasmine, Sweet Jasmine' forever."

She began the tune and I joined. When we finished, Pearl began again in the Yangchow accent, and I followed. We sang in both Soochow and Nanking accents, too.

"Do you have a favorite Chinese opera?" I asked after we exhausted all our accents.

"*The Butterfly Lovers!*"

"That is my favorite too!"

"The Ming dynasty version or the Ching dynasty version?" Pearl asked. I was surprised at her knowledge. "The Ching version, of course." She nodded and then we began.

> *I live by the Yangtze River near its source,*
> *While you reside farthest down its course.*
> *You and I drink water out of the same stream,*
> *I haven't seen you though daily of you I dream.*
>
> *When will this river water cease to run?*
> *When shall I not love you, the way I do?*
> *I only wish our two hearts would beat as one,*
> *And you wouldn't disappoint me in my love for you.*

Hand in hand we walked along the riverbank. I asked if she was allowed to sing Chinese opera at home.

"Are you kidding?" she mocked. "Absalom allows no other sound than God's."

I asked if she got along with her parents.

"My parents use a fork and knife; I use chopsticks."

*   *   *

Both Absalom and Carie were out when we arrived, so Pearl gave me a full tour of her home. The house was a three-room bungalow made of brick and wooden boards. The middle room served as a living and dining area. On each side were bedrooms. Pearl shared hers with her baby sister, Grace. Her parents' bedroom had a big wooden bed. The sheets were washed white and made of coarse cloth. The stains on the wall showed a leaky roof. The place was extremely clean. Even the worn-out furniture glowed. Pearl pointed out the pink curtains. "Mother made them herself with fabric from America." On the side of the house there were two large ceramic jars containing water from the river. I was surprised that the family lived just like us.

"Mother leaves our door open all year long," Pearl said.

"She will receive anyone who knocks?"

"My parents love any opportunity to introduce Jesus Christ."

"But Carie cares about people, doesn't she?"

"Yes, my mother does, a great deal, unlike my father, who cares only about God."

"I don't know about leaving the door open all the time," I said. "Beggars might get in and it would be hard to get them out."

"People who show up are 'too poor to afford a string to hang themselves with,' in my mother's words. 'Foreign Mistress, Carie TaiTai,' they call her, and beg for food."

"Your mother has to put up with a lot."

"This is nothing compared to what she has been putting up with from her husband." Pearl told me that Carie had tried to convince Absalom to leave China in order to save her dying children.

"Does your mother still want to leave China?" I asked.

"No, she gave up." Pearl paused and then went on. "The visitors Mother truly enjoys are sailors from America. She bakes cookies for them and they love her for it. After food and wine, Mother and the sailors sing 'Afar from Home' together. They all laugh and cry at the same time."

*   *   *

As Pearl predicted, Carie was pleased the moment she found out that I was willing to join her children's choir. She took me to the piano and I sang "Amazing Grace."

Carie showed me how to steal breaths when hitting the high notes. I learned not to strain my voice. To instruct me, Carie began to sing other songs. I loved Carie's voice although I had no idea what she was singing. I promised to come again for lessons. Carie believed that my voice would change for the better with practice. After a couple of months, I did improve. I was able to carry the high notes effortlessly. I could imitate Carie's voice, and I also had the ability to memorize a song once Carie had sung it. Soon, Carie invited me to sing at Absalom's Sunday service. I sang the song clearly with emotion as if I understood the lyrics.

Pearl was proud. Her face glowed when Carie said, "I thank God for Willow!"

Absalom was also impressed. "Keep up the good work for the Lord," he encouraged.

I knew in his heart Papa didn't care much about God although he pretended that he did. I figured that I could do the same. What I loved was to sit by Carie as she played the piano. Carie never quizzed me regarding my knowledge of God. I was grateful that she didn't mind that I sat quietly. She said that a child ought not to miss the joy of music. She would sing a tune that came to her mind. I would hear seasons in Carie's voice. The sound of spring was like the Yangtze River filling up the creeks. Her sound of summer was like the sun's touch. Autumn was colors that vibrated and heightened my senses. Her voice of winter was deep, a story of snow.

While sitting by Carie I felt happiness. But once in a while the words would fill my heart with sadness. It would happen in the middle of my practice. I would choke and break down. Carie would put her arm around me.

"Let's take a break," she would suggest. "I'll play you my favorite tune."

Carie's music never failed to cheer me up. When Carie was in a good mood, she would sing duets with me. I loved the sound we made together. If I began to get an idea about heaven, it was through singing with Carie.

"Willow, how I wish that I could take you to see America," Carie said one day.

Carie spoke about her homeland. She said that she didn't mean to live in China forever. It was her duty as a Christian wife to follow Absalom to China and set up her tent in the small town of Chin-kiang. It was not her choice, she emphasized.

I asked Pearl if she shared her mother's feelings.

"Well, China feels more like home to me than America," she replied matter-of-factly. Pearl hadn't been to America since she was three months old. "America is my mother's real home and she says it's mine too." She paused and then added, "America is where Mother comes from and where she wishes she could return."

"What about you?" I asked.

"I have no idea where I will end up eventually."

I asked if she missed America. She laughed. "How could I miss something I have no idea of?" I asked if she knew her relatives in America. "I know their names," she replied, "but I don't know them personally. My parents talk about my aunts, uncles, and my cousins. They are strangers to me. The only people I know besides my parents and sister are your people. I am afraid that one day my father will decide to return to America. I can't imagine leaving China."

I looked at her, trying to picture the moment of such a departure.

"In a way it is sad that my mother is not like her husband," Pearl resumed after a while. "Absalom's home is where God's work is. He doesn't care where he lives, be it America or China. My mother lives with a broken heart. As far as she is concerned, her life is as an exile. She holds on to her piano, because it is from her home."

I had noticed the way Carie cared for her piano. Its legs were in slippers—Carie raised the piano from the packed earth to protect it from moisture. In Chin-kiang water came into the rooms at the end of each rainy season. Wooden furniture had to be put on bricks. We laid planks from room to room when the water was too high. Carie's biggest concern was that mold would eventually destroy her piano.

We practiced for the Christmas performance. Carie had translated the lyrics from English to Chinese. Although I was literate in neither language, I liked the English version better. I told Carie that the sound of "Silent Night" in Chinese was not as beautiful as in English. Carie replied, "The beauty of a song shouldn't matter as much as its message."

Absalom had his highest attendance ever—the children's singing drew people in from the streets on Christmas Eve. For the first time, I saw a big smile on Absalom's face. To celebrate, he got rid of his fake Chinese queue and let his shoulder-length brown hair hang down. It took the crowd a while to get used to his new Western-man look. Papa told NaiNai that Absalom needed the success. He had returned from a rough tour recently. While Absalom was preaching in a neighboring village, he was beaten by folks who had never seen a foreigner in their lives and who thought that Absalom was there to do harm. Dogs were let out to chase him away.

Pearl showed me Carie's yard. "Mother is determined to create an American garden. She brought plants from America. This is dogwood and that is a Lincoln rose, Mother's favorite."

"This looks like a Chinese butterfly flower." I pointed at the dogwood. "And the Lincoln rose must be a cousin of the peony."

"I am sure there is some sort of connection. Mother said God created nature the same way he did humans. What we see is God's generosity."

"Do you really believe in God, Pearl?" I asked.

"I do," she said. "But you know me. I am also Chinese. Part of me can't talk to my parents, not that they care."

"Do you get confused too?" I asked carefully. "I mean, about God?"

She kicked a rock off the road. "It hurts me that God doesn't respond to my mother's prayers."

"Is your mother mad at God?"

"Mother is angry at Father, not at God," Pearl explained. "She is still unable to accept the deaths of my four brothers."

"Is that why she doesn't preach, even though her Chinese is much better than Absalom's?" I asked.

Pearl nodded. "Mother wants to have faith in Father's work, but she can't convince herself. She told me that she has a hard time staying on the sunny side."

"Your mother shows the goodness of God to us."

"Mother says that she helps others because it helps in healing herself."

"A woman hides her broken arm inside her sleeve," I told Pearl, repeating something NaiNai had said. "Your mother abandoned her parents for her crazy husband."

Pearl and I discovered that God had a strange way of making things work for Carie. At first she wasn't able to get people to join Absalom's church, but when she started to help the locals, attending their sick and dying, administering Western medicines for humans and animals while refusing money or gifts, the locals began to crowd the church.

Carie was concerned that I had become a distraction to Pearl's study. Absalom disagreed. He told her, "Pearl is doing a great service to the Lord when she takes the opportunity to influence her friend."

To encourage my friendship with his daughter, Absalom gave me gifts such as a picture of Christ by his own hand. Absalom put Pearl to work with me using his own translation of the Bible. We fooled around instead. Pearl had a hard time concentrating on doing God's work. Only when we saw Absalom's shadow passing by the window did we recite the Bible in dramatic, loud voices.

Carie set new rules for Pearl about spending time with me. She was only allowed to play after she completed her studying. Carie taught Pearl at home herself. Pearl was also given Chinese lessons by Mr. Kung, a chopstick-thin Chinese man in his fifties. I sat by Pearl's door and waited patiently. I noticed that Pearl often went ahead of Mr. Kung. She finished the novel *All Men Are Brothers* before the lesson even started. Pearl had told me that the novel was about a group of poor peasants who were driven into desperate situations and became bandits. In the story, they seek justice and become heroes. Mr. Kung was impressed that Pearl had memorized the novel's one hundred and eight characters, but he criticized Pearl the way any Chinese teacher would. "A truly smart person . . ." Mr. Kung paused and smoothed his goat beard with his thumb and first finger before continuing, ". . . is the kind of person clever enough to hide her brilliance."

"Yes, Mr. Kung," Pearl answered humbly, and winked at me.

Papa celebrated the day Absalom made him a "Clergy."

"I thought my best luck would be to become the church's gateman." Papa wept as he sat on the doorsill.

NaiNai was overwhelmed with happiness. "Promise me, son, you will honor Absalom by weathering the storms with him."

Papa promised like a son of true piety. He told NaiNai that Absalom had started training him to be in charge of the Chin-kiang church.

"What will Master Absalom do when you take over?" NaiNai questioned.

"Absalom will work on expansion. He plans to go deep into the countryside."

Papa told NaiNai that although he felt honored, he was having difficulty committing himself to God.

"Absalom has assigned a dog to be in charge of catching mice," NaiNai sighed. She worried that her son would let Absalom down.

Papa tried his best to play the part. He said that he would never admit that he was in it for the money. Papa told NaiNai that his promotion came as a result of Absalom's fight with another man of God.

"Is there another God's man?" NaiNai and I asked.

"A new missionary who called himself a Baptist," Papa explained.

"Is Absalom a Baptist as well?" we asked.

"No, Absalom is a Presbyterian."

Regarding the difference, Papa said that he was confused himself, although Absalom had explained it to him.

"As far as Absalom is concerned, Chin-kiang is his territory," Papa concluded.

The Baptist was a red-haired heavy fellow with one blind eye. He often came by our church and told the crowd that Absalom had it all wrong. He pointed out, for example, that Absalom only sprinkled the heads of his converts when he ought to soak their heads in the water.

This made sense to the Chinese. The logic was that if a little water was good for the soul, more water should be better, and that a deep soaking would be the best way to go.

Absalom was convinced that the Baptist was here to destroy his work by snatching away his converts. "He is planting doubts in their heads about me," Absalom complained to Papa.

I didn't know how to deal with the Baptist when I met him outside the church. By walking away, I would insult him. So I waited until he finished his preaching about immersion.

Our encounter upset Absalom. He vowed revenge.

NaiNai predicted rather gladly, "The fisherman profits when a crab and a lobster are locked in a fight." By fisherman, she meant Papa.

Papa agreed. "I heard Absalom shout at his wife," he reported, mimicking Absalom. " 'I have taught, labored, and suffered all the troubles of instilling the fundamentals of Christianity into the heathens! It is nothing short of religious thievery when my future members would be added to the Baptist's glory!' "

"Is it that serious?" NaiNai wondered.

"Oh, yes, for Absalom," Papa said. "How otherwise would I receive my promotion as a Clergy? Absalom is no fool."

"You'd better not meddle," NaiNai warned.

Papa smiled. "I would benefit more if their fight continues."

NaiNai shook her head and said, "Being a crippled donkey walking on a broken bridge—you are going to fall sooner or later."

"I am no longer the same rotten character you think," Papa said. "I'll not be the one to bring Absalom's church into contempt. Absalom will win."

"I just want to be able to have a clean conscience when I die." Tears filled NaiNai's eyes.

Papa took out a string of copper money and laid it by NaiNai's pillow. "Absalom paid me for your medicine, Mother."

NaiNai cupped her face in her palms and began to weep.

"Where is Absalom now?" I asked Papa.

"He is touring the countryside. Perhaps he is in the middle of conducting a study class."

"Does he teach?"

"Yes."

"What does he teach?"

"Absalom teaches Bible history, philosophy, religions, Greek, and Hebrew. He spreads the Gospel."

"Does he take women disciples?"

"No, Absalom's disciples are men only."

"How far does he travel?"

"As far as he is able to reach." Papa paused for a moment and then added, "The man is ambitious. I have little doubt that his Christian God will conquer China one day."

Papa told me that he was amazed by the fact that educated Chinese youths were willing to follow Absalom.

"Absalom has converted even Chinese Muslims." Papa scratched the back of his head in disbelief. "I believe it is the way Absalom wages the war of God that attracts young people. He is absolutely committed and stubborn. A zealot, so to speak. The young worship his energy and determination. More than anything else, he sells God's victory. People want to follow a strong man, a leader."

I asked Papa, "How can you be a Clergy if you don't believe in God one hundred percent?"

"Keep your voice down, my daughter." Papa was embarrassed. "Be the keeper of my secret. According to Absalom, God will call."

"Have you been waiting?"

"Yes, I have, and I must be patient."

"I hope you mean it."

"I do," Papa swore.

The winter of 1899 was brutally cold. Sky and hills merged in one bitter whirl of wind and snow, which was rare in southern China. In the mornings the valleys were silent under their blanket of whiteness. The weather helped Papa achieve the attendance he had promised Absalom. Attracted by the church's warm fire, the poor gathered under the portrait of Jesus Christ and prayed.

The way Papa preached the Bible was different from Absalom. Papa told it the way he would a Chinese story. He prepared his material carefully so that it would always have a suspenseful beginning and a satisfying end.

When Absalom returned from his trips, he was bothered by Papa's exaggeration and invention. Especially when Papa compared Jesus to the Chinese folk heroes, even the fictional Monkey King. Papa argued that the Monkey King had the same kind heart as Jesus. Papa's aim was to do whatever it took to keep the audience coming back.

"Stick to the Bible from now on," Absalom ordered Papa. "Emphasize that the journey of the faithful will be over a lifetime of poverty and sacrifice."

Papa convinced Absalom to at least allow him to mention Buddhism. "I'll use the concept as a tool to ease people toward Christianity," he promised. Answering Absalom's doubts, Papa said, "Nobody likes to be told that their religion is bad and silly."

People attended the church, but no one agreed to the conversion. Calling on his wits, Papa became inventive. Inspired by the local fortune-teller, Papa copied drawings from the Bible onto cards with which he played with the locals. The rewards for joining the church and obeying God would be good harvests, sons, and longevity. For punishment, Papa described scenarios borrowed from the Chinese hell, where men and women were chopped to pieces and fed to beasts.

Pearl burst out laughing when Papa exchanged the names of Chinese gods with Christian saints. For example, Guan-ying as Mary.

"Absalom will tear out his hair for this one," Pearl said.

I asked if she missed her father when he was away. She said that she didn't. "I don't know him enough to miss him." She adored Papa and thought that he was funny and creative. Pearl especially enjoyed the New Year's couplets and riddles Papa created. The phrases were from the Bible. Papa gave Bible Sticks for people to draw—an idea he stole from the Buddhist temple, where drawing fortune sticks was part of the worshipping ceremony.

Absalom continued to complain, and even threatened to fire Papa. But he was impressed with the results. Church attendance soared. The Chin-kiang church was now known throughout the province, although there were still not enough converts.

Pearl and I were told by our fathers to influence our playmates. I didn't feel comfortable talking about a foreign god. Pearl shared my feelings. We bribed our playmates with games and food in exchange for promises that they would show up at the church on Sundays. The trouble was that once the children became too familiar with Papa's Bible stories, they wanted different stories or they would stop coming. In the meantime, spring arrived—and the laborers left for home to work in the fields.

Papa worried that when Absalom returned from his latest trip, he would find the numbers down. Papa didn't want to lose his job. Every night, Papa worked hard on refreshing the Bible stories.

For several Sundays, Pearl and I sat in the back of the church listening to Papa speaking to an almost empty room. Pearl didn't seem to be bothered by the declining numbers. She continued to bury her face in her books.

I wondered what we would do if Papa lost his job. NaiNai's illness had worsened during the winter. The medicine no longer had any effect. NaiNai was reluctant to call for a doctor for fear of going deeper into debt. At the thought that I might lose NaiNai, tears came to my eyes. As I raised my chin to push back the tears, I noticed something strange was happening to the church's ceiling. The beams were covered with brown-colored spots. I went to Pearl and pointed out what I saw. She wondered if the spots were bugs.

For the next few days we watched. The bugs did not move. A week later we found that the bugs had swelled and were turning into green leaves.

"The leaves are growing!" Pearl and I looked at each other and were excited.

In a week, the green leaves took up the entire corner of the ceiling. They began to spread over to the window and then to the top of the doorsills. We called all our friends to come and look. They came. They went home and told their parents about the green miracle on the church's ceiling.

Eventually we learned that the green growth was willow sprouts. The beams had been made of willow trunks. Although the trunks were stripped bare, the warm spring had brought them back to life.

The news that the foreign god was showing signs of his existence brought people rushing back. Papa called the church's ceiling God's Garden. The place was packed the day Absalom returned. The willow beams were flourishing. The new sprouts were five and seven feet long. With the breeze from the window, the leaves swayed like dancers' sleeves across the room.

With Absalom by his side, Papa read from the Book of Revelation. The crowd listened while enjoying the miracle of God at work. Bees, butterflies, and birds flew in and out of the room and drove the little children wild.

Chapter 5

An opera troupe, the Wan-Wan Tunes, arrived. For the Spring Moon
Festival it would play *The Butterfly Lovers*. The moment Pearl and I
heard the news, we could barely contain ourselves. Pearl begged Carie
for permission to join me and NaiNai, who said it was the last show she
wanted to see before she died.

We dressed up for the performance. I wore a blue floral cotton gown
and Pearl wore a purple silk dress embroidered with pink butterflies.
Pearl carefully stuffed her curly hair under the black knitted cap. From
the back, we looked like twin sisters. We made necklaces with fresh
jasmine buds. Hand in hand, we walked toward the riverbank where the
performance was to take place.

The stage was next to the riverbank. It was an abandoned temple with
four columns. The crowd began to gather at sunset. Some people came
with boats and others watched from rooftops. There were also people
watching from a faraway hillside. With Pearl and me on either side
of NaiNai, we pushed through the crowd. We settled near the stage.
NaiNai took out roasted soy nuts for Pearl and me to share as we waited
for the curtain to open.

The drums finally began. Our hearts raced. We cheered with the
crowd. "*Wan-Wan Tunes! Wan-Wan Tunes!*"

The curtain moved aside. The stage warmers entered. A string of
cartwheels followed. The chorus singers introduced the story. A moment
later the actors appeared. The star actor, who played the male lover, the
handsome Liang, was a girl. She wore heavy makeup. She was dressed

in a splendid sun-colored costume with long jade beads. Her voice had what opera fans would call a copper sound to it, considered the highest quality for a young male voice. Her Wan-Wan tune brought joyful tears to NaiNai's eyes.

My eyes followed Liang's every move. His lover, Yin-tai, was a supreme beauty. The actress was wrapped in a long-sleeved pink silk costume. She moved like a goddess stepping from the clouds. Although her breath seemed a little labored, her voice was sweet.

The evening deepened. The stage was brightly lit with lanterns. In front of our eyes, the love story unfolded. The lovers proclaimed their passion and fought the feudal force that tried to separate them. Pearl and I both wept at the end—the lovers had taken their own lives in the face of society's brutality.

Later on, Pearl would tell me that she had learned the Chinese version of *Romeo and Juliet* before she knew the name Shakespeare.

The dead lovers came back to life as butterflies. They reunited and lived happily ever after. It was a tragedy with a happy ending. Spreading their giant wings, the lovers danced and sang:

> *Dreams possessed me*
> *I wandered and finally was where you were*
> *We sat on the veranda*
> *And you sang the sweet old air*
> *Then I woke*
> *With no one near me*
> *The moon shining on*
> *Lighting up dead petals*
> *Making me think that you have passed and gone*

After the performance, we escorted NaiNai home. Pearl and I went back to the stage and waited at the exit, hoping to steal glances at the actors. We were fascinated that the entire cast was female. A turtle-faced, bald-headed lady was in charge of the girls. She had played the evil rich man in the opera. Pearl recognized the actor who had played Liang and the girl who had played Yin-tai, her partner. Without makeup and costume, she looked bone-thin. She went and sat on a stool. Her head rested against the wall. She was pale and looked ill. Liang helped her remove her boots and then folded the costumes and packed them into cases.

We learned that the troupe lived in two boats docked by the lower bank. This was where the night soil and trash were dumped. Although the air stank, we didn't want to leave until the turtle-faced lady threatened to send for our parents.

Pearl and I talked about the opera on our way back. We entertained ourselves with the Wan-Wan tune and the opera's theme song. We danced as the butterflies, swinging our arms up and down.

The next afternoon Pearl met with me again. We visited the troupe before they departed for the next town. We witnessed something we didn't expect: The troupe girls were forced to practice their acrobatic skills on the stone pavement. Pearl and I felt fortunate that our parents had not sold us.

Finally we located Liang, who was washing a bucket by the water.

Pearl introduced herself and expressed our admiration.

Liang gave a grateful nod but lowered her eyes. We saw tears running down her cheeks.

"What happened?" Pearl asked. "Where is your friend, Yin-tai?"

"She is sick."

"Maybe she is just exhausted," Pearl comforted her. "Give her a day to rest. I'm sure she'll recover."

"No, there is no hope."

"What do you mean?"

"She is dying of tuberculosis," the actor sobbed. She pulled over the clothes she was washing and showed us a bloodstain.

Pearl and I were shocked.

"Isn't she supposed to perform tonight?" we asked.

"The performance has just been canceled." The actor broke down. "The doctor said that she wouldn't make it through the night."

We didn't know what else to say.

The beautiful actress died. Having no money for a proper burial, the turtle-faced lady dumped the body into the river. Since the girl had been sold to the troupe at a young age, neither her parents nor any relatives had been notified about her death. After Pearl told Carie what had happened, she called Absalom and Papa. Both men went to the river and brought the body back. Absalom conducted a modest ceremony and the actress was buried in the back of the old church. NaiNai, Wang Ah-ma, and Lilac washed the young actress and dressed her in the dress I had worn to the opera. I was comforted to see that she fit my dress perfectly.

Liang came for the farewell. She was sorrow-stricken. For a moment my mind went back to the stage scene where he expressed his undying love for her as she lay dying.

Pearl couldn't stop weeping. Weeks later, she went to Absalom demanding an answer. "Why didn't God do something?"

Absalom told her that "one has to work to earn God's protection."

The distressed Pearl came to NaiNai. She took her to the Buddhist temple and asked to read a chapter from the Buddhist scripture. The title was "Heavenly Deaths and Circle of Life." Afterward, Pearl and I burned incense and prayed for the actress's soul.

"I am learning what is gay as well as what is terrible," Pearl said, as if to herself. "I'll accept the Buddhist notion that all that is truthful is beautiful."

Dysentery claimed countless lives during the Year of the Rat. NaiNai was among the sick. The local doctor refused to let Absalom and Carie treat NaiNai with their Western medicine. He insisted that the effect of the Chinese herbs that he prescribed would be disturbed.

Papa spent all his savings. NaiNai continued to get worse. I was with Pearl in the hills when a neighbor came and told me that NaiNai was about to depart. By the time I reached NaiNai's bed, she was almost unconscious. "Carie . . ." she kept calling.

I flew from the house and went to Carie. Without saying a word, Carie picked up her medicine box and came.

"My mother is possessed by evil spirits," the panic-stricken Papa warned. "If you touch her, bad luck will follow you home."

"What a shame that my husband converted you!" Carie was disgusted. "You certainly don't sound like a Christian." Opening her medicine box, she ordered Papa, "Stay away."

Taking out her needle and tube, Carie administered a shot for NaiNai. "The dose will do the job," she said. "Let me know if it doesn't. I'll fetch the doctor at the embassy."

By midnight, NaiNai was asking for water. At sunrise, she said that she was hungry.

While Papa got down on his knees to express his gratitude to Carie, Absalom said that it was God's will that NaiNai lived.

"It has nothing to do with my wife," Absalom insisted. "It's the church members' collective praying that God answered."

If Papa was a fake Christian, he changed at that moment. So did NaiNai, who officially said good-bye to the little Buddha statue in her room. She replaced it with a clay figure of Christ—a gift from Absalom.

Still, some things would never change. In NaiNai's Christian heaven, angels took the form of peach flowers, butterflies, and hummingbirds. God himself lived in a Chinese landscape where lakes reflected clouds and bamboo and pine covered the mountains. What amused Pearl and me the most was that NaiNai's Christian God traveled on the backs of deer and rode a crane if traveling great distances.

By the time I turned eleven, Pearl knew almost everyone in Chin-kiang. Our favorite person was the popcorn man, who made it to our town the first week of every month. The man spoke a northern dialect and his skin was the color of coal. Dirt thickened his hair and he wore the same canvas clothes with patches on top of patches year after year. Although he never smiled, he couldn't have been a nicer fellow. His fan-shaped nose was forever smeared with coal dust. Pushing his little cart, he wandered from village to village.

On the popcorn man's cart was a cannon-shaped cooker made of iron. The firebox was made of tin cans. Connected to the bottom of the firebox was a wooden bellows with an aluminum pipe. A crate of firewood was on the side. On top of the wood sat a cotton sack. We got excited when the man started to heat up the cannon. We watched the flames shoot high. We kept our distance after adults warned that the cannon might explode.

Pearl and I stood by the popcorn man and watched for hours on end. He rotated the cannon with his left hand and worked the bellows with his right. The man needed no clock to tell him when it was time to pop the corn. When he felt that the temperature was just right, he picked up the cotton bag and covered the cannon with it. Using an iron pipe, he pried the cannon open. The sound of an explosion followed. This was what the children had been waiting for.

"Pop!" the man would shout right before the explosion.

While small children covered their ears and some closed their eyes, Pearl and I enjoyed the sound of the explosion. Following the sound came a delicious smell. The cotton sack was instantly full. To us, it was pure magic—a can of corn or rice could be made many times its original size.

Pearl and I jumped for joy the day Carie finally agreed to give us a can of dry corn. It was already dark and the popcorn man was gone. We caught him and begged him to pop the corn for us. The man shook his head and said that the stove was already shut down. We begged and begged. We offered to help him.

We were thrilled when he finally agreed. I worked the cannon while Pearl pulled and pushed the bellows. The flames blazed. Pearl kept looking at the popcorn man—she didn't want the cannon to explode. About ten minutes later, the moment arrived. The man took over.

We heard the grand sound of the explosion. It felt as if we might go deaf.

That night, the popcorn tasted better than ever.

It became our passion to follow the popcorn man. We were like two fools, said Carie. Her rice jar was our target. Before long, Carie found out that we had been gradually emptying her grain storage. When the popcorn man came, Carie showed up. She called him a crook. Her opera-like voice was heard by the entire town. Carie grabbed the popcorn man by the arm and demanded that he leave.

Pearl and I were embarrassed. We each held Carie back as the man collected his things.

Carie yelled, waving her fist, "Don't you ever come back and steal from my children!"

The man hurried away, dragging his cart.

For days Pearl and I were sad. We could not forget the popcorn man. We felt guilty about ruining his business.

Chapter 6

Absalom had been working hard to convert the town's newcomer, Carpenter Chan. He was sixteen years old and originally from Canton. He limped a bit. He told Absalom that he had been beaten by his former employer. He had no job and was homeless and in debt. Absalom took him under his wing, hiring Chan to build his church in exchange for shelter and food. Absalom knew exactly the kind of church he wanted. He had a plan and he had purchased the land. It was a leveled lot on the main street near the market.

What Absalom didn't expect was Carpenter Chan's stubbornness and peculiar sense of style. Although the man was smart, he was incapable of following Absalom's design because he found it ugly. Chan had grown up building Chinese temples and was proud of his craft. His ancestors were among those who built the Forbidden City for the emperor. Carpenter Chan's speciality was Tokung, the traditional interlocking wooden structure. He was frustrated that he was not given an opportunity to use his skills. Carpenter Chan took every opportunity to convince Absalom to alter the design. He told Absalom, "The best Chinese architecture always has the Tokung style. It is a symbol of power, wealth, and nobility."

"I'd like to have none of that." Absalom was determined. "The church is a place where souls gather under God. No soul is above or under any other. Instead of power, wealth, and nobility, I'd like you to demonstrate simplicity, humbleness, and warmth." Absalom wanted his new church to follow a Western design, to be inviting instead of intimidating.

"Why won't you let me offer Jesus the best of my abilities?" Carpenter Chan was confused. "I should build him a temple instead of a house."

Nail by nail, Absalom and the carpenter fought. Carpenter Chan was polite and obedient, but the moment Absalom turned his back, he put back what he was ordered to take down.

Absalom threatened to fire Carpenter Chan. He demanded that all the windows be changed. "Make the frames narrower with pointed arches," Absalom ordered Chan and his crew. "Or I'll have you walking, all of you!"

Carpenter Chan was miserable when he eventually complied. To him, the rough stone façade was an insult to his reputation.

Absalom called the work a masterpiece, and he praised Carpenter Chan for his fine skills.

When Carpenter Chan started to work on the interior, he invited his friends, the local artists and sculptors, for ideas.

"I understand that you are masters of rendering Chinese gods," Absalom warned them instead of greeting them. "But I don't want my Entrance Jesus to look like the Kuang-yin Buddha. You are forbidden to make Jesus's expression vicious like the Chinese gate god. Do not show his teeth. As for my Worshipping Jesus by the altar, I don't want him to look like the Chinese kitchen god. Heaven forbid—do not make Jesus fat."

By the time the Jesus was presented to Absalom, he had a Buddha belly.

"No Chinese would worship a god who mirrors a bone-thin coolie," Papa advised.

Absalom was upset. He took up the scraper and carved the fat off of Jesus's belly himself.

At Sunday church, Carpenter Chan met Lilac, the egg lady. He fell in love with her at first sight. She liked him but was troubled by his limping. Knowing that she was already a converted Christian, he converted himself to please her. It made Papa happy, because he could add one more number to his book. In the meantime, Absalom began another project—to create a school. Carpenter Chan was hired to build an addition behind the church.

Papa was put in charge of the fund-raising. While Absalom was impressed by Papa's effectiveness and enthusiasm, he was irritated by his methods. Papa told the local businessmen that an investment opportunity had arrived—God would reward them with fortune and prosperity.

Under Absalom's nose, Papa inflated the numbers for the church attendance. He became bold. He signed up the walk-ins as church members and put out more food to attract beggars from neighboring villages.

"See the rug you walked on when entering this church?" Papa would open his preaching with the same sentence. "That's the rug my daughter Willow tried to steal before she was saved by God. Yes, the same God who will change your life too."

Pearl wouldn't tell me what was bothering her. NaiNai suspected that something was going on inside her family.

"Absalom is in big trouble," Papa came home and told us. "He is being investigated by the Christian headquarters in America."

"What did he do?" NaiNai asked.

"He was suspected of cheating."

"On what?" I asked.

"On his conversion numbers," Papa sighed.

We went silent. We knew that Papa was guilty.

"Maybe you should stick your head out for him," NaiNai said.

"The problem is that Absalom doesn't exactly know what I've done. He believes in my work so much that he recommended the investigators talk to me directly."

"Oh, no!" I was afraid for Papa.

"You are going to let Absalom down." NaiNai shook her head.

Under the candlelight Papa's slanting eyes narrowed into slits. He sighed and sighed.

"How could you do this to Absalom?" NaiNai wiped her tear-filled eyes.

"I only meant to help," Papa responded. "Half of the people I helped convert are for real."

"Absalom can certainly count on me for a solid member," NaiNai agreed. "Son, I want you to make it right for Absalom."

Papa went door-to-door to talk to the converts. "We must be prepared to protect Master Absalom," he urged, describing the investigation. "Act like a real Christian when questioned. Try your best to memorize the key elements, such as Jesus bore mankind's guilt down into the depths of the Jordan, and that Jesus inaugurated his public activity by stepping into the place of sinners."

Papa wouldn't let people sleep until they could respond with the correct answers. By midnight everyone was exhausted. They kept giving Papa the wrong answers.

"What did Jesus say to the crew of the ship?" Papa drilled again.

"I don't remember . . ."

"*Take me and throw me into the sea!*" Papa shouted out for them.

"What does the word *baptism* mean to Jesus?" Papa kept pounding.

"His death!" people chanted. "Jesus's own death!"

The next morning Pearl arrived.

"It didn't work," she reported. "Absalom has been fired."

"It can't be true," cried NaiNai.

Pearl burst into tears. "A new minister is on his way as Father's replacement."

Papa was shocked.

"How is your mother doing?" NaiNai was concerned.

"Mother is in distress. She told me that Father is going to lose his salary."

It took Carie a while to make us understand what had happened. Absalom had never paid much attention to his accounts. Papa had led Absalom to believe that he kept an accounting book. The trouble was that Absalom was unable to produce the book. Papa had spent all the church funds without bothering to make a detailed record. He had been taught by Absalom that as long as the money was spent doing God's work, he had the right. To help increase the conversion numbers, Papa had loaned most of the church money to families whose homes had been destroyed by floods and storms.

"Is your family going to starve without Absalom's salary?" I asked Pearl.

"I don't know," Pearl replied. "Mother has already told the servants that she might not be able to keep them."

"The town will not let its pastor and his family starve." NaiNai turned to Pearl. "Tell your mother that you have my invitation to move in and live with us."

For the next few weeks, the town of Chin-kiang united in defending Absalom. The investigator from the Christian headquarters accused Papa of being a man of corruption with a history of theft. Absalom responded by saying that God had restored Papa's soul. "Since his conversion, Mr. Yee has been a model Christian for the community." Absalom acknowledged that his work needed improvement, but he refused to admit that he had been misusing the church funds.

The new pastor arrived on a boat from America. He was a young man with red hair. He had a small head and a white face. If Absalom were a lion, this man would be a goat. He didn't want to speak to Papa, who tried to negotiate.

"God doesn't negotiate," the new pastor told Papa.

At the next Sunday service, Papa presented a petition to the new pastor. It was signed by the entire town of Chin-kiang. It requested Absalom's reinstatement or all the church members would leave.

The young pastor could hardly believe what he read. When he avoided the subject and started to preach, people got up and left. Children swarmed after the young pastor. "Absalom! Give us back Absalom!" they shouted.

The young man reboarded the same boat he came on and went back to America. He never returned.

Before the month ended, Absalom was reinstated.

A celebration was held at the church. Donations spilled from the paper box. Absalom was also asked to host the wedding between Carpenter Chan and Lilac. Within a year, a set of twins was born. Carpenter Chan and Lilac asked Papa to think up names for the boys. After discussing it with Absalom, Papa named them Double Luck David and Double Luck John.

The town of Chin-kiang was peaceful and quiet until Carpenter Chan got in trouble with a powerful warlord.

Although he was only in his early twenties, the warlord was famous along the Yangtze River. His nickname was Bumpkin Emperor. His territories included most of the canals in Jiangsu province. He had two sworn brothers, whom the locals nicknamed General Lobster and General Crab. Until now, their main enemies had been other warlords.

It happened when Bumpkin Emperor entered the town and took a fancy to Lilac. He claimed that Carpenter Chan had stolen his mistress. The two men had a fight and Bumpkin Emperor swore revenge.

Under Papa's questions, Lilac confessed the truth. She had had a one-night affair with the warlord and agreed to be his concubine before she met Carpenter Chan.

"Absalom knew my story," Lilac said to Papa. "He told me that God would forgive and protect us as long as we accepted Jesus as our savior and we did! I thought my troubles were over."

Papa comforted Lilac and Chan, telling them to place their trust in God.

Bumpkin Emperor returned the next day with his troops. He threatened to burn down the church if he was refused Lilac.

Papa was out of his wits because Absalom was not in town. Absalom was away on a preaching tour. Papa was given three days to turn over the couple.

Panicking, Papa sent a messenger to find Absalom.

Pearl and I visited Carpenter Chan and Lilac, who had hidden themselves in the back of the church. Believing that they would not survive, the couple huddled together and sobbed. Pearl had an idea when she learned that Bumpkin Emperor was extremely superstitious.

"I feel like I know this type of character from *All Men Are Brothers*," Pearl told Carpenter Chan. "Please tell me the gods he worships."

"Bumpkin Emperor worships gods and ghosts of all kinds," Carpenter Chan said. "He invites a ba-gua master to tell him what to do before engaging in battles. He burns incense and kowtows to not only Buddha, but also to the sun god, moon goddess, god of earth, god of war, god of water, god of thunder, god of wind and rain, and even the god of animals. Bumpkin Emperor believes in supernatural powers and fears the revenge of any god."

The three-day ultimatum had passed. Bumpkin Emperor arrested Lilac and Carpenter Chan and held a public rally. He was set to have Carpenter Chan beheaded.

It was the first time Pearl and I saw Bumpkin Emperor up close. He had a pair of big frog eyes, orange skin, and meatball cheeks. His head was pear-shaped. His dark-brown uniform was made of wool with lace sticking out from both shoulders. There were medals pinned on his breast. Carrying a sword, he stood in the middle of the town square. Behind him stood a squad of his soldiers.

Pearl and I walked toward Bumpkin Emperor. Pearl carried a bucket of ink. For the first time, she was without her knitted black hat. Under the bright sun her curly golden hair shone like autumn leaves.

No one paid attention to Pearl at first. All eyes were on Bumpkin Emperor. Carpenter Chan and Lilac were tied with their hands behind their backs. Bumpkin Emperor announced Carpenter Chan's beheading.

The executioner was called to choose his ax.

Lilac fell to her knees. She crawled toward her lover.

The crowd begged Bumpkin Emperor.

Papa and NaiNai prayed for God's mercy.

The soldiers drove the crowd back.

In my ear, Pearl whispered, "Now!"

Raising the bucket, she poured the black ink water over her head.

"Angry spirit!" I shouted.

Pearl pretended to be possessed by evil as she ran toward Bumpkin Emperor with ink dripping from her face.

The crowd gasped. "Angry spirits!"

"Black blood!"

Pearl landed in front of Bumpkin Emperor. She waved her arms and kicked her legs, knotting herself into a ball, and groaned as if being tortured by invisible spirits.

"What is this?" Bumpkin Emperor asked loudly. "Who are you?"

Kicking her feet, Pearl uttered a string of words no one understood.

"Speak! Who are you?" Bumpkin was visibly nervous.

NaiNai turned to Bumpkin Emperor and said, "You must have done something to offend the gods."

The warlord got down on his knees in front of Pearl. "Can I help you, whoever's spirit you are?" He tried to steady his shaky voice.

"I must speak to the one who is in charge," Pearl murmured in a husky voice, her eyes tightly shut. "I must speak to the general himself."

"I am the general," Bumpkin Emperor rose.

Pearl began to speak English.

"What, what is she rumbling about?" Bumpkin Emperor became tense. "Which god are you representing? Is she talking to me?"

"Yes." I told the warlord that I could be his translator.

"What is she saying?" Bumpkin Emperor turned to me.

"She said, 'The fire is at your door.' "

"Fire at my door? What does that mean?"

"In the name of the Holy Spirit . . ." Pearl continued.

"Holy Spirit?" Bumpkin Emperor was confused. "Mother of a mule, I don't understand!"

"Would you like me to stop?" I asked.

"Of course not," he said. "Carry on, dammit!"

"Well, she is not making sense."

"Do the best you can to make her words into sense!"

I began acting, bending down to get close to Pearl. "Yes, I heard you . . . Went out to him? All the country of Judah? Wait a minute." I turned to the warlord. "She said, 'All the people of Jerusalem are going toward the river to confess their sins . . .' "

Confused, Bumpkin Emperor cried, "Which god is this?"

I shook my head.

"A powerful God," Papa said, raising his arm to point at the sky. "Perhaps the true God."

"What is his name? Tell me, please!" Bumpkin Emperor begged.

"Angel," Pearl uttered.

"His name is Angel," I translated.

"I have never heard of such a god," Bumpkin Emperor responded. "Is he new?"

"He is ancient," Pearl continued. "He's been here since the beginning of time. Only the wise can hear him. He is mad at you."

"What . . . what does he want from me?" Bumpkin Emperor's voice grew weak.

Pearl went silent.

"The God no longer wants to speak to you," I translated. "The God is leaving."

"Please! Don't go!" Bumpkin Emperor was scared. "Ask what business he had here! If he is a foreign god, who is his patron in China?"

"I was invited by the Dowager Empress of your country," Pearl began to speak in Chinese. "I was escorted here by the Imperial Minister-in-Chief Mr. Li Hung chang . . ."

Before Pearl ended her sentence, Bumpkin Emperor fell down and kowtowed, hitting his forehead on the ground. "Your Majesty, I mean no offense! I . . . I deserve to die three thousand times! Please, forgive me!"

Again, Pearl closed her eyes.

"Please don't leave! Grant me a chance," Bumpkin Emperor begged. "Your Majesty, I am asking for a last chance!"

"Release Carpenter Chan and his lady," Pearl spoke with an imperial tone. "And leave Chin-kiang right away."

"Yes, Your Majesty, I shall depart instantly."

"Well, let us have no doubt that God sent Pearl to save you," Absalom said to Carpenter Chan and Lilac. "My daughter is no angel, but she is a good Christian."

Later, Pearl told me that she didn't like what her father said, although she was happy that the trick worked.

"I am sure your father loves you," I comforted my friend.

Pearl shook her head. "To tell you the truth, I am jealous of those whom he baptizes. He offers affection to strangers, to you, NaiNai, your papa, Carpenter Chan, Lilac, and almost everyone in the town. He will never spare affection for his own children. He is always cold with me."

"Absalom loves you, Pearl."

"I don't feel it. My mother doesn't feel his love either. Absalom shuts himself in the study so that he can be with God without any distraction!"

"Your father is proud of you, or he wouldn't say that you were a good Christian."

"Absalom cares about Chinese people so much that he's willing to risk his life for them. In the meantime, he believes that they are heathens and he is their superior. He lives to convert people. He even wants a chance with the warlords."

"Absalom wants to convert Bumpkin Emperor, General Lobster, and General Crab?" I laughed.

"Yes, and their fish wives, shrimp siblings, and snail concubines."

"That's impossible!"

"Oh, yes, God works miracles, hah, hah, hah!"

"Papa will believe whoever saves his ass."

"My father is a nut and your father is a crook."

We laughed and put our fathers out of our minds.

We walked to the outskirts of town, where someone was getting married. We joined the children who had been invited to the wedding to help inspire fertility. We were given nuts and seeds to throw at the new couple. The groom was a young peasant who was already drunk. He meant to thank the guests but instead he threw up. The bride was dressed in a bright-red embroidered costume. Her face was covered with a piece of silk. Pearl and I admired the costume and the bride's glittering hair ornament. When the band started the wedding song, we joined in.

Buddha sits on a lotus pad,
Beautiful fingers orchidlike.
Sun goes down and moon comes up,
May your life be peaceful and tranquil.

Mud walls and straw pillows,
Fruits, seeds, and many sons.
Happiness and longevity,
May you have the spring and all its fair weather.

CHAPTER 7

The Boxer Rebellion hadn't hit Chin-kiang until the first years of the new century. It had spread like a wildfire. Peasants from inland came wearing red turbans. They believed that foreigners were destroying China. It didn't occur to me that Pearl and her family were foreigners. Pearl didn't like Westerners. She had witnessed opium addicts in our town and had criticized the white folks and their opium trade. As far as she was concerned, the Boxers' fight would have nothing to do with her.

But times had changed. There had been incidents where foreign missionaries had been murdered in the northern provinces. Carie made sure that Pearl dressed like a Chinese girl and wore her black knitted cap at all times.

Pearl came to me one day and told me that Carie had been talking about their departure. "Mother said that a ship will come and it will take us all back to America."

Pearl's words devastated me. I didn't know how to respond.

She looked disturbed and nervous.

"But . . . you don't know anything about America!" I said.

"Mother said that America is a place where I would belong," Pearl said matter-of-factly. "At least I will look like everyone else. I am sick of wearing this damn black knitted cap! I'll burn it the moment I arrive in America."

"But you said that you don't know anyone in America," I insisted.

"I don't."

"Will you still go then?"

"I don't look forward to leaving, however much Mother tries to reassure me."

"To leave China is Carie's wish, not yours!" I tried to sound calm, but it was impossible. I felt like crying. "You will not be able to find a friend like me in America!"

"Perhaps not, although Mother promised that I would."

"She is tricking you." I gave a cold laugh. "You'd be a fool to believe that."

"But I can't stay if Mother decides to go."

For the next few weeks the departure became the only thing we talked about. But the more we talked about it, the deeper our sense of doom became. We ran up and down the hills and laughed, pretending that it was not going to happen. But time and time again we were reminded. For example, Wang Ah-ma became depressed because Carie told her to prepare to go her own way. The pregnant Lilac and Carpenter Chan came to visit Papa and NaiNai to update them on the murder cases involving foreign missionaries.

Pearl and I learned that more people had joined the Boxers. The swelling numbers began to demand that the Imperial government throw out foreigners and shut down their businesses in China forever. When they didn't receive the government's response, they began to mob foreign banks and buildings and destroy the national railways. Our neighboring Christian churches were disrupted. Foreign missionaries were taken from their homes and publicly tortured. When the news reached us, Pearl and I realized that our days together were numbered.

Pearl began to talk more about her "real home" in America, while I became cynical and irritable.

"Real home?" I sneered. "I'll bet that you won't even know where your front door is." I asked Pearl if she knew the feng shui of her American home and was pleased that she had no answer.

"Your house could be facing the wrong direction. Bad luck will stick to you forever!"

"What if I tell you that I don't give a damn if my American home has the wrong feng shui?" She picked up a rock and threw it into the valley. "It'll be my mother's home, not mine!"

"But you will be living in it. You will be alone and miserable because you know better!"

"I will have the company of my cousins!" she countered.

I laughed and said that her cousins might know her name, but they would have no idea who she was and what she liked. "They won't even care. To them you'll be a total stranger!"

"Stop, Willow, please," she begged.

We sat in silence and tried not to weep.

The news regarding the Boxers got worse. They were seen in Soochow, which was less than a hundred miles from Chin-kiang. Carie tried to convince Absalom to temporarily relocate. Absalom wouldn't consider it.

"I won't abandon God's work" was Absalom's answer.

Carie threatened to leave on her own and said that she would take Pearl and Grace with her.

"Mother told me that I must learn to trust in God and accept my destiny," Pearl said. We held each other's hands and sat on top of the hill. We watched the sun set without speaking another word.

It felt like living in a bad dream. I imagined Pearl's American house. According to Pearl, it was built by her grandfather. Pearl's description of the house was word for word from Carie. "It is large and white with its pillared double portico set in a beautiful landscape," she told me. "Behind the house are rich green plains and mountains."

I also imagined Pearl's relatives, who all had milk-white faces. I imagined them receiving her warmly. They would hug her as if they knew her. They would say, "How are you, my darling? It's been so long . . ." Pearl would be surrounded with clean sheets and soft pillows. She would be served plenty of food, but not the kind that she liked. No more Chinese food, of course. No more Chinese faces. No more

Mandarin, or stories, or Peking operas. No more "Jasmine, Sweet Jasmine."

"I suppose I'll get used to it." Pearl gave out a long, deep sigh.

She would be forced to adapt. She had no other option. She would forget China and me.

"We might not recognize each other if we meet again," Pearl teased.

It was not funny, but I played along. "We probably wouldn't even remember each other's names."

"I might lose my Chinese."

"You will."

"Perhaps not," she said. "I'll try my best not to lose my Chinese."

"Maybe you'll want to. What's the use of Chinese in America? Who would you speak Chinese to? Grace? She's too young. You two don't play together. Maybe you will when you get to America. You won't have a choice."

She turned her head and stared at me, her blue eyes big and clear. Tears began to well up.

"You'll be drinking milk and eating cheese." I tried to cheer her up.

"And I'll turn into a big fat farmwife," she responded. "My belly will be the size of a Chinese winter melon, with breasts like round squashes."

We laughed.

"I could be married, you know," I said. "NaiNai has already been approached by matchmakers. I could end up marrying an old, greasy rich man and be his concubine. He could be a monster and beat me every night."

"Wouldn't that be awful?" She looked at me seriously.

"Awful? What would you care? You will be gone by then."

Pearl's hands reached out for me. "I'll pray for you, Willow."

I pushed her away. "You know I have a problem with that. You haven't been able to prove to me that your God exists!"

"Then pretend that he does!" Pearl's tears fell. "I need you to believe in him."

We decided to stop talking about the departure. We decided to celebrate our time together instead of wallowing in sadness. We went to see a troupe on wheels called the Great Shadow Art Show. It featured the Drunkard Monkey King and the Female Generals of the Yang Family. We had a wonderful time. Pearl was fascinated by the handmade shadow figures. The figures were created from scraped and sculpted cattle hides. The troupe master was from mid-China. He invited Pearl and me backstage, where he demonstrated how the figures worked. The actors hid under a large curtain, each holding a character with four bamboo sticks. The figures were able to tap their feet, dance to the rhythm, and fight a martial art battle while the owner sang in a high-pitched voice our favorite Wan-Wan tune.

By early fall a children's game was becoming popular. It was called Boxers and Foreigners. It was played by the rules of traditional hide-and-seek. The boys wouldn't let Pearl and me join because we were girls. All day long Pearl and I sat on top of the hill sucking milkweeds. We watched the boys with envy. One morning Pearl came to me wearing an outfit of Western clothes she had borrowed from the British ambassador. It was a camel-colored jacket with copper buttons in the front and an open neck. The sleeves were wide at the elbow and tight on the wrists. The pants were made of brown wool. "It is their daughter's horse-riding pants," Pearl explained.

When I asked why she had dressed up, Pearl replied, "We shall play our own game of Boxers and Foreigners." She showed me a red-colored scarf. "This is your costume. Tie it around your forehead. You'll be the Boxer and I'll be the foreigner."

To make herself look more the part, she took off her black knitted hat and let her waist-long hair fall freely.

I became excited. I wrapped the red scarf around my forehead like a turban.

With wood sticks as our swords, we charged down the hill. The boys were stunned by Pearl's appearance.

"A real foreign devil!" they cried.

Soon children begged to join us. Pearl became the leader of the foreign troops, while I was the chief of the Boxers.

We threw rocks, ran around the hills, and hid in the bushes. In the afternoon, my group climbed onto the roofs of houses while Pearl led a door-to-door search for us. We roamed through the streets until it was dark.

When it was time to round up the Boxers, my group let Pearl's people tie our hands behind our backs. My group lined up to be executed. Pearl offered each of us an imaginary cup of wine, which we drank before reciting our last wish. When the shots were fired, we fell to the ground. We remained dead until Pearl announced that it was time to round up the foreigners.

My group chased until Pearl and her people were captured. We tied the foreigners together like a string of crabs and paraded them through the streets. People were invited to watch the execution. Pearl had great fun shouting in English. The villagers were shocked at first, then they applauded and laughed with us.

CHAPTER 8

At Sunday service Absalom announced his family's departure. "God will prevail" were his farewell words to the crowd. He promised to return as soon as he settled his family in Shanghai.

"Monkeys will scatter when the tree falls," Papa said. He was worried.

Led by Absalom, the converts packed the church's valuables and hid them within their own homes. Carie's piano was a big problem. There was no way to hide it. Papa volunteered to go to Bumpkin Emperor and his sworn brothers for help. The warlords were enemies of the Boxers.

The first thing Papa said to Bumpkin Emperor was "A smart rabbit digs three holes for security. If I were you, I wouldn't miss this opportunity to make friends with the foreign god." Papa went on to tell how the Western fleets had recently destroyed the Chinese Imperial Navy.

Bumpkin Emperor took Carie's piano and hid it in his concubine's mansion.

Carie was relieved. She thanked Papa. For the last time, she trimmed her roses and cleaned her yard. Watering each of her plants, she broke down. She sat on the dirt and wept.

Pearl and I exchanged farewell souvenirs. I gave her a pink silk fan painted with flowers. Pearl gave me a hairpin with a silver phoenix. She would be leaving in ten days, perhaps sooner.

I shut my eyes and told myself to go to sleep that night. But my eyes stayed open. I tossed until dawn. NaiNai told me to forget about Pearl and to spend time with other girls in town. Over the next few days I tried, but without much luck. People didn't care to be my friend. Since I'd begun to attend the church school, I had changed. I didn't like the town girls, whom I considered narrow-minded and shallow. I couldn't help but compare them with Pearl, who was kind, curious, and knowledgeable. The town girls fought over food and territory, and they fought among themselves. They could be best friends and worst enemies and best friends again all in one day. They often singled someone out to be the enemy of the moment. Then they attacked her by embarrassing her. I avoided them because I knew that Papa and NaiNai's past would be used to torment me.

Unlike peasant daughters, who were too burdened and exhausted to have time to themselves, the Chin-kiang town girls had time on their hands. Many of their parents were shop owners and merchants. They loved to pretend to be big-city girls. But they knew very little about the big cities, like Shanghai, where Carie once lived before Pearl was born. The Chin-kiang girls looked down on peasants. They made fun of their uncivilized habits and forgot that they were not much different.

I had long accepted the reality that I was considered an odd character among the town girls. Catfighting didn't suit me. Since I had become Pearl's friend, I had been the target of these girls. The fact that Pearl and I were so close drove them mad. They watched us with jealousy and envy. Now I was having trouble. I couldn't break into the town girls' social circle. I feared that people would say I had been abandoned.

I played cards with the town girls one afternoon. My heart ached for Pearl. She would be here only a few more days and I wanted to be with her. I forced myself to concentrate on the cards. One girl cheated and I caught her. She argued and denied everything. She didn't mean aggression, nor did she say anything to provoke my anger, but I attacked her. I stopped the game and called the girl a liar. Step-by-step I exposed her tricks. The cards flew from my hands. The girl was embarrassed and exploded. No one was able to break us apart until Pearl arrived.

Pearl knew it was not my character to fight with others. She knew that I was troubled by her departure. She carefully wiped the blood off my forehead with her handkerchief. The spot on my left cheek where my opponent had scratched me with her fingernails swelled. Looking at me with her gentle blue eyes, Pearl sighed.

"I don't need you here," I said.

"Does it hurt?" she asked.

"No."

"It's not like we won't see each other forever," she said in a soft voice.

"But when? When will you come back?" I cried out.

She was unable to answer.

It was a clear day when Pearl's family boarded a steamboat that came from the upper Yangtze River. The townspeople filled the pier to see them off. Papa, NaiNai, Carpenter Chan, Lilac, and their twins, Double Luck David and Double Luck John, and a newborn son were among the crowd. Absalom had recently baptized the boys and named the newborn Triple Luck Solomon.

Absalom made Carpenter Chan promise to continue his work on the second floor of the new school until the job was finished. Reciting from the Bible, Absalom encouraged him, "*It will be the offer of a sacrifice made by fire which ye shall offer onto the Lord.*"

Carpenter Chan nodded and gave his word.

Wang Ah-ma begged Carie to take her with them.

"My husband's mind is set," Carie told her tearfully. "You must go your own way. We no longer have the money to keep you."

"I'll work for free!" Wang Ah-ma stuffed her mouth with the corner of her blouse to avoid crying aloud. "I'll cost you no money. I have no one else, no place to go. You and the children are my family."

The actors from the Wan-Wan Tunes opera troupe came. Many of them, including the nasty turtle-faced lady, had become Christians to Absalom's credit. "Actors travel," Absalom once told Papa. "They will be perfect to spread the Gospel."

The actors wished Pearl's family a safe journey and sang their new aria, adapted from the Bible.

> *Surely goodness and mercy*
> *Shall follow you all the days of your life,*
> *And here we shall remain your faithful servants*
> *We shall dwell in the house of the Lord forever.*

Pearl promised to return, but she and I both knew that it was wishful thinking. The Boxers were moving toward the coast and might reach Shanghai soon. America would be the place where Carie and her family would eventually end up.

Pearl and I struggled to find pleasant farewell words, but it was impossible.

We bade good-bye and embraced silently.

The steamboat pulled away from the pier, creating big ripples in the water.

I waved as my tears ran.

The ripples went away. The water became calm again.

I stood on the empty pier and a Tang dynasty poem Pearl used to recite came to mind.

> *My friend left the Mansion of Crane for the South where fish would bite*
> *Hazelike willow down drift, petals scattered in full flight*
> *Her boat disappears where the waves meet the great river*
> *The bright moon is over the sky's dome*
>
> *Wild geese fly by mountains and pavilions ancient*
> *Have you achieved the smile after red sorghum wine sweet*
> *Wear the blossoming chrysanthemums full in my hair*
> *Draw the bamboo curtains over the windows and dream for the night*

Part Two

CHAPTER 9

The day I was engaged to be married, I was fourteen. I had no say in the decision. The town's matchmaker told Papa, "The only medicine that will help your mother regain her health will be news of Willow's marriage."

I wanted to reach Pearl desperately, but our lives had taken separate paths. Pearl had enrolled in a missionary middle school in Shanghai. Her life was a world away from mine.

"Shanghai is like a foreign country," Pearl wrote. "The international military forces maintain peace here. My father is waiting for things to calm down in the countryside so that he can return to Chin-kiang. At this moment, he is translating the New Testament. At night, he reads out loud from the original Greek text and Pauline theology. He also chants intonations of Chinese idioms. Mother has fallen ill. She misses her garden in Chin-kiang."

Although I wrote back, I was too ashamed to tell my friend that I would soon be married to a man who was twice my age. I felt helpless and close to despair. Pearl's letters showed me that there were other possibilities in life, if only I could escape. Now I understood why I loved *The Butterfly Lovers*. The opera allowed my imagination to take flight. In my daydreams, I escaped the life I was living to live the life of a heroine.

The more dowry that arrived from my future husband, the worse I felt. It didn't seem to occur to Papa and NaiNai that I deserved better. Papa was angry when I begged to go to school in Shanghai. NaiNai told me that for a small-town girl, "the more she fancies the outside world, the worse her fate will be."

*　　*　　*

I had written to tell Pearl that her bungalow home had been set on fire when the Boxers raided the town. To save the church, Papa had replaced the statue of Jesus Christ with the sitting Buddha. Papa told the Boxers that he was a Buddhist and that the church was his temple. To strengthen his lie, Papa dressed like a monk. The converts chanted the Buddhist sutras as the Boxers inspected the property. It was not hard because all the converts were former Buddhists.

Papa begged Bumpkin Emperor to help protect the church. "The foreign god will return the favor," he promised. "God will save a seat for you in heaven. You will be reunited with all your dead family members and have an extravagant banquet."

Papa's tricks didn't last. Once the Boxers discovered that the "monks" were Christian converts, they were slaughtered. A member of the Wan-Wan Tunes opera was dragged out in the middle of their performance and killed in front of Papa's eyes.

Carpenter Chan and Lilac were on the Boxers' list to be beheaded. They barely escaped.

Papa was the last convert to flee the town. On the morning of the Chinese New Year, the Boxers caught him. A public execution was to be held in the town square.

Papa begged the Boxers to let him live. He admitted that he was a fool.

The Boxers laughed and said they needed to show the public that the Christian God was a hoax. "If your God is real, call him, because we are going to hang you!"

Papa fell upon his knees and hailed, "Absalom!"

Although Papa didn't believe in God, he believed in Absalom. When a voice answered Papa's call, everyone was stunned. The voice came from the riverbank. A tall figure jumped off a boat. It was Absalom! His hands were above his head waving a piece of paper. Behind him were Bumpkin Emperor, General Lobster, and General Crab.

"Old Teacher!" the converts screamed.

The Boxers carried on. They slipped the noose around Papa's neck.

"Stop the execution!" Absalom halted in front of the Boxers. "Here is the copy of Her Majesty Dowager Empress's decree! Her Majesty has signed a peace treaty with the foreign troops! The eighth item in the treaty says, *Foreign missionaries and their converts are to be protected.*"

Five more years would pass before Pearl and I would see each other again. By then I was nineteen and Pearl was seventeen. Our reunion happened soon after our ruler, Dowager Empress Tsu Hsi, died. It was said that she had exhausted herself putting out the wildfire that was the Boxer Rebellion. The new emperor she appointed was only three years old. The nation went into a long period of mourning for the Dowager Empress. Nothing had changed locally, although the country was said to have become a headless dragon.

I went to the pier to greet Pearl and Carie the day they returned to Chin-kiang. I was nervous because my appearance had changed. My dress and hairstyle indicated that I was a married woman. Instead of a braid, I wore a bun in the back of my head. In letters, I had avoided mentioning my married life to Pearl. What was there to say? The moment I entered my husband's home, I found out that he was an opium addict. The matchmaker had lied. His fortune had been squandered long ago. The family was a fabulously embroidered evening gown chewed by moths. He was in so much debt that the servants had fled. My husband had borrowed money to pay for my dowry. The marriage was my mother-in-law's idea. It was "one stone for two birds." Her son would get a concubine and she would get an unpaid servant.

My existence was about serving my husband, his mother, and his elder wives and their children. I cleaned beds, emptied chamber pots, washed sheets, and swept the gardens. I had to sneak out to see Pearl and Carie. My husband would never have given me permission had I asked.

Pearl had grown into a stunning beauty. She was tall and slender and dressed in Western clothes. She carried the air of a free spirit. Her smile was full of sunshine.

"Willow, my friend, look at you!" she called from a hundred yards away with arms wide open. "What a pretty lady you have become!"

"Welcome home" was all I could utter.

Laughing radiantly, Pearl hugged me. "Oh, Willow, I missed you so much!"

Papa, Carpenter Chan, and others came. We helped carry the luggage to Absalom's newly rented house. It was a former merchant's home located on the top of the hill.

"What a beautiful house!" Pearl marveled. "Father, how have you allowed us such luxury?"

"It is a haunted house," Absalom explained. "No locals will take it. The rent is very cheap. I took advantage of the opportunity since I don't believe in Chinese ghosts."

As soon as Pearl settled in, we took off to climb the hills. Pearl's younger sister, Grace, wanted to join us, but Pearl and I flew away together. Pearl told me that Shanghai was very flat and that she had missed the mountains and hills. She had been itching to go on a hike. She spoke about ideas I had never heard of. She described a world I could only imagine. Her Mandarin vocabulary was more sophisticated. She told me that she was getting ready for college in America. "After that, I will travel the world!"

I didn't have much to share, so I told her how we had survived the Boxers. In the middle of my story, I stopped.

"What's wrong?" Pearl asked.

"Nothing."

"Willow," she called gently.

I told myself to smile and to turn away from dark thoughts. But my tears betrayed me.

"Is it your marriage?" she asked, her hand reaching for mine.

My marriage was not uncommon for a Chinese girl, but it was too much for Pearl.

I told Pearl that on my husband's good days he smoked and gambled; on his bad days, he would take out his anger on me. He would beat me and sometimes rape me. I had to be obedient toward my mother-in-law. As far as she was concerned, it was my fault that the family was going down the drain.

"This is slavery!" Pearl concluded, her features twisting into an expression of anger.

Pearl told me that she had worked with girls in Shanghai who had been forced into abusive marriages or prostitution. "You don't have to hide your broken arm inside your sleeve anymore, Willow," she said.

My husband got himself a new concubine. It surprised me because I knew he didn't have any money. He ignored me when I questioned him. Tradition gave a man the right to dispose of his wife at will. To protest, every morning I went and stood by the village well that everyone shared. I shouted out the terrible things his family had done to me. But I received no sympathy. The village elder criticized me and said that I should commit suicide.

Standing up for myself only gave me a bad reputation. Papa considered me selfish, while NaiNai called me foolish. I didn't feel completely deserted because I had Pearl's support. I went to Carie and offered to help with the school and with setting up the new clinic. Besides teaching me English, Carie trained me and other girls to become nurses.

Pearl and I continued to spend time together, but our friendship was no longer the same. The more she looked forward to college in America, the less we could say to each other. She was sensitive and knew how I felt about my own future.

I didn't believe she would return to China after college. She seemed less sure now too. After all, it had been Carie's long-held wish to return to America.

Absalom was not interested in Pearl's departure, nor was he sad that she might never return. Absalom was more excited about his upcoming preaching tour farther inland.

Papa was a different person when he was with Absalom. He respected and worshipped him.

"You can tell just from Absalom's face that he is no ordinary human being," Papa told the Sunday crowd. "Absalom experiences a radiant joy when he lifts his hand to bless you. You can feel that God is with him."

Pearl again admitted that she was jealous of the Chinese converts who received Absalom's affection. It was one of the reasons she wanted to go away. She told me that she was even unhappy about the donkey Papa had bought for Absalom. "The animal has enabled Father to take farther and longer trips."

"But your father is happy," Papa told Pearl.

Although Pearl agreed, she said, "Sometimes I don't think he is my father. He will tolerate others interrupting his sermon with a question, but never me."

"Will you consider marriage?" I asked Pearl. "And if so, when?"

She laughed. "I'll see what happens when I get to America."

Pearl said that she had already started missing China. "I may have been saying that America is my real home, but I doubt that it is true."

Pearl knew that revealing her thoughts would disturb Carie, so she kept them to herself. "I never intended to defy my ancestors or Western culture," she told me. "It is just that China is what I know."

Carie had been in a good mood although she had been ill. She was happy to be able to grow roses and have a garden again. She said that with Pearl gone she would have more time to sit in the garden and read her favorite Western novels. Carie didn't want Pearl to know that she dreaded her departure.

Pearl was not fooled by her mother's cheerfulness. She knew that her mother wept behind her back. Pearl worried that Carie might need her when she was in America.

I assured Pearl that I would take care of her mother and would keep her informed about Carie's health.

Chapter 10

October 23, 1913

Dear Pearl,

How happy I am to learn that you have been well and are in good health. Your mother is weak although, as always, she shows good spirits. She finally listened to me and has quit teaching. I took over her classes. Can you believe it? I also wanted to tell you that I have begun your Charles Dickens books.

I am not sure if your mother told you what happened to Absalom. He went too far inland and got stoned by mobs again. Thank the Lord he is fine. Two of your father's Chinese disciples died, I'm sorry to report. Papa has been running the church for Absalom. He is much improved at preaching. Absalom is so pleased with him that he has started to take even longer preaching tours, although his absence makes your mother unhappy.

I also have this sad news to share: NaiNai passed away last month. Through Absalom's efforts she finally accepted the conversion. Papa insisted on waiting for Absalom to conduct the burial ceremony. Papa believed that God would favor Absalom's wishes regarding NaiNai's next life. Papa didn't want to take any chances. We all thought it was impossible because Absalom was so far away. Only a few months ago, Absalom had refused to return even when Carie called him about her own worsening condition, so we had little hope.

Well, Absalom showed up. He rode the donkey all day and night. The animal collapsed! NaiNai is so fortunate, because her journey to Heaven was blessed by Absalom. To a Chinese person, a good death is more important than a good birth.

Carie lives alone now after she sent your sister to Shanghai for schooling. Absalom resumed his tour the day after NaiNai's burial. He wouldn't stay for Carie. Of course, this is nothing new to you.

Papa has achieved several new conversions. These came from some of the people he invited to NaiNai's burial. They liked Absalom better than their head monk at the Buddhist temple. There is trouble though. One of the men has more than one wife, and the other is an alcoholic. Absalom has disqualified them before, but Papa faked the papers. Will Papa never learn? He gets carried away in his desire to please Absalom.

March 7, 1914

Dear Pearl,

Your mother shared your letter with me. Congratulations on your new popularity. In just one year you've gone from being unable to make friends to being Captain of the class. I'd also like to congratulate you on winning the highest honor in the writing competition. It seems that you have made good use of your Chinese background. By the way, do people in the West know Confucius?

Your mother may have already told you what happened to me. I was a few months pregnant when I walked out on my husband. I felt terrible carrying his seed. I thought about taking the Chinese herb medicine to abort the fetus. My mother died taking that herb and you can imagine how scared I was.

But about three weeks ago I began to bleed. I went to your mother for help. Before I developed enough courage to tell her the truth, she figured it out. The blood wouldn't stop. She knew that I must be miscarrying. She said that I could have died if I hadn't come to her. All I could do was cry. She took me to the British Embassy doctor. I was unconscious when the doctor finished. I am fine today and that is the good news. The bad news is that I might not be able to have children in the future. This has made me sad beyond words.

I have been taking piano lessons from Carie. She was right that music could help me heal. It brings me closer to understanding God. I have wanted to learn piano ever since we were children. It's truly a dream come true for me.

Carie has put me in charge of the elementary students. Did she tell you that our church school has expanded? We will soon have a middle school. Instead of three classes, we now have five. The school has become so popular that some locals have even signed up their daughters. You must remember how difficult it used to be to get peasant families to support their children's education. This year, we had to deny a number of applicants due to lack of space. Papa addressed the problem to the governor of Jiangsu, who in turn promised a parcel of land to expand the school. Carpenter Chan will be the chief builder.

December 2, 1915

Dear Pearl,

You won't believe this: I am writing you from Shanghai. This is what happened: My husband abducted me. As far as he was concerned, I was still his property. He didn't tell me that he had sold me. Remember, I had wondered where he got his money to buy a new concubine?

Anyway, I ran away and hid in the church. My husband and his hired men chased me. They beat up Papa when he refused to tell them where I was hiding. Eventually, they found out. They broke into the church at night and took me. It was Carie who sent a message to Absalom. Without delay, Absalom appealed to the governor. He said that my abduction was a violation of the treaty law. The next day the governor ordered my husband to either free me or be arrested and beheaded!

I didn't feel safe, because I suspected that my husband would look for another way to kidnap me. Papa saw suspicious men hanging around our house. Carie thought that it would be a good idea for me to leave Chinkiang for a while. She made introductions for me at the Christian School for Women in Shanghai. I was offered a scholarship. All I can say is that I am truly blessed by God.

March 24, 1916

Dear Pearl,

Who would believe that the "Paris of the East" is built on sand? The city's old name even says it. "Shang-hai-tan," meaning a sandbank at the *mouth of our great Yangtze River. Emperor Guangxu considered it next to worthless, I've been told. His imperial opinion must have lessened the sting when he was forced to give it up to foreigners after losing the Second Opium War. What a lot the English, French, and Germans have done with that sandbank, my new home!*

I shouldn't be singing about Shanghai as if you knew nothing about it. I well know that you once lived here. In fact, I often picture you here, imagine where you may have gone, what places you liked best. But forgive me, I can't help but share my feelings with you because I have no one else.

The Christian school is perfect for me. I have been taking as many classes as I can. The teachers have all been very helpful, sometimes even staying after class to answer my many questions. I never knew that there were so many books, so much to learn.

The students are nice, too. At first I was shy and awkward around them. I felt like such a country bumpkin. I didn't even know that the Manchu dynasty had been overthrown! So many other things! But isn't it wonderful that we no longer have an emperor, that China will soon become a republic!

My first weeks at the school now seem like a lifetime away. I feel more at home now and have begun to make some friends. Not like you, of course. But there are some brilliant people here and there is an electricity in the air. The most interesting people are the artists, writers, journalists, and musicians. They form a loose group that gathers at certain bars and restaurants in the city, talking and drinking and arguing for hours on end. I seem to be falling in with these people more and more. I find it exhilarating, so different from the life we knew together in Chin-kiang.

Dr. Sun Yat-sen is among us. He has been single-handedly leading the New Republicans to change China. He is a Christian and a Cantonese by origin. Before he became a revolutionary, he was a physician. He was educated in the West and studied political science. He went to Japan to study how the Mingji Reform has changed the country. In 1911, Dr. Sun returned to China and succeeded in stirring up a military uprising.

Pearl, as you can tell, my universe is expanding at the speed of light. If it wasn't something I had promised Carie, I would have skipped Sunday church. My stomach is full, but my mind is hungry.

I miss your mother, and I'll forever be in her debt. Two days ago I went to visit Grace to deliver your mother's package. Your sister is turning into a fine young lady. She is sweet, but a little shy compared to you. Oh, how I wish you were here with me.

September 2, 1916

Dear Pearl,

It's been six months since I last wrote you. Things have kept speeding up. I have been involved with the National Party of China. Most of our members are followers of Dr. Sun Yat-sen. Although I'll always have faith in God, I find myself open to other ideas. I must now leave for a meeting and will continue to write when I return.

October 27, 1916

This letter is taking too long. My life is in fabulous chaos. I don't know day from night anymore. China is undergoing a political transformation.

December 13, 1916

Pearl, I must share with you my sorrow, China's sorrow: Dr. Sun Yat-sen has been diagnosed with cancer. He is not expected to live. The man who will succeed him is Chiang Kai-shek. We are not sure if he is trustworthy. His record shows that he has been an opportunist. Unfortunately, there is no other candidate equal to him in military experience and connections. He has been the Commander-in-Chief of China and claims himself a disciple of Dr. Sun. The fact is that he is the only man who can control the warlords and who is committed to Dr. Sun's cause.

January 28, 1917

Dear Pearl,

I must inform you about Carie's condition. I am sure she has been hiding the truth from you. I visited her last month. It was lovely to be back in

Chin-kiang, to see all the familiar faces. But I was taken aback when I called on your mother. She could no longer get out of bed. Apparently, her health took a turn for the worse when she went back to work at the school soon after I left for Shanghai. She told me she didn't want you to return to China to help care for her. She worries about you constantly. Are you really planning to return?

Before I came back to Shanghai I accompanied Carie to the Deng Family Village, where she purchased a burial plot for herself. I have no idea why she picked that place. We didn't speak of her reasons. I only sensed that she is so deeply disappointed in Absalom that she doesn't care to be with him in death. But the place is beautiful and serene although remote. It broke my heart that she is quietly doing this. Am I betraying Carie by sharing this information with you? Carie can't stand the thought that she might not be there to receive you when you return.

April 15, 1917

Dearest Pearl,
How wonderful it is to learn that YOU ARE ENGAGED, and that you are on your way back! My good God! I was deeply surprised to learn this momentous news, the more so because I haven't heard a word from you for so long. Of course you have my blessing. In your letter to Carie you said that "the decision to register for the marriage" was for the "convenience of traveling." But do I misunderstand something? Should "convenience" be the reason for marriage? Forgive me for being overly cautious—my own marriage almost ruined my life. But I suspect that your mother's condition only gave you an additional reason to hurry the happy plans for your marriage.

I am grateful to Carie for sharing your letters and photos. I understood immediately what brought you and Mr. Lossing Buck together. A mutual love of China, for one. How lucky to find someone with a lifelong interest in China in America. And of course you were impressed with Lossing. A Cornell degree, his professorship at Nanking University, and his commitment to helping the Chinese peasants. His agricultural expertise will be greatly appreciated here. He certainly is handsome. You two make a beautiful couple! What a wonderful idea to have the wedding ceremony in Chin-kiang.

I feel that you ought to learn your mother's feelings. Although she wishes that you were with her, she doesn't want you to follow in her footsteps. She prefers that you make your life in America. I certainly don't share those feelings, but I thought that you should know.

Another letter of yours arrived today. I understand that you and Lossing have applied as a couple to the Presbyterian Board of Foreign Missions, and that Lossing was granted the appointment to China as an agricultural missionary. Forgive me for being selfishly joyful, but this is more wonderful news. I can't wait to see you again.

I have been thinking about returning to Chin-kiang. Life in Shanghai has been exciting, but I feel like a lotus pad floating on the surface—rootless. Every day I speak about helping my country, but in truth I have achieved little of significance. I have been working menial jobs just to cover living expenses. My days are spent discussing politics and shouting for reform. The Republican Party provides a forum for exhibiting one's debating talent. It is best suited for those who love the sound of their own voices.

I fear I am turning into a teahouse revolutionary. Increasingly, I am aware of how different I am from my comrades. They have been scholars and students all their lives. I have learned much in the last two years, but at heart I am still a girl from the small town of Chin-kiang. I have lived outside the world of books. I have worked, sometimes only to put food in my stomach. It has made me impatient with idealists and dreamers, however well intentioned. Many of my comrades can't be prevented from rushing to their own destruction. How can they save their country when they themselves are lost?

You have written to suggest that I "meet people where they are." I am trying. I have always envied your ability to find healing in people's very presence. You see humanity and kindness in all people. I see the same thing only rarely. Your mother is an example.

You are a different creature than your parents. I understood when you said that you "live in many mansions." I am trying to bring down the walls of my own culture. Being a Chinese woman, I am prone to certain sentiments. I try not to be as sour as our famous Chin-kiang brown vinegar. I love my country, so much so that I hate her for not being all I want her to be.

I am thinking about establishing a local newspaper when I return to Chin-kiang. I am counting on your contributions.

Love,
Willow

The Nanking railroad station had stood as a witness to wars and sorrow. Built in 1894, it had gone through destruction and restoration several times. The station had a small waiting room and a ticket booth.

Carie wasn't really healthy enough to travel, but she wanted to be there when Pearl got off the train. The prospect of hosting her daughter's wedding had given her new energy.

The manager of the train station was a Christian. He invited Carie to rest inside his little ticket booth. "Although it is March, madame, the cold air outside might make you sick."

Carie didn't want to go inside until the man told her that the train was going to be late.

We waited. After two and a half hours, we heard the sound of the approaching train. Excited, I ran outside.

The old steam engine puffed smoke and made terrifying sounds. My heart raced in anticipation. It had been four years since Pearl and I had last seen each other. I knew that I was not the same person she had left behind. I wore a fashionable navy blue jacket with a low collar and a matching skirt. I had on a pair of black leather boots.

The train came to a stop. Passengers started to come out. I spotted my friend instantly, although something felt amiss. It had never occurred to me before that Pearl was a foreigner. She stood out among the Chinese crowd. She was accompanied by Lossing Buck, who was tall and brown-haired. I watched Pearl search the crowd, and her eyes stopped on me.

"Willow, is that you?" Pearl cried. "I can barely recognize you, a fashionable Shanghai lady!"

"Pearl!" I embraced her. "This *is* you—I'm not dreaming!"

Pearl turned around and introduced Lossing Buck.

We shook hands, but my eyes wouldn't leave Pearl. Her blue jacket and tight skirt made her look like a model in a Western magazine. The design of her clothes showed that she was proud of her full figure. I remembered that she used to feel awkward about her developing breasts.

Lossing was about Pearl's age, twenty-six years old. He had a long face with a big square jaw. He had a thin-lipped mouth and a high nose. His large eyes were deep set and brown. He was friendly and apologized that he didn't speak Chinese.

"Where is Mother?" Pearl asked.

"She is in the ticket booth waiting for—" Before I finished the sentence, I saw Pearl's smile freeze as her eyes looked past me. Shock flooded her face. I turned and saw that Carie had come outside of the booth.

Later on Pearl told me how crushed she felt the moment she saw her mother. I should have warned her that Carie had shrunk to the size of a child.

Carie had powdered her face and rouged her cheeks and lips. But it didn't help. She looked gravely ill and ghostly. Her missing side teeth made her cheeks look hollow, as if she were permanently inhaling. Her skin was dry and waxy. She insisted on painting her eyebrows herself. They were visibly uneven. The right eyebrow was higher than the left.

"Mother!" Pearl cried, throwing herself at Carie.

Smiling, Carie addressed her daughter as her tears ran. "God is good, my daughter."

Carie stood straight, as if her illness was gone. "Let's go," she said. "Your father is waiting in Chin-kiang." She told Pearl and Lossing that she had already made all the arrangements for their wedding.

On the train back to Chin-kiang, Carie fell asleep on Lossing's shoulder. I sat with Pearl across the aisle and insisted that she share the story of her romance. She had met Lossing on a ship. She told me Lossing had been on a Chinese-language tour, and Pearl was returning to China from America via Europe. During the voyage, they had several weeks to become acquainted.

"How did he court you?" I asked.

"With his China studies," she said, laughing. "Lossing's academic work outlines what he plans to do in China. The title of his degree thesis is *Chinese Farm Economy and Land Utilization in China*. Lossing's plan is to live in China and conduct experiments that will help the peasants."

It was easy for me to imagine how my friend had been swept off her feet.

"When Lossing told me that Chinese peasants would be freed from their backbreaking labor if his methods succeed, I fell in love with him. Lossing was fascinated by my life growing up in China. When he realized I spoke so many Chinese dialects, he proposed right away."

"When did you say yes?" I asked.

"Just after I found out that Lossing's Chinese would never get him anywhere. He is tone-deaf. How can you be tone-deaf and learn Chinese?"

"So he needs you."

"I need him, too. I haven't been able to fall in love with any man in America, to tell you the truth." Pearl said that she had made efforts to date, but she had felt like a foreigner in America. "I spoke English, but I didn't understand the culture. I felt out of place and confused. What we would consider rude in China, Americans consider attractive. My relatives thought that I was strange and I thought that they were strange. On the surface, I got along with everybody, but inside I was lonely. For the entire four years I felt that way. I was afraid that I might never like a man enough to marry him. In the meantime, my Chinese mind told me that I'd better hurry or I'd end up an old maid."

"Lossing's timing is perfect," I commented.

"Yes, China brought us together. God has answered my prayers. Lossing and I couldn't be more blessed!"

For Pearl's sake, I hoped that she was right.

I sensed that Pearl had given up America to come back and care for her mother. I asked if it was the truth.

She admitted that Carie was an important reason why she returned. "I love America, but not enough to stay," she said.

"You can go back to America anytime you want, can't you?"

"That's true. But Lossing is like Absalom. He is determined to die in China." She laughed. Her eyes were radiant with cloudless pleasure.

The first time I witnessed Pearl and Lossing's differences was at their wedding. Pearl was wearing a Western wedding gown, while Lossing wore a dark suit. Pearl held a bouquet of flowers picked that morning from Carie's garden. As Pearl was led to the church, the town's children sang American songs Carie had taught them. Afterward they sang the Chinese wedding song, which delighted Pearl because she used to sing the song as a child.

Buddha sits on a lotus pad,
Beautiful fingers orchidlike.
Sun goes down and moon comes up,
May your life be peaceful and tranquil.

Mud walls and straw pillows,
Fruits, seeds, and many sons.
Happiness and longevity,
May you have the spring and all its fair weather.

Lossing didn't care for the song. When our friends from the Wan-Wan Tunes troupe came to congratulate the couple and performed the popular musical *The Pig's Wedding*, Lossing became upset.

While Pearl felt honored, Lossing felt humiliated. He didn't like the pig bridegroom, although the character was a hero in the classic Chinese novel *Journey to the West*. I could tell that Lossing's offense and lack of humor bothered Pearl, but she didn't make a show of it.

Carie had planned the wedding to the last detail. Besides Papa, Carpenter Chan, Lilac, and many of her other Chinese friends, Carie invited the English consul, the embassy doctor, their wives, and her other missionary friends. Carie didn't expect the entire town of Chinkiang to invite itself. However, the Chinese believe that a good wedding must be packed, and the townspeople felt that Carie's daughter deserved everyone's blessing.

Pearl wanted me to be the hostess. She didn't care that I had been married before. But all the women in town, myself included, thought it was a bad idea. I was considered abandoned by my husband, and therefore I was bad luck for a new bride. Instead Pearl asked me to hire the local chefs and pick the size and color of the melons and fruits that would be piled throughout the entrance and hallway. It was important in Chinese custom to invite all the gods by displaying the symbols of festivity and fertility.

Seeds, nuts, and fruits were thrown at the couple as soon as Pearl and Lossing were pronounced husband and wife. The church courtyard was overflowing with cheerful people. I helped Carie as she gave candies to people and thanked them for coming.

Led by Papa, the crowd paraded through the town. We arrived at Absalom and Carie's house. The new couple's room was on the second floor. The pink curtains and the beautiful Persian rug were from Carie's own room. The banquet was to be held downstairs, where nine courses of Chinese dishes would be served.

Pink-cheeked and in a red Chinese dress, Pearl came downstairs and served tea. She lit cigarettes for the elderly and placed jasmine buds in the palms of young children. Outside, there was the sound of firecrackers. This was to invite good omens. The local band started to play.

Lossing said in English that he didn't want to play clown and be pushed around by a Chinese crowd. He wanted no part of what he called their "silly games." It was no use that the locals kept cheering. Pearl ended up apologizing for Lossing.

Told by their parents to help inspire fertility, children hid themselves under the wedding-night bed. They were chased away by Lossing.

Lossing was disgusted when he saw all the chopsticks reaching toward the same plate. He said he would rather starve.

When Pearl encouraged Lossing to taste her favorite Chin-kiang sesame candy, Lossing pointed out the seller's dirt-filled fingernails and gave Pearl a lesson on how disease spreads.

Pearl was confident that Lossing would soon get used to the Chinese culture. She never doubted that she could create harmony in her marriage. She had faith in Lossing's ability to understand. "After all, he graduated from Cornell," she told me.

At Lossing's request, Pearl accompanied him into the countryside. Lossing began his agricultural project by surveying the land. Pearl became his personal assistant, interpreter, guide, interviewer, field secretary, and footman. She got up at dawn and worked with Lossing in the fields until nightfall.

As I had feared, it didn't take long for Pearl to lose her enthusiasm. She found herself fighting the widening gap between herself and her husband.

"Conflict is a sign of a healthy relationship," she said when I asked about her marriage. It pleased her that Lossing was getting what he needed. Pearl wanted to fulfill the role of a good wife. She made it her duty to be pleasant and cheerful.

"Lossing carries far too heavy a burden," she told me. "His well-being depends on me." She wouldn't admit that he didn't even notice what she cooked for him. Unlike the Chinese, who lived to eat, Lossing ate to live.

While Carie accepted Lossing, Absalom began to have trouble. He disapproved of Lossing's interference with the way Chinese peasants did their business. The two fought often and finally quit speaking to each other.

Pearl was right that there were similarities between Absalom and Lossing. Absalom's mission was to save Chinese souls, and Lossing's mission was to fix Chinese farming methods. Absalom believed that the Christian God ought to be the only God. Lossing believed that his farming method was the best.

But Pearl had her doubts. She said to Lossing, "The Chinese have survived, farming for thousands of years, on the same land and by the most skillful use of fertilizers and irrigation. They produce extraordinary yields without modern machinery!"

The couple moved away soon after Lossing's proposal was approved by the governor of Anhui province. Lossing didn't take the governor's advice to move after the winter. He couldn't stand Absalom another minute.

Reluctantly, Pearl followed Lossing. They moved to a town north of Chin-kiang called Nanhsuchou, in Anhui province. Pearl didn't want to leave her mother behind. I asked Pearl why Lossing had to go to the poorest province in China. "Why can't he find a better place to conduct his project?"

"The farmers of fertile southern land are satisfied with their ways," Pearl explained. "They are not interested in Lossing's experiments."

The governor of the poor province supported Lossing's ideas because he had little to lose. The governor would gain all the benefit if Lossing succeeded. What Lossing needed was the commitment of the farmers to follow his methods. To make it all work, the governor promised to compensate the farmers if Lossing's experiment failed.

After a few weeks, I went north and visited Pearl to see how she was faring. Her new home was a two-room cottage. It had previously been occupied by a Christian missionary family. Pearl's door and windows didn't keep out the dust. No matter how hard she cleaned, within hours the inside of her house would be covered by a new layer of dust. Pearl's neighbors were Chinese peasant families. They lived in horrible poverty. Pearl told me that she was grateful for the roof over her head.

"Moisture seeped through my walls last month," she said. She showed me the mold that grew underneath her bed and between her mats and sheets. "I have to always be careful when opening the chamber pot." She tried to sound lighthearted. "I never know what could be hunting for food in there. It could be a giant spider or a grandmother stinkbug."

The second time I visited Pearl, she shared with me the exciting news that she was pregnant. "I am finally released from my official duties for the agriculturalist."

"The agriculturalist" was what Pearl had started to call Lossing. "I thought when I got married I would no longer have to take orders like I did from my father when I was a child."

As a way to escape her troubles, Pearl began to write. She found comfort in writing. She told me that her imagination was the only place where she could be herself and be free. I knew she had a zest for stories. Charles Dickens was her inspiration. I remembered the first time we met that she held in her hand a black leather-bound book, which she later told me was *A Tale of Two Cities*. She loved *Oliver Twist*, *Bleak House*, and *The Pickwick Papers*. She read the stories so many times that she could practically recite them. She had always enjoyed writing and had won awards for her work when she was at Randolph-Macon Woman's College in America. She knew that she had to keep her writing a secret. Absalom had made it clear to her that serving God was the only purpose of living. Lossing made Pearl feel guilty for pursuing anything of her own interest. He wanted her to continue to be his interpreter and was upset when she refused. Pearl joked, "Am I conditioned to a man's dominance?"

Using pregnancy as an excuse, Pearl wrote whenever Lossing wasn't around. She no longer complained about Lossing's long trips that took him away for months at a time. She learned to be alone and to keep discontent locked inside herself.

Pearl confessed to me that she feared she was becoming Carie— in exile in her own home. As she made friends with the neighboring peasants, her writings began to fill with their stories.

"It's a shame that China's intellectuals prefer fantasy over realism," Pearl wrote to me. "It's easier to close one's eyes on disease and death."

I wrote back and told her that my newspaper, the *Chin-kiang Independent*, had finally launched. Pearl promised to contribute a monthly column. Using a Chinese man's name, Wei Liang, she discussed politics, economics, history, literature, and women's issues. Her articles were well received. Although the distribution was pitiful, we felt proud that we had a voice of our own.

Early in 1920, the light began to go out of Carie's eyes. She was in and out of consciousness. Pearl rushed back from Nanhsuchou. She sensed that her mother might not live to see her grandchild.

CHAPTER 12

The *Chin-kiang Independent* would have to close after a year. No matter how hard I pushed, the newspaper was not selling enough copies to make ends meet.

Papa offered to be the sponsor under two conditions. The name must be changed to the *Christian Chin-kiang*, and the contents would need to promote Christianity.

"If I spend Absalom's money, I must sing God's songs," Papa insisted. "No reporting that would make Jesus lose face."

I told Papa that I couldn't accept his offer. In fact, my newspaper was in the middle of investigating a scandal regarding Chinese converts who continued to practice the worst of traditional Chinese customs. I had been interviewing wives whose Christian husbands kept purchasing new concubines.

Papa was upset because he, too, was having affairs with different local ladies, which he kept a secret from Absalom. Papa asked, "Why do you have to pick the teapot that isn't boiling?"

"My readers are entitled to the truth," I replied.

"No money from the church then."

"So be it."

I took the matter to Pearl, whose care of her mother was doing wonders. She was confident that the newspaper could survive. We discussed strategy and made adjustments to target the young intellectuals.

Pearl took another male-sounding pen name, Er-ping, meaning "An Alternative View." She began to write about China's place in the world.

She introduced Western history, the industrial revolution, different models of government, the concept of political democracy, and the world's important schools of philosophy and art.

Pearl's analysis and essays generated great interest. Her eloquent Chinese impressed the readers so much that no one suspected that Er-ping was a Caucasian and a woman. The number of subscribers increased. My advertising space was sold without a struggle.

My own writings improved because Pearl edited my drafts. I practically lived in the printing factory, which was located near the town's border. From my window, I watched the construction of the future Chin-kiang Christian Hospital, a two-story brick building funded by Absalom's church.

Although Pearl was eight months pregnant, she didn't get much rest. Besides helping me with the newspaper, she had to play the role of a peacemaker between her parents. The conflict between Carie and Absalom intensified. Carie could no longer stand Absalom. She forbade Absalom from ever visiting her.

"You go and save your heathens" were her last words to him.

Pearl spent nights at her mother's bedside, sitting in a rattan chair. I would come and relieve her at dawn for a few hours. On some nights, after the day's newspaper was out, Pearl and I would take walks, as we had when we were younger. Carie would be sound asleep as we ventured into the moonlight.

We discussed everything from China to America, from my former husband and mother-in-law to her troubled marriage.

"How is your agriculturalist?" I asked.

"Well, he is turning into a disillusionist," Pearl replied. "Lossing resents the attitudes of Chinese farmers. He feels less sympathy toward their misery because they are closed to his ideas. His efforts didn't succeed and the farmers quit his experiments."

"Were you surprised?" I asked.

"No, and I don't blame the peasants," she replied frankly. "They have good reason to see Lossing as a foolish man. Chinese peasants know what their land is capable of producing and how to do it. Lossing believes that if his method works in Iowa, it must work in Anhui."

"What about the government's offer of compensation?" I asked.

"The peasants no longer want to practice Lossing's methods even with compensation."

"So what is Lossing going to do?"

"He has been looking for a way out. Two weeks ago he received an invitation from his former professor, who is now the dean at the College of Agriculture and Forestry at Nanking University. The dean offered a teaching position and Lossing accepted it. To hell with the farmers in Nanhsuchou."

"So you are moving to Nanking?"

"What choice do I have?"

"What about your mother?" I asked.

"I'll see her," she replied. "Thank God for the railway."

One day I ventured to ask Pearl if she and Lossing still loved each other.

Tears welled up in her eyes. "For heaven's sake, I am carrying his child. Even if I don't need him, the child does."

Carol Buck was born on March 4, 1920. Although it was a smooth birth, a tumor was discovered in Pearl's uterus. The doctor insisted that Pearl go to America to have the tumor removed, which she did. It was a long journey that took four months. As a result of the surgery, Pearl could no longer have children. The news crushed her. She wrote, "I am grateful to have the opportunity to lavish my affection abundantly on Carol."

Pearl and Carol followed Lossing to Nanking. "We simply abandoned Nanhsuchou," Pearl reported.

To Pearl's dismay, Nanking was in the middle of a war. Different Chinese warlords and political factions were fighting for dominance of the city and outlying regions.

"I was shaken when bullets whistled across my garden," she wrote. "I tried to help the civilian casualties. One woman was shot in the stomach and died in my arms. I felt powerless."

Carie longed to spend time with her granddaughter. Painstakingly, Pearl made arrangements. She took the train and visited as much as possible. To hold the baby in her arms, Carie struggled to push herself out of the bed. Carol was a milk-skinned, chubby, and beautiful child.

Motherhood brought Pearl profound happiness. The birth of Carol also saved her marriage. She no longer complained about Lossing. Instead she talked about her handsome new home in Nanking with all its lovely trees and a bamboo grove at the far end of the garden.

Pearl applied for a part-time job teaching English at the university's night school. She was pleased that with only their two small salaries she and Lossing were able to afford servants. "Believe it or not, we have three," she said. "One takes care of the laundry and the garden, one does the cooking, and one helps me with Carol. It's hard to believe that I now have extra time on my hands. I have been writing every chance I get and I have just completed a new novel!"

None of us had any sense of the tragedy that was looming. Carol showed no sign that she was a victim of phenylketonuria, but Pearl would soon find out. It was an inherited metabolic disease that would lead Carol to suffer severe mental retardation.

Pearl started to come to Chin-kiang less frequently. By this time, Carol had had her first birthday. When Pearl did come, she didn't stay long. She had to leave before Carie had had enough time with Carol. Pearl grew tense when watching Carol play. I noticed that although baby Carol looked healthy and was sweet, she didn't talk when she was supposed to.

Without any warning or word, Pearl stopped coming. After a two-month silence, she came without Carol. She made excuses when her mother questioned. She sat with Carie and tried to look cheerful, but I could tell it was an act.

Carie had her bed moved next to the window, where she could better see the trees and mountains. She was silent most of the time while Pearl held her hand. She said nothing when it was time for Pearl to leave.

Carie stared out into the darkness after Pearl was gone. To cheer her up, I told her about the Chin-kiang Christian Girls' Choir. "I have been teaching the girls all the songs you taught me," I reported, "and we have been rehearsing for the Christmas Eve performance."

Carie enjoyed my news, but deep down she missed her daughter and granddaughter.

Months went by and Pearl didn't visit. Then I received a letter from her. It broke my heart. Doctors had confirmed her worst nightmare—Carol would never grow up mentally. In her letter, Pearl begged me to keep the news from Carie. "Tell Mother that I will come as soon as I get a chance and I promise that I will stay longer next time."

Carie sensed that her end was approaching. She called me to her bed. She wanted to visit Kuilin in Guangxi province before she died. "Would you accompany me, Willow?" she asked.

I made arrangements immediately. I wrote to Pearl, who was in America with Lossing getting treatment for Carol, that her mother was determined to make the trip. We arrived in Kuilin by train after five days. Sitting on a chair on a bamboo raft, Carie floated down the Li-jiang River. With tears in her eyes, she gazed over the ink-painting-like landscape. The clear, smooth water mirrored the green mountains against a cloudless sky.

"I am ready to die now," Carie said quietly.

"No, you cannot," I responded. "You haven't heard Carol call you Grandma yet."

She shook her head slightly. "Carol might never be able to."

That was when I realized that Carie had known all along what was happening. She had tried to take away Pearl's burden by pretending to know nothing. She had seen too much death and illness over the years to be fooled.

"But why aren't you fighting?" I wept with my cheek against the back of her hand. "You have always been a fighter. You fought for your children, your own fate, and everybody else's. I remember the way you scrubbed my hair with soap trying to get rid of the lice."

Carie gave a weak smile. "I am too tired."

I understood the reason Carie had come to Kuilin. It was her way to help Pearl. If she wasn't home, Pearl wouldn't have to rush back to Chin-kiang.

"You have been hard on yourself, Carie," I said.

"Nothing is hard when I have you by my side." She smiled.

I asked if there was anything else that I could do for her.

She was silent for a while and then uttered, "Be there for Pearl after I'm gone."

CHAPTER 13

Carie died the day before Christmas. Pearl and I were with her till the end. Carie's last wish touched me deeply. All her belongings were to be sold and the funds given to her lifelong maid and friend Wang Ah-ma, so that she could retire and return to her provincial town. The funeral was held on Christmas Day. Absalom performed a simple ceremony, the same ceremony he offered the locals. We were stunned that Absalom didn't do more for his wife.

The casket was lowered slowly into the ground. Behind Pearl and Absalom, the entire town of Chin-kiang stood. Grief-stricken, Wang Ah-ma fainted. The Chin-kiang Christian Girls' Choir sang "Amazing Grace." Playing Carie's piano, I made a promise to myself to maintain Carie's grave like a Chinese daughter would.

Hundreds of candles were placed in cut-off gourds filled with sand. Members of the girls' choir lit the candles and prayed for Carie's spirit. The candles were then placed on lotus pads and set free to drift with the current. Slowly the candles floated into the canal and then the Yangtze River. We prayed that Carie's spirit would travel across the Pacific Ocean and reach her birthplace in America.

Absalom was upset when Lilac proposed hosting a "tofu banquet" to honor Carie. It was the Chinese Buddhist tradition. The wish came from people who felt deeply indebted to Carie. Papa reminded Absalom that the majority of the provincial people, whose lives Carie had touched and helped, were not Christians.

Lilac told Absalom, "We would like to send off old spirits and greet new ones so Carie may gain favors in her next life, not only with the Christian God but also the Chinese gods."

Papa explained to Absalom, "It is an honor only people of high standing and wealth can afford."

"No!" Absalom frowned with his eyebrows and said firmly. "That is against the Christian principle. An elaborate funeral is wasteful. Carie did nothing more than her Christian duty."

Pearl tried to convince her father that by honoring Carie, the people were honoring the Christian God. But it was no use.

An idea proposed by Carpenter Chan and his friends to build a memorial gate for Carie was also dropped. In order to allow the tofu banquet to take place, Papa fabricated an emergency in a neighboring village church. It sent Absalom on his way out of Chin-kiang.

The tofu banquet lasted a week. It was held in Carie's name. It symbolized her thanks to all who came to help her complete the transition from one life to another.

People traveled long distances to attend the ceremony. Staying up all night, I helped Lilac soak and cook the soybeans. We ground the beans and made a variety of tofu dishes, including tofu chicken, tofu duck, tofu fish, tofu ham, tofu bread, and a big tofu cake.

Pearl received families dressed in traditional mourning costume, white from head to toe. The white cotton robes were matched with white hats pinned with white flowers and white shoe covers. Pearl had no idea that her mother had so many friends.

I was called the Other Pearl because Carie, in many ways, had adopted me. I sang the crying tune with the crowd. It was Chin-kiang's tradition to mourn this way. The tune asked the gods to hear our complaints for taking Carie away too soon.

Carpenter Chan and his crew built makeshift gates that guided the crowd to Carie's grave. Wood carvings of protective gods stood on top of each gate. Every gate had its own title, which stood as a symbol of blessing for Carie's next life.

The first gate was titled Sleeping Seeds, which stood for winter; the second was Flower Buds, which meant spring; the third was In Full Blossom, representing summer; and the last gate, Harvest and Fruits, was for the fall. Carie was assured all four seasons in her next life.

As people passed through the gates they kowtowed. Children were told to beg the gods to guard Carie's spirit. The Wan-Wan Tunes troupe played *The Celebration* and the mourners entertained gods of the universe. First was the god of death, who was believed to have ordered Carie's departure from earth. He was entertained to make sure no mistakes had been made. Next were the demons that were believed to have escorted Carie. They were asked to "be gentle with the sorrowful spirit." Third was the Heavenly Judge, who was in charge of counting Carie's virtues and deciding her future. The message from the mourners to him was "Please be fair and kind." Food and wine were offered to this god to assure a receptive mood.

Pearl was grateful that the local people thought to honor her mother with their ancient traditions. She participated in the piety ceremony, where she lit incense at Carie's altar and prayed for the comfort of her mother's spirit.

I asked Pearl where her husband was.

"Lossing is an American . . ." Pearl said. "And he has been very busy."

I sensed she was upset.

"Lossing should have been here for you, if for no other reason."

Pearl appeared hurt, although she explained, "I told him that he didn't have to come if he was busy."

"Pearl." I made her look at me. "What is going on?"

Reluctantly, she replied, "Lossing complains that I am too demanding. He didn't even think that I should come. He wanted me to stay in Nanking and take care of Carol."

I shook my head.

"Carol is not getting better …" Pearl broke down. "I don't want to believe what I see. But I am forced to. My daughter doesn't talk and doesn't respond to me. I have tried to teach her, but I am not reaching her … Lossing thinks it is my fault. And I think it's my fault, too … I didn't make Carol right in the first place. I don't know what happened … Lossing is devastated. He can't believe that she is his child. He left us last week, again, for a field trip in the north. Maybe it's for the better—we don't have to fight endlessly … Lossing will be gone for three months, maybe longer. I am afraid that he won't return …"

"Lossing will return," I comforted her. "He is Carol's father. Give him time."

"You don't know the truth of our marriage, Willow. It hasn't been working. Carol's trouble is like salt on top of a wound. I thought I could take it. I don't mind Lossing taking his anger out on me. But when he is mean to Carol, I …"

I let her sob on my shoulder.

"I can't see myself living with him anymore," she continued. "Carol doesn't know what is wrong. She doesn't deserve her father's cruelty."

"You need Lossing at this moment," I said.

She agreed. "We need money to pay Carol's doctors in America."

Pearl's searching for Carol's cure would eventually end. After years of disappointment, she would accept her fate. Pickled in sorrow, she began to imagine her own accidental death and contemplated suicide. I wrote her as much as I could.

Pearl told me that writing had become her salvation. It was the only way that she could take her mind off her daughter. If she couldn't fix Carol, she could fix the characters in her novels.

After Carie's death, Absalom traveled deep inland, sometimes a year at a time. As a result, more Christian churches were established. Carpenter Chan followed Absalom. He brought his wife and children with him.

Papa continued to be responsible for the Chin-kiang Christian community. His recent achievements included the conversion of the richest man in Chin-kiang, the head of the famous Chin-kiang Vinegar Company. Receiving handsome contributions, Papa transferred the money to Absalom, who in turn funded Christian schools inland.

Besides being publisher and editor of the newspaper, I was also in charge of the Chin-kiang Christian Girls' Middle School. I followed Carie's original curriculum and added Chinese history, science, and mathematics.

I wasn't aware of the *Chin-kiang Independent*'s popularity until I received a letter from the *Nanking Daily* offering me a position as its editor.

I accepted the offer without hesitation because I had always admired the *Nanking Daily*. The paper was as prestigious as the *Shanghai Daily*, and its readership reached all of southern China. The offer would expand my horizons and also enable me to reunite with Pearl.

As if our childhood had returned, Pearl welcomed me to Nanking. We climbed the famous Purple Mountain together. Beneath our feet spread the city of Nanking. Temples, shrines, and the tomb of the fourteenth-century Ming emperor were scattered over the mountainside. The city had a twenty-four-mile-long wall and nine elaborately decorated, forty-foot-high gates. Running beside the city was the Yangtze River, which flowed on to Chin-kiang.

"I love the winding cobbled streets and the little shops glimmering with candlelight at night," Pearl said. "I adore the flickering oil lamps that light the streets. I can't help but imagine the family life of the people within these ancient walls."

After I settled into my small apartment near the newspaper office, we began to visit each other regularly. Pearl lived in a three-room brick house. It was modest compared to the residences of other foreigners. The house belonged to the university compound occupied mostly by faculty. Lossing had been living here for four years now. Like Carie, Pearl tended to her garden. Besides roses and camellias, there were tomatoes and cabbages.

I was pleased to see Carol again, although I was sad to witness her condition. She was five years old. I tried to communicate with her, but she did not respond. I also saw Lossing. His skin was whiter than I had remembered. He taught in the classroom, where he felt that he was wasting his time. He longed to return to the field.

"Please, Willow, stay for dinner," Pearl insisted one evening. "It will be no trouble for me at all. The servants do everything for three bags of rice at the end of the month. It makes me feel guilty even though almost every white family in the city enjoys such help. My chef is from Yangchow, but he can also cook Peking and Cantonese style."

It was at the dinner table that I witnessed the couple fight. Lossing needed Pearl to be his translator for his new field experiment, but Pearl refused.

"I no longer know who this woman is." Lossing turned to me, speaking half jokingly. "She certainly doesn't need a husband. She is having an affair with her imagined characters."

"Perhaps writing eases her anxiety." I tried to make peace.

Lossing interrupted me with laughter. "No, you don't know her, Willow. My world is too small for this woman. Vanity and greed are the true demons here. And yet if Pearl has ambition, she has little skill or training. She wants to be a novelist, but she has no academic training and no material. She is lost as a mother, and she is bound to lose if she tries to make it as a writer."

Pearl stared at Lossing, disgusted.

Lossing ignored her and continued, "It is destructive when a hobby turns into an obsession."

"Stop it, Lossing," Pearl said, trying to control her anger.

"You have a responsibility," Lossing went on. "You owe this family!"

"Please, stop."

"I have the right to express myself. And Willow has the right to know the truth."

"What truth?" Pearl's eyes were burning.

"That this marriage is a mistake!" Lossing said loudly.

"As if we even have a marriage!" Pearl responded.

"No, we don't," Lossing agreed.

"You have no right to ask me to give up writing," Pearl said.

"So you have made up your mind." Lossing looked at her. "You have decided to ignore my needs and abandon this family."

"How have I abandoned this family?"

"You disappear mentally when you write. We don't exist. I know I don't. You refuse to work with me to support this family. You well know that without your help I can't do my job. You treat your writing as if it is a job, but all I see is an amateur at play. Let me remind you, I am the one who earns the money, who pays for the rent, all the living expenses, and Carol's doctor fees!"

"Writing helps me stay sane." Pearl was on the verge of tears.

"It doesn't seem to be helping on that score."

Pearl struggled to compose herself.

Lossing carried on.

Pearl looked defeated. She got up and went to the kitchen.

From the living room, I heard Carol's screaming and the maid's voice, "Put it down!"

"I am only talking common sense," Lossing said to me. "I can understand that Pearl wants to write novels to escape her life. But who wants to read her stories? The Chinese don't need a blonde woman to tell their stories, and the Westerners are not interested in China. What makes Pearl think that she stands a chance of succeeding?"

Chapter 14

Taking the *Nanking Daily* job proved to be the best decision I ever made in my career. I was surrounded by people who were intelligent and open-minded. Our staff competed with the *Peking Daily* and the *Shanghai Daily*. I often brought work home that I couldn't finish in the office. After a year, I had moved to a new place, a little bungalow located outside the ancient city gate. It was close to the woods and mountains. The fresh air, the views, the privacy—all of these did me good. Clearing the weeds, I discovered that I actually had a garden. I planted roses, lilacs, and peonies. It pleased me that I would be able to bring fresh flowers to Carie's grave site by the time of the Spring Memorial Festival.

Pearl continued her teaching at Nanking University. We celebrated our birthdays together. We had reached our midthirties and we joked and teased each other about our lives. I was still legally married to my former husband, since China didn't have such a thing as divorce. I had no idea how many new concubines my husband had married and how many children he had. I asked my father if he, as the head of the church, would make an announcement to disassociate me from the man.

Papa didn't think that it was necessary. "Out of sight, out of mind," he said. "Your husband has been telling everyone that you are dead. I am getting tired of explaining to people that you are not dead."

I asked Papa if he would like to come to Nanking so that I could take care of him. He declined. He said that he was God's foot soldier. The church was his home, its members his family.

Pearl, on the other hand, talked the head dean of Nanking University into offering Absalom a nonpaying position teaching a course on Western religion. Pearl convinced the seventy-three-year-old Absalom to slow down, to move to Nanking and live with her. He finally agreed.

Following Absalom, Carpenter Chan and Lilac also moved to Nanking. They found a modest place a mile from Pearl's house. Carpenter Chan believed that Absalom would need him, for he "will never stop expanding God's kingdom."

Lilac was convinced that it was her husband's commitment to Absalom's causes that brought her happiness. Lilac was one among hundreds of Absalom's followers.

I said to Pearl, "Absalom feels content enough to quit risking his life going inland."

"Remember the beginning, when Absalom preached on the streets of Chin-kiang?" Pearl smiled.

"Oh, yes. Everyone thought he was mad."

Pearl tried to get Carol to say the one word she had been teaching her all week. But Carol would not deliver. It drove both of them crazy. The Chinese servants had been feeding Carol relentlessly, for they believed that the fatter the child, the better the health. Although mentally handicapped, Carol developed a strong body. One day Carol hit Pearl on the forehead with a stone paperweight.

Blood crawled down Pearl's face like an earthworm. Carol, unaware of what she had done, went on playing. Pearl sat on the floor, quietly wiping the blood from her forehead.

Lossing, meanwhile, made peace with reality. He avoided Pearl and Carol. He spent long hours working in his office, even on Sundays.

Pearl's refusal to give up on Carol aggravated the strain in their already suffering marriage. Pearl called Lossing a coward when he tried to convince her that there was no point in fighting God's will.

Pearl often expressed her anger in Chinese. Lossing understood but couldn't respond fast enough. Pearl would say, "Maggots don't just breed in manure pits, they breed in expensive meat jars too."

When Pearl yelled, "Only the toes know when the shoe doesn't fit," it was unclear whether Lossing understood her meaning.

Fighting with her husband and caring for her daughter consumed Pearl. She no longer paid attention to her appearance. She wore the same wrinkled brown jacket and black cotton skirt every day. More and more, she looked like a local Chinese woman. With her hair tied up in a bun, she walked in a hurry with a stack of books under her arm.

Eventually Pearl quit making demands on Carol. I often found Pearl sitting quietly, watching her daughter. Her expression was infinitely sad.

At the university, Pearl was a beloved teacher. The fact that she was a native Chinese speaker made her the most popular foreign instructor on campus. She was promoted and became an official university staff member. Besides English, Pearl taught American and English literature. Pearl was sincerely interested in her students. She loved it when they compared their lives to those of the characters in Charles Dickens's novels. Pearl taught older students, too. As they practiced their conversation skills, Pearl learned about their families and their lives outside of school.

Pearl shared with me one of her students' stories. "This happened only three months ago," she began. "A massacre took place in the town of Shao-xing. A group of young Communists were beheaded by the nationalist government. Their bodies were chopped up, ground, and made into bread stuffing. The bread was advertised for sale at the local bakery! Can you believe that, Willow? What a way to scare people into submission!"

Pearl discovered that her servants had been hiding something from her. "Last night," she came to tell me, "I followed a noise to the back of my house and found a woman living there with her newborn baby. The woman was my age, perhaps younger. Her name was Soo-ching. She told me that she had been living there for six months and had given birth to her son only days before."

"She begged you to let her stay?" I asked.

"Of course."

"What did you say to her?"

"I didn't know what to say. I can't kick her out. The strangest thing was that this beggar lady named her son Confucius."

I was not surprised. It could have been my name too. When Papa was a beggar, he decided that if I had been born a boy, he would have named me after Confucius, or Mencius, or the ancient Chinese philosophers Lao Tse or Chuang Tzu.

"Will you publish such stories if I write them?" Pearl asked. "I mean the stories of real people?"

"Personally, I'd love to. But I'm not sure if the newspaper would agree," I responded.

"Why not?" Pearl asked. "They are moving, human stories. Readers would be interested and the stories might do some good."

"Yes, perhaps. But the paper has a tradition of publishing only what will inspire, not what will depress. Remember, this is the *Nanking Daily*, not the *Chin-kiang Independent*. Our funding is from the government."

"What is the purpose of a newspaper if not to tell the truth?" Pearl said. "People will get a false picture of what is truly happening in China."

"Read the alternative papers published by the Communists if you want the truth. I have books by Lu Hsun, Lao She, and Cao Yu."

Pearl couldn't wait. She came to my home and borrowed the books I recommended.

Though I continued to attend church regularly, great changes were happening in the outside world, and my job brought me into their midst. For Pearl, her reading soon expanded beyond my recommendations and helped push her marital troubles to the back of her mind. Her enthusiasm returned. She was once again the Pearl I used to know.

*　　*　　*

112

We discussed works by Lu Hsun. Pearl's favorites were *The True Story of Ah Q* and *The Story of Mrs. Xiang-Lin*. Although the author's criticism of society was sharp and original, we didn't love the stories. Pearl's trouble with Lu Hsun was that he depicted his characters as if he were standing on a roof looking down.

"The peasants he portrays are all narrow-minded, stubborn, and stupid," Pearl pointed out.

"Well, it was considered revolutionary that he even made peasants his subjects," I commented.

Pearl and I both loved Lao She and Cao Yu. Among their best were *The Big House, Full Moon*, and *The Marriage of a Puppet Master*. We favored *Full Moon* in particular for the author's sensitivity. The story was about a single mother who was driven into prostitution. Although her daughter tries to avoid following in her mother's footsteps, she ends up succumbing to the same fate.

Pearl liked the story but resented the novel's bitter hopelessness. She preferred stories that offered hope in the end, however tragic. "The character must believe in himself, and he must have the stamina to endure."

"Beautiful, heart-wrenching tragedy has been central to the Chinese tradition for thousands of years," I reminded her. "Both novelists and readers relish what you call hopelessness."

"That is not always true," Pearl challenged. "The novel *All Men Are Brothers* is the best example. The poor peasants were forced to become bandits. But the novel is filled with energy. There is no bitterness to it. To me, this is the Chinese essence!"

"Chinese critics don't share your opinion," I argued. "They say *All Men Are Brothers* lacks sophistication. They consider it folk art, not literature."

"That is exactly why things must change," Pearl shot back. "Everyday life has a power of its own. And it's important to pay attention to it. Look at Soo-ching, the lady who delivered her son in my backyard! I bet she bit off the umbilical cord like the character Er-niang in *All Men Are Brothers*! I didn't see her pity herself. She was ready to go on.

That poor lice-infested beggar lady! I think her a worthy subject, even heroic!"

I remembered the first time Pearl and I discussed the Chinese classic *Dream of Red Mansion*. I was sixteen and had just learned to read. Pearl didn't like the novel, especially the hero, Pao Yu.

"Have your views changed regarding *Dream of Red Mansion*?" I asked.

"No. Pao Yu is nothing but a playboy," Pearl replied.

"By Chinese estimations, Pao Yu is a rebel and an intellectual prince," I said, smiling. "The popular view is that Pao Yu deserves more respect than an emperor."

"What do you mean by popular? The people who hold such views are only a tiny minority."

"Well, that minority rules the literary world."

"Are you telling me that the majority, who happen to be peasants, don't count in China?" Pearl was annoyed.

I had to agree with her that it was not right.

Dream of Red Mansion was a classic, Pearl admitted. "But it is an ill beauty, so to speak. It is about escapism and self-indulgence. I am not saying that the novel doesn't deserve credit for criticizing the feudalism of the time."

"I am glad that you acknowledge that. It is important."

"However," Pearl continued, "the novel, in its essence, reminds me of Goethe's *Sorrows of Young Werther*. The difference is that Werther fell in love with one girl, Lotte, while his Chinese counterpart Pao Yu fell in love with twelve maidens."

"In China, educated men still spend their lives imitating Pao Yu."

"Drinking clubs and brothels have become the only source of inspiration. What a pity!" Pearl went on. "I think it is a crime that there is no representation in literature for the greater part of the Chinese people."

CHAPTER 15

Days of drizzle announced the coming of spring. Camellias blossomed. Leaves shone glossy green. Heavy with moisture, massive flowers began to plop to the ground. I was working late at night when I heard a knocking on the door.

It was Pearl without an umbrella. Her hair was drenched and she looked devastated.

"What happened?" I let her in and closed the door.

"Lossing . . ." Unable to go on, she passed me a piece of wadded paper.

It was a letter, a hand-copied ancient erotic Chinese poem.

"It's not his handwriting," Pearl pointed out.

"From a female student, you think? Where did you find it?"

"In his drawer. I went to his office looking for an address. I was writing to his aunt, who had some questions concerning Carol."

I was stunned. "Do you think that Lossing is having an affair?"

"How could I think otherwise?" Tears welled from her eyes.

"Where is Lossing now?"

"I don't know."

"Does he know that you know? How long could this have been going on?"

"I haven't paid attention to anything else but Carol."

"Who is this girl?"

"I think I know who she is. Her name is Lotus, a first-year student in the agricultural department. I ran into her several times at Lossing's office."

"Is she pretty?"

"I don't remember . . . that she was particularly pretty. She was the translator he hired for his fieldwork. He has taken trips with her. I was foolish to trust him." She took the towel I offered and wiped her face. "I can't say that I didn't see it coming."

I sat down with her and made tea. "What are you going to do?" I asked quietly.

"If I didn't have Carol, I'd leave now," she answered. Her eyes became tearful again.

"The trouble is that you don't earn enough money."

"No, I don't."

I thought about Pearl's mother and the way she had felt trapped all her life.

"Would you put up with him for Carol's sake?" I asked.

Pearl's hands went through her wet hair. She bit her lower lip and shook her head, slowly but firmly.

"The reality is . . ."

"Listen, Willow. Last month I succeeded in placing two essays, in *South East Asia Chronicle* and the *American Adventure Magazine*. Although the payments weren't much, it gave me hope."

"Pearl, look, it's difficult for anyone to make a living these days. It's doubly hard for a woman. You know that."

"I am not going to let anything stop me." She was determined. "My gut feeling tells me that writing is my best chance. I must try."

"With your Chinese stories?"

"Absolutely. I believe in my Chinese stories. No other Western author can come close to what I offer—what life is really like in the Orient. For God's sake, I'm living it. The Chinese world cries out for exploration. It's like America once was—fertile and full of promise."

Pearl and I made a new discovery: the poet Hsu Chih-mo. In the summer of 1925, Hsu Chih-mo was called "the Renaissance Man" or "the Chinese Shelley." Promoting the working class's right to literacy, he became the leader of China's new cultural movement. Pearl and I were strong supporters of Hsu Chih-mo.

"*A bush at the foot of the mountain can never enjoy what a pine would . . .*" I shared with Pearl from Hsu Chih-mo's essay titled "On Universe." "*To touch the fantastic rolling clouds the pine must hang dangerously from the cliff.*"

In return, Pearl sent me a section of his essay "Morality of Suicide," enclosed with her own note: "Let me know if you don't fall in love with the writer's mind."

> *What is wrong is that these suicides embody the values of our society and set our moral standard: a village girl who drowns herself instead of yielding to her abusive mother-in-law; a businessman who hangs himself to escape debt; an Indian who sacrifices himself to feed crocodiles and a minister who drinks poison to demonstrate his loyalty toward the emperor.*
>
> *We dishonor the integrity of the individual by honoring these deaths. We make death sound glorious. In my opinion, the people who commit suicide are not heroes but victims. I offer them pity and sympathy but not respect and admiration. They are not martyrs, but fools. There are other types of suicide, which I think are truly glorious and worthy—such as that of the characters in Shakespeare's* Romeo and Juliet. *Their deaths touch us because we identify with their humanity.*

The wind was harsh. Gigantic pines stood solemnly against the gray sky. Pearl and I sat with the city view below our feet, discussing Hsu Chih-mo. We knew a lot about him already. He earned a degree in law at Peking University. Then he went to England to study economics but instead earned a degree in literature. Next he attended Columbia University in America and majored in political science. What interested us most was his graduate thesis, *The Social Position of Women in China.*

Pearl recited Hsu Chih-mo's poem titled "Cancer in Literature."

> *The language smells of a dying room*
> *Rotten, filthy and stinky*
> *Anxiety and struggle*

No means of escape
Youthful enthusiasm
Hope and ideal
Grass grows through concrete
To reach sunlight and air

"You are falling in love with Hsu Chih-mo," Pearl teased.

I wished that I could deny it. I took an assignment in Shanghai so that I could attend Hsu Chih-mo's poetry reading. I was excited to find that he was everything I had imagined. He was a six-foot-tall, handsome northern Chinese. He had silky, curly black hair. His leaf-shaped eyes were gentle, although his gaze was intense. Under his Mongolian high-bridged nose was a sensuous mouth. He read passionately. The world around me disappeared.

I entrust
The poplar catkins have all fallen
I entrust
The cuckoos confuse nights with days
And cry "It's better to return!"

To the bright moon
I entrust an anxious heart
Who says you are a thousand miles away
I entrust
Moonlight will shine on you
I entrust
The frost kisses the marshland's tender reeds

I followed Hsu Chih-mo and bought tickets to his lectures. I dressed for him and hoped that our paths would cross. He didn't appear to notice me, but I felt rewarded just to be able to see him.

In Shanghai I learned that I was among thousands of women who dreamed of Hsu Chih-mo. We threw ourselves at him like night bugs at a light.

Pearl told me that Hsu Chih-mo was a constant subject of gossip columns. His affairs with three different women had made headlines in the *Shanghai Evening News* and the *Celebrity Magazine*. The first was his wife by an arranged marriage. She was the daughter of a wealthy family in Shanghai and followed Hsu to England. The couple committed the unthinkable: They issued a public letter claiming that their relationship was loveless and wrong. Chinese society was stunned by the word *divorce*. Cynics believed that Hsu had abandoned his wife to pursue other women. The wife returned home to give birth to their son and continued to live with and serve Hsu Chih-mo's parents.

It was said that the beautiful Miss Lin was Hsu Chih-mo's second lady. She was an American-educated architect and the daughter of Hsu's mentor, a professor of Chinese literature in England. Miss Lin was said to be torn between Hsu Chih-mo and her fiancé, a famous scholar of Chinese architecture. After much publicized drama, Miss Lin chose her fiancé over Hsu Chih-mo. Hsu Chih-mo's third lady was a courtesan from Peking. He married her in an effort to save her from opium addiction and alcohol. Their marriage was troubled from the start. It had been a staple on the front pages of newspapers and magazines.

Pearl sent me a telegram while I was still in Shanghai. My heart took flight with every word: *"Hsu Chih-mo is scheduled to visit Nanking University. He is accompanying Tagore, a poet from India. You'd better hurry because I have sent Hsu Chih-mo an invitation to give a talk in my class and HE HAS ACCEPTED!"*

CHAPTER 16

The roles of host and guest were reversed from the beginning. Hsu Chih-mo was getting more attention than his distinguished guest, Tagore. The two stood shoulder to shoulder onstage in front of a podium. Tagore read his poem *Gitanjali* as Hsu Chih-mo translated. Listeners packed the hall. Students applauded at each of Hsu Chih-mo's sentences.

Looking like a brass temple bell, Tagore was wrapped in a brown blanket. Although he was only in his fifties, the Chinese thought him older because of his chest-length gray beard. In contrast, Hsu Chih-mo was slender, youthful, and stylish. One could easily tell that he was what the crowd had been waiting for. He was the reigning prince of Chinese literature.

Tagore grew increasingly uneasy as the students cheered Hsu Chih-mo. Turning to Hsu Chih-mo, Tagore said, "I thought the crowd was here to see me."

"Yes, sir," Hsu Chih-mo assured him. "The people have come to celebrate your work."

Pearl and I sat in the front row. I wore my silver Shanghai-style coat with a crimson silk scarf. Pearl had arrived late. She wore her wrinkled brown jacket and black cotton skirt and was in a pair of Chinese peasant shoes. Her socks were so worn they hung loose at her ankles. From the disarray of her hair, I knew she'd just had a problem with Carol.

"I can't believe it. You didn't bother to dress up," I whispered in her ear.

She cut me off. "Just be glad that I am here."

I wouldn't let her off easily. "It's Hsu Chih-mo, for God's sake. How often do we get to meet with a celebrity?"

She gave me a tired look.

"What?" I asked.

"Don't."

"Say it." I held her elbow.

"Fine." She turned and whispered in my ear, "I wouldn't have minded missing Hsu Chih-mo. Tagore is the one I came for."

"How about I take the young one and you take the old?" I teased.

"Shush!"

The duet on the stage continued. Hsu Chih-mo translated Tagore's last poem:

I am only waiting for love to give myself up at last into his hands
That is why it is so late and why I have been guilty of such omissions
They come with their laws and their codes to bind me fast
But I evade them ever
For I am only waiting for love to give myself up at last into his hands
People blame me and call me heedless
I doubt not they are right in their blame

"Tagore is lucky," I whispered to Pearl.

Nodding, she agreed. "Hsu Chih-mo is particularly good at reconstructing Tagore's sentences into Chinese."

"Tagore doesn't seem to fully appreciate it."

Hsu Chih-mo continued,

The market day is over and work is all done for the busy
Those who came to call me in vain have gone back in anger
I am only waiting for love to give myself up at last into his hands

Pearl and Hsu Chih-mo stood together in front of her class. She had invited the poet to speak to her students the day after his appearance with Tagore. This was before they knew what was going to happen—long before historians wrote about this moment.

I could tell that Hsu Chih-mo was surprised by the excellence of Pearl's Chinese. Except for her Western features and the color of her hair, Pearl was Chinese in every way.

"My apologies for the humble reception, but our hearts are sincere." Pearl smiled and gestured to one of her students to come pour tea for Hsu Chih-mo.

"Long Jing from Hangchow," Pearl said, taking the tea to Hsu Chih-mo. She bowed lightly after placing the cup in front of him.

In retrospect, it was I who didn't see that Hsu Chih-mo was attracted to Pearl the moment he laid eyes on her. Her ease and confidence caught him.

"Where are you from?" Hsu Chih-mo asked Pearl, ignoring the class.

In a perfect Chin-kiang dialect, Pearl replied, "The pig is from River North."

He understood her joke and laughed.

Many southern Chinese called coolies, drifters, beggars, and bandits River North Pigs, because they came from the northern, unfertile part of the Yangtze River and were poor and a lower class. With this joke, Pearl revealed two facts about herself. First, she was a native. Second, she identified with the people. If she had wanted, she could have spoken perfect Mandarin with an Imperial accent.

During the class Hsu Chih-mo discussed his effort in translating Tagore.

Pearl was charming, although her questions were daring. She challenged Hsu Chih-mo on the Indian rhythm compared to the Chinese. She also asked him to explain the art of his translation, especially the difference between being "faithful in appearance" and "faithful in essence."

Infatuated with Hsu Chih-mo, I was blind and deaf to what was truly happening between him and Pearl.

"What influenced you to become a poet?" a female student raised her arm and asked.

"Craziness," Hsu Chih-mo replied. "My mother said that I was a spooky child. My eyes were open and my lips uttered strange words at night. Poetry to me was like rocks and cards were to other boys."

A male student with glasses asked, "You are called the Chinese Shelley. What do you make of that?"

"It doesn't mean anything to me." Hsu Chih-mo smiled. "But I am honored, of course."

"What do you do to make your poems successful?" Pearl asked.

Hsu Chih-mo thought before he replied. "I feel very much like a tailor making a pair of pants. I first study the fabric so I know how to cut it. A good pair of pants takes a great deal of fabric. I make sure that my cuts go with the grain instead of against it."

A loud voice came from the back of the room. "Mr. Hsu, what is your view of the literary movement in our society today?"

The question threw a boulder into a calm pond. Hsu Chih-mo was stirred. "It disturbs me that our country debates whether or not the Chinese language should be made accessible to the peasants!" His voice resonated. "As we all know, the emperor we overthrew thirteen years ago spoke a private language, which nobody but he and his tutor understood. Our proud civilization and heritage become ridiculous when our language is used to create not communication and understanding, but distance and isolation."

As the editor in chief of the *Nanking Daily*, I created, sponsored, and produced the news program *China Literary Front*. The program was syndicated across all of China. I was able to travel, dine, and converse with some of the brightest minds of our time. But what I enjoyed most was my time with Hsu Chih-mo. He was guarded at first, but I earned his trust. By the end of our work together, we had become good friends. I asked him about the inner force that drove him.

"The inner force is far more important than talent," Hsu Chih-mo revealed. "Writing is my rice and air. One shouldn't bother picking up a pen if that is not the case."

"That is exactly the case with my friend Pearl Buck," I said.

"You mean the River North Pig?" He smiled remembering her.

"Yes."

"What has she written?"

"She has written essays, poems, and novels. She is my special columnist. I'll send you copies of her articles if you are interested."

"Yes, please."

As we continued talking, Hsu Chih-mo asked how Pearl and I had become friends.

The problem with people who end up digging their own grave is that they often have no idea they are digging it. Such was my case as I told Hsu Chih-mo stories about my friend.

After Tagore went back to India and Hsu Chih-mo returned to Shanghai, I felt inspired and enlightened. Against my better judgment, I gave in to my emotions. If I had never believed in fate and coincidence before, it wouldn't be long before I did. When the Nanking University board asked me to help invite Hsu Chih-mo to come back and teach, I did everything within my power to make it happen.

Pearl didn't think that Nanking University stood a chance of getting Hsu Chih-mo. "He has been teaching at Peking University and Shanghai University," she reminded me. I decided to play a card that at the time I thought was brilliant. As friends, Pearl and I together wrote Hsu Chih-mo a personal invitation.

A few weeks later, Hsu Chih-mo responded and said he was on his way.

CHAPTER 17

After Hsu Chih-mo's arrival, the center of China's literary society shifted from Shanghai to Nanking. Nanking University became the main stage of the New Cultural Movement. I hosted weekly events featuring journalists, writers, and artists from all over the country. I was so busy that I ate my meals standing up. I hadn't had time to visit Pearl for weeks, so one evening I decided to drop by.

She surprised me with the news that Lossing had moved out.

"He is living with Lotus," Pearl said in a subdued voice.

"What about Carol?" I asked.

"Lossing said that Carol wouldn't know the difference. He insists that she doesn't even know that he is her father."

I tried to comfort her. "The important thing is that you are doing the best you can."

She shook her head.

"You have your own life to live, Pearl."

"Carol doesn't deserve this. Her own father abandoning her . . ."

"Carol may not be aware . . ."

"But I am!" she almost shouted.

I went quiet.

She began to sob.

I walked to the kitchen to get her a cup of water.

"Pearl," I said gently. "You have to comb your hair and dress yourself, and you have to eat."

"I would like to simply slip away, to die," she responded. "I need to be released from this trap."

"Have you been writing?" I asked.

"I can't do anything else but write. Here." She tossed me a stack of pages. "From last week. Two short stories."

I glanced at the titles. "The Seventh Dragon" and "The Match-maker."

"You have been productive, Pearl."

"I was going crazy until I started typing."

I asked if there was any interest from publishers.

"No. One editor from New York was kind enough to send me a note of explanation after rejecting my manuscript. What he said was no news to me. Lossing has been telling me the same thing all along."

"That Western readers are not interested in China?"

She nodded.

"Well, perhaps they are only accustomed to stories of little merit. It may take time to convince them that what you write is different," I said. "Have you tried Chinese publishing houses?"

"Yes."

"And?"

"I made a fool of myself," she sighed. "The right-wing Chinese houses want pure escapism, while the left-wing want nothing but Communism and Russia."

"And you don't care about either of those?"

"No."

"Unfortunately, you still need money."

"Unfortunately."

I invited Pearl to come with me to a New Year's party hosted by the *Nanking Daily*. Pearl didn't want to go, but I insisted.

"Hsu Chih-mo will be there." I could hardly contain my excitement.

"Too bad he is your interest—not mine."

"He's the only one who hasn't read you. He told me he wants to read your work."

"I am not going."

"Please. I don't want to look desperate."

"Desperate? Oh, I see."

"Will you come?"

"Okay, I'll go for tea only."

Hsu Chih-mo stood on a chair waving his arms. "Ladies and gentlemen, I want to present my best friend, the great hope of China's new literature, Dick Lin! He is the seventh translator of Karl Marx's *Communist Manifesto* and the editor of the *Shanghai Avant-Garde Magazine*." Hsu Chih-mo was dressed in a Western black silk suit with a Chinese collar and Chinese cotton shoes. His hair was neatly combed from the middle to the sides.

The crowd cheered. "Dick Lin! Dick Lin!"

Dick Lin, a short and broad-shouldered man with black-framed glasses, came to shake hands with Pearl and me. He was in his thirties. He had a pair of lizard eyes and a crooked nose. The corners of his mouth drew downward and gave him a serious, almost bitter expression.

"I admire your work at the *Nanking Daily*," Dick blurted out to me. "How about working for us?"

Though I was flattered, I was taken aback by his directness.

"You will be guaranteed your own page plus the weekend edition," Dick continued. "You can run it any way you want. We'll match your current salary and add a bonus."

I turned to Pearl. My eyes said, "Can you believe this man?"

She smiled.

Dick turned to Pearl and began to speak English with a Chinese accent. "Welcome to China," he said, bowing with exaggeration. "It is my honor to meet you! Hsu Chih-mo tells me that you came to China in diapers. Is that true? No wonder your Chinese is flawless. Do you know Chinese is a very dangerous language for foreigners? One slip in tone and 'Good morning' becomes 'Let us go to bed together.' "

The debate was moderated by Hsu Chih-mo. The topic was "Should novelists write for people or write as people?" The discussion soon became heated.

"A novelist's duty is to wake society's conscience," Dick insisted. "He must make the peasants learn shame—I am talking about those who bought and ate the bread made of the bodies of the revolutionaries!"

The crowd clapped.

"China is where she is because our intellectuals are selfish, arrogant, decadent, and irresponsible," Dick continued. "It's time for our novelists to demonstrate leadership . . ."

Pearl raised her hand.

Hsu Chih-mo nodded for her to speak.

"Have you ever thought," she said, "that it might be the author's choice to write *as* the people? No matter how you justify the horror of an act like the one you just used as an example, the fact is that China's majority is made of peasants. My question is, Don't peasants deserve a voice of their own?"

"Well, you must pick a worthy peasant to portray," Dick responded. "Like harvesting a fruit tree, you pick the good apples and throw away the rotten. Again, you have an obligation toward society, which needs a moral compass."

"Does that mean you won't publish authors who write with the voice of the real people?" I asked.

"Personally, I won't."

"Then you are denying representation to ninety-five percent of China's population." Pearl's voice was pitched.

Holding firm in his view, Dick declared, "We deny these small-minded, ill-mannered characters a voice."

"Who will you publish then?" I asked.

"The authors who are committed in their fight against Capitalism," Dick replied. "In fact, we are aggressively seeking to publish works by authors that represent the proletarian class. We'll assure these authors' success."

"Dick wants to change the world," Hsu Chih-mo teased.

"Shouldn't it be up to the readers?" Pearl challenged.

"No," Dick said. "Readers need guidance."

Smiling, Pearl disagreed. "Readers are smarter than we think."

"Mrs. Buck." Dick lowered his voice, although it was still loud enough for the room to hear. "I was the editor who rejected your manuscript. I am sure you have tried other publishers without success. My point is that we, not readers, decide."

Pearl got up and quietly walked out of the room.

I rose and followed her.

Outside in the hall, Pearl rushed toward the door. Hurrying my steps, I suddenly heard footfalls behind me. I turned and there was Dick Lin, coming my way.

I paused, thinking that he might wish to apologize for his rudeness toward my friend.

"Willow," he called out as I stopped. "Willow, when can I see you again? I would love to buy you a cup of tea sometime."

I sneered and turned, making my way toward the door.

Hsu Chih-mo's wet hair fell across his face. He stood in front of me by the garden door. His hand reached up to his face to wipe away the rain. "I come to apologize to Pearl for my friend if he has offended her."

I said, "Pearl Buck has told me that she no longer wishes to be part of the Nanking literary circle."

"Dick didn't mean to attack." Hsu Chih-mo insisted that he have a chance to speak with Pearl face-to-face.

I stood looking at him and wanted time to stop. My emotions churned and I started to feel sick inside. I kept telling myself: The man has no interest in me! But my heart refused to listen. My eyes luxuriated in the sight of him.

Hsu Chih-mo looked away uneasily.

"I will pass the message," I said like a fool.

Pearl sat by the table and drank her tea as if she was lost in her own thoughts. I had torn her away from her writing and brought her to my house so that Hsu Chih-mo could talk to her. I was sure that Pearl would leave as soon as he delivered his friend's apology. I waited impatiently for my own private time with Hsu Chih-mo.

"Dick is oblivious." Hsu Chih-mo leaned forward, holding his cup in both hands. "He is combative by nature, but he is good-hearted. He is a genius. To have a conversation with him is like planting seeds together. Wisdom will sprout once you allow sunshine. Only those who appreciate honesty can enjoy Dick. He is passionate about what he believes."

"So you are here to deliver Dick Lin's message?" Pearl's eyes were on the tree outside the window.

"No," Hsu Chih-mo said so gently that it was as if he had merely breathed. "I come to deliver my own message."

She didn't ask to know.

He waited.

I found myself tortured by the fact that he tried to get her attention, tried to get her to turn her head.

CHAPTER 18

Many years later, after Hsu Chih-mo's death and after Pearl had become an American novelist and had won both the Nobel Prize and the Pulitzer Prize, she wrote about him.

He claimed me with his love, and then he let me go home. When I arrived in America, I realized that the love was with me, and would stay with me forever.

He used to sit in my living room and talk by the hour and wave his beautiful hands in exquisite and descriptive gestures until when I think of him, I see first his hands. He was a northern Chinese, tall and classically beautiful in looks, and his hands were big and perfectly shaped and smooth as a woman's hands.

I sat in the same room with Pearl and Hsu Chih-mo. It was my home, but I felt like a ghost.

Dick Lin was no longer their topic of discussion.

Hsu Chih-mo was talking about a famous musician, a blind man named Ah Bing who played the erhu, a two-stringed violin.

"Ah Bing is a perfect example of someone who created his art *as the people.*" Hsu Chih-mo's tone was rushed, eager to get his point across. "Before Ah Bing became an artist, he was a beggar—something the critics choose to ignore. Ah Bing spent years wandering the streets of the towns of southern China. He dressed in rags and was bitten by hungry dogs. He became famous because his music moved people.

Listening to his erhu was like hearing him tell the stories of his life. He made my heart weep and made me want to be a good human being. He didn't set out to inspire or guide . . ."

"What do you imagine occupied Ah Bing's mind when he played?" Pearl asked.

"I have asked myself the same question." Hsu Chih-mo's hands gestured like birds in the air. "Did Ah Bing think that he was creating a masterpiece? Was he impressed with himself? Did he think that he was claiming an important place in Chinese music history?" Hsu Chih-mo turned to look at Pearl as if asking for her opinion.

"More likely, he was thinking about his next meal," Pearl responded.

"Precisely!" Hsu Chih-mo agreed.

"Ah Bing wanted only to please the passersby for a penny or two," Pearl continued. "Hunger drove him. I imagine him apologizing for being a bother. At night, he slept below the ancient walls or outside the train station . . ."

"Yes, and yes," the poet Hsu Chih-mo echoed. "During his waking hours, he played his erhu to forget his misery."

"Ah Bing would take up his bow. Sorrow would pour from his strings . . ." Pearl followed.

"Yes, Ah Bing, the greatest erhu player that ever lived. His music is considered the symbol of the Yangtze River. It starts at the bottom of the Himalayas and flows like water across the vast plains of China to the East Sea and out into the Pacific Ocean."

They spoke as if I were not in the room, as if I didn't exist. I could feel the force pulling them closer. It was strong. They were my real-life Romeo and Juliet, the Butterfly Lovers. I sat behind Hsu Chih-mo in the corner of the room by the shadow near the curtains. I held my breath and dared not stir. Moment by moment I saw love take root in their hearts. They blossomed like flowers. It was fate.

I was amazed to be both witness to and victim of a great love. I was touched by their birth of feeling but sad beyond description because my heart withered.

"I share Ah Bing's joy in the warmth of springtime." Pearl's voice came gentle and soft. "I smell the sweet scent of jasmine and I see all beauty under the sky. Ah Bing's love of life touches a commoner's heart. My favorite is 'The Fair Maiden.' His longing for her is endless and deep. His musical depiction of the sunshine in a girl's eyes brings tears to my eyes."

Hsu Chih-mo turned toward Pearl and their eyes locked on each other.

"It was in music that Ah Bing escaped the life he was living." Hsu Chih-mo's voice was so quiet he was almost whispering.

"Yes," Pearl uttered. "Through music Ah Bing became the hero he desired to be."

They stopped.

The sound of a teakettle boiling came.

"Excuse me." I got up and went to the kitchen. I tried to press back my tears.

I emptied the teapot and refilled it with cold water. My hands were shaking.

After a time, I heard Hsu Chih-mo say, "That is how I felt when I read your manuscript."

I didn't hear Pearl's response.

I looked out the window. The sky was dark gray. The sound of the mountain creek was clear.

"I have to go," I heard Pearl say.

I tried not to think that Hsu Chih-mo stayed because he felt sorry for me. I invited him for dinner and drinks. Alcohol went to our heads and we became animated. I joked about my marriage and he his. Hsu Chih-mo spoke of his confusion with feminism. I asked about his infamous love life.

"Don't tell me that you hate it," I said.

"I do, believe it or not."

"Come on, you are living every man's fantasy!"

"Willow, my friend, you have had too much to drink. A cold shower would do you some good." Hsu Chih-mo shook his head.

I let him know that I was upset that his thoughts were still with the one who had left.

"You are attracted to Pearl Buck." I turned to him and made him look at me. "Don't even attempt to lie."

He smiled. "What makes you think that?"

"Can you tell me that it is not true?"

He lowered his eyes. "I am a married man."

"I am drunk." I threw my cup at him. It missed. "Now get out!"

I would have felt better if Pearl and Hsu Chih-mo had admitted their attraction to each other. Their denial and resistance made it worse. Pearl avoided Hsu Chih-mo at the university. She went to Lossing and persuaded him to move back home, which he did.

Pearl buried herself in her room and wrote feverishly. She sent out her manuscript *East Wind, West Wind* and finally found a small American publisher willing to take on the book. She was happy, even when the book didn't sell well. She didn't care. She couldn't stop writing.

She started another novel. She let me see a few pages a day from her rough draft. I ended up reading the entire manuscript. It was *The Story of Wang Lung*, a title later changed to *The Good Earth*. I could see the shadows of villagers whom we both knew. Pearl described a world I was familiar with but had never encountered in Chinese literature. She changed my perspective. She made me see things I intuitively knew to be true.

"I am doing this behind her back," I told Hsu Chih-mo when I shared Pearl's manuscript with him. I asked him to help find the manuscript a home so that Pearl could earn an advance.

Hsu Chih-mo promised to try.

I must say that I brought this upon myself—if Hsu Chih-mo hadn't already been in love with Pearl, this would have pushed him over the edge. Hsu Chih-mo believed that Pearl was a true artist, the Ah Bing of literature.

We went on being good friends. Finally, after much beating about the bush, Hsu Chih-mo asked if I could pass along a letter to Pearl Buck.

It was a thick letter.

I told Hsu Chih-mo that I would think about it. The truth was that my jealousy of Pearl was growing by the day. And I was hurt by the fact that she had never even made an effort to attract him.

Pearl was the only faculty member who voted against the renewal of Hsu Chih-mo's teaching contract. She refused to explain her action to the others.

"He wasn't telling the truth when he said that money was the reason he applied," she said, frying cabbages in her wok. "He needed to pay off his wife's debts, so he jokingly claimed. He fooled everyone on the committee but me."

"Did you read Hsu Chih-mo's comments about your new novel?" I asked.

"I did."

"What do you think?"

"What do you expect me to say?"

"Did they please you?"

"Yes, very much so. It was generous of him."

"Do you think he understands what you wrote?"

"He is the only other Chinese person besides you who understands my writing."

"There is a big difference between us. Hsu Chih-mo's credentials give him the power to influence others."

"I didn't say I couldn't use his help."

"Then why do you keep rejecting him?"

She closed the lid on the wok and turned away from the stove. "I am confused about my feelings for him." She paused before continuing. "He inspires my confidence and creativity, but . . . I am terrified at the same time."

"Are you falling in love with Hsu Chih-mo?" I watched her eyes.

"I feel like I am about to tumble down a hill."

"Yes or no?"

"Willow, please."

"Don't you think you owe me at least a clear answer?" I couldn't help raising my voice. "I am not blind and deaf as you assume. I have been poisoned by the air you two breathe. I am a strong woman capable of handling my own crisis. I am honest with myself. I have the courage to chase after my own dreams. Unfortunately, I can't force a man to fall in love with me. By God's grace, I have been blessed with everything else but the love of a man. One thing is clear: As long as you are in the picture, I don't stand a chance with Hsu Chih-mo. What can I say? Bad luck? Or do I tell myself, Okay, you can't have him but your best friend can? To tell you the truth, my heart is not that big."

"What would you like me to do?" Pearl said apologetically.

"I want you to stop lying to me!"

"Willow, I didn't lie to you. I have never lied and never will."

"Oh, donkey shit! 'I am confused about my feelings for him,' for example. Are you, really? You know exactly what is going on! You know you are in love with Hsu Chih-mo. You know you can't run away from him, though you tried and tried like a rabbit running from a forest fire."

"All right, I sinned. How do I make it right?"

"Admit the truth. Can't you see that I need a shoulder to cry on?"

I accepted Dick Lin's invitation for tea. We met at a small teahouse at the foot of the Purple Mountain. It was a warm autumn afternoon. I was in my blue coat with a black silk scarf.

Dick wore a French-style collarless jacket and a matching French hat. The moment we sat down he started to talk about himself.

"I worked in the fields with my parents before I was five," he began. "My father was determined to get me an education although he was a poor peasant. I went to school naked like other boys in the village. The new teacher was from the city, and she didn't expect to see a bunch of bare-assed monkeys. She screamed the moment she stepped into the classroom."

Dick had an abundance of self-confidence. He demanded his audience's attention.

I studied his features as he talked without pause. It was a strange picture of harmony. The lizard eyes went well with the crooked nose. The thin-lipped mouth fit the small chin. Although I didn't like him at first, I began to warm up to him, to his openness, his childlike enthusiasm, and, most of all, his will to believe in dreams.

"I traveled after I escaped my village," Dick continued. "My father chased me and beat me. He even pushed me into the river trying to drown me. I went abroad as a student worker. I lived in France for three years. I worked during the day and went to school in the evening. In Paris I experienced Communism firsthand."

Dick laughed and then paused to observe me.

I tried to be present, but it had been a long day and my mind began to wander. I nodded and asked, "So, what brought you back to China?"

"I didn't miss my family, but I did miss my country," he went on. "I was twenty-two. Never before had I felt so strongly that I could do something to help change the world, to reverse the inequity between the rich and poor . . ."

Although he lacked the grace of Hsu Chih-mo, I found myself listening.

"I could have been silent and remained unaffected." He looked at me, eager for a response. "I could have imitated an ancient sage and hid myself away in the mountains. Instead I chose to lead a purposeful life and fight for the people."

His tone was charged with energy. I was strangely moved.

The clouds drifted low to the ground and the crowns of pine trees spread like beggars' arms. Dick and I followed the trail leading to the top of the Purple Mountain. I thought about asking him to reconsider publishing

Pearl's novel. But the moment he said he would do anything for me, I changed my mind. I didn't want to be beholden to him.

Pearl deserves honor, not mercy, I thought.

Dick said that he was nervous whenever he was near me. He complimented and flattered me. I wished that his words were coming from Hsu Chih-mo. I wondered where Hsu Chih-mo was and what he was doing. Was Pearl's name written in the sky of his mind? For the past few months, Hsu Chih-mo had made visits to Shanghai to be with his wife. Each time he returned to Nanking, he would be even more depressed. When I asked about his wife, he would reply, "My wife lives in her opium den. She doesn't talk unless it is to ask me for money."

The gossip publications following Hsu Chih-mo revealed the massive debts his wife owed. The latest reports had the former courtesan spending time with a wealthy patron. Hsu Chih-mo was said to be fighting with his wife over money and her drug habit. One source said that Hsu Chih-mo had gone back to his former architect mistress. The public had become obsessed with the drama.

"It's time for you to think about taking Hsu Chih-mo as a lover," I said.

Stunned, Pearl turned to me. "You are crazy, Willow."

"Why not?" I went on. "After all, Lossing is with Lotus."

"No," she said bluntly.

"Hsu Chih-mo . . ."

"Stop, would you? I don't feel like discussing Hsu Chih-mo."

"But I do."

She was quiet.

I felt sick with myself, but couldn't stop.

"I am not a fool, Willow," I heard Pearl say. "I can see . . ."

"Then answer my question."

"I don't know how to answer your question. As you know, we both are married. Frankly, I don't enjoy this kind of joke. Or . . . is it a joke?"

"What do you think?"

"It is pure Chinese that you indulge in this game of cruelty. This is how you drive away misery. But is it working? Are you less miserable than yesterday?"

"You speak like your father, wearing God's clothes!" I responded. "You can't face the truth!"

"I am trying to act decently. I am your friend."

"Then damn your decency!"

"Fine!" She came to face me. "You want the truth? Here it is! Yes, Hsu Chih-mo and I are in love with each other! And yes, we will go to bed together, tonight!"

CHAPTER 19

I accepted Dick Lin's offer to be the editor of his magazine. I made up my mind to move to Shanghai for good.

Pearl was devastated.

A month before I left, Hsu Chih-mo paid me a visit. He pleaded with me to save his relationship with Pearl. "She fell apart after learning about your departure. She told me that she would view me as an enemy if I continued to visit her. She's engaged in a war with me."

I refused to talk to Hsu Chih-mo. I had done enough for him.

Confused, he said, "I'll come back when you are in a better mood."

After he left, I couldn't escape the sound of his voice praising Pearl. "Pearl and I are soul mates!" "*The Good Earth* is like no other novel I have ever read. It's a masterpiece!" "It takes a humanitarian to be a good novelist." "She denied that love has passed between us!"

Before I could say hello to Shanghai and to Dick Lin, I knew that I must settle my past accounts and say good-bye to Nanking. Yet the shadows of Pearl Buck and Hsu Chih-mo followed close upon me.

Dick promised me independence. He said that he would always be there for me if I needed him.

"You are coming to Shanghai," he said in his letters, "and that is all that counts."

Dick was confident that I would grow to love him.

I warned him that I was taking advantage of him.

"You don't owe me anything" was his response.

Dick told me that Shanghai had been the red cradle ever since the Communist Party had been created in 1921. Although the party was still considered a guerrilla group, it was becoming the major opposition force against the ruling nationalist government. Dick played an important role in the party. He had become Mao Tse-tung's chief adviser and he ran the party's bureau of propaganda.

I was not terribly interested in the new world Dick described. I didn't care whether or not the Communists would win China. What I cared about was having a place in Shanghai where I could tend to my wounds and try to start my life again. Dick made it convenient.

"You used to be a tiny creek and now you are part of an ocean." Dick was as happy as a goalie after catching a ball.

The day of my departure was approaching. I wasn't living a lie, yet I wasn't living truthfully either. Pearl and Hsu Chih-mo had called a cease-fire and had finally become lovers. I took credit because I had helped. My home was their love nest. There, they were able to escape the prying eyes of the public. But I was wrong about myself. I was consumed by envy and jealousy.

Pearl knew me too well to feel comfortable with the situation. She even refused to show up when Hsu Chih-mo gave me a farewell dinner. On the one hand, I was comforted by the fact that Hsu Chih-mo didn't know that I was in love with him. On the other, I suffered when he shared with me his feelings for my friend. "I am in love" was written all over his face. It hurt me, but Hsu Chih-mo couldn't stop talking and I couldn't stop listening.

Hsu Chih-mo was convinced that Pearl was more Chinese than he was. He was infatuated with her perspective, her Chinese habits, her love of camellias. He was especially thrilled when she cursed in Chinese. He loved "the Chinese soul under the white skin."

Hsu Chih-mo told me that he used to play with peasant children when he was young. "My family were small landowners, so I was surrounded by peasant children. But I had no understanding of them when I played with them. I only knew that I was the young master and they were my slaves. They were not my equals as human beings. My family owned them or hired them. All Chinese schoolboys have the same attitude. When they become adults they look down on peasants. But Pearl believes that all spirits are equal before God. This respect for her subjects makes her work wonderful. In her, one hears the voice of a peasant as a human being."

I drank and toasted with him.

Hsu Chih-mo confessed, "Pearl makes me happy. I never know what she is going to say next. She's brilliant, cunning, and funny. The mix of the Chinese and American cultures in her fascinates me always. I find myself looking forward to her thoughts."

"What about love?" I asked.

"What about it?" He blinked.

"Does she . . . love like a Chinese woman?"

Hsu Chih-mo's lips stretched into a big smile. "That is my secret."

"Share with me a little, please."

"I must go, Willow."

"How dare you destroy the bridge after crossing the river!"

I imagined the hands she described, his hands, touching her. Pearl told me that she had woken up from her foolishness. I asked what she meant. She said that Lossing vanished from her mind the moment she was alone with Hsu Chih-mo. She was afraid she was becoming obsessed with Hsu Chih-mo. "I used to think that what I went through with Lossing happened in every marriage. I write about romance because it hasn't existed in my life."

"And romance is frightening?"

"I am afraid of what that knowledge will do to me."

"So this may be more than just an affair?"

"I don't know anymore. Hsu Chih-mo is a green refuge in the desert of my life. Because of him, I am more patient with Carol and tolerant of Absalom. I am no longer disgusted with myself. My despair has left me. I have even been thinking about adopting a little girl. In fact, I've already begun the process. And yet ..." She stopped for a moment before continuing. "It is hard to see that Hsu Chih-mo and I would have a future together."

"Because you are both married? Or because you are too different as individuals?"

"All I know is that I am in love with him, and that common sense has deserted me."

"Hsu Chih-mo will continue to pursue you."

"He doesn't understand my responsibilities. He doesn't understand that I will never be free because of Carol. He told me that he lost his own son at the age of five. He was able to dig himself out of his own sorrow. But I can't. I am not like him. For Carol's sake, I must stay with Lossing ... for the money."

"Will you give up Hsu Chih-mo?"

"Do I have a choice?"

"Your mother used to say that life is about being forced to make choices."

We both went quiet. "I am watching life escape before my eyes," she said.

The air was filled with the sweet scent of summer blossoms. I had come to the riverbank to say good-bye to the city of Nanking. I knew that under the cover of darkness, in the shadow of the magnolia canopies, Hsu Chih-mo and Pearl walked the streets of Nanking. Pearl had told me that the place they most often frequented was a local restaurant called Seven Treasures. Her favorite was Chin-kiang mushroom noodle soup.

Lossing had moved away again with Lotus. He had accepted a new position as the head of the agricultural department at a university in southwest China. Hsu Chih-mo was free to visit Pearl, although in secrecy. The love she could not let go of revived Pearl, and she changed. She began to pay attention to the way she dressed and she joined a dance class at the university. She went with Hsu Chih-mo to collect fresh camellias during the early spring. Inspired, Hsu Chih-mo published a poem titled "The Camellia Petals on My Pillow."

Rumors spread and the public assumed that Hsu Chih-mo had gone back to his former mistress. The newspapers competed to predict Hsu Chih-mo's next move.

I didn't answer Pearl's request for a chance to say good-bye.

I felt that we had said enough to each other. I didn't want to hear the name Hsu Chih-mo again. I left quietly. The pier was crowded. I boarded the steamboat and stood by myself. As the boat began to pull away, I got a surprise.

Pearl ran down the stone terrace toward the water.

I didn't think she would be able to find me.

She slowed and finally stopped. Behind her, people waved, cheered, and shouted.

Then she found me. Her eyes. I knew she saw me because she stood completely still, gazing in my direction. She wore an indigo-colored Chinese outfit. Her hair was in a bun. The sun shone down on her. She looked like Carie.

I wished that I could shut my eyes.

The porters let go of the ropes. The steamboat began to pick up speed.

"Farewell!" the crowd on the pier cried.

One wife shouted at her husband affectionately, "Hey, you idiot and soon-to-be-beheaded. Don't forget to save firewood after lighting the stove!"

The husband laughed and yelled back, "Hey, dumb wrinkleface, you'd better remember to come home or you will find me spending all your savings on a concubine!"

I wept, wishing that my arms were around Pearl. By leaving I meant to escape my own misery, but I had ended up punishing her.

The departure would preserve what we had, I hoped.

Yet could I truly leave?

The water gap between us widened. People screamed back and forth in a contest of comic insults.

Then, in a Chin-kiang tone, I heard Pearl yell, "I am not a bird but a mosquito—too tiny for you to use a rifle on!"

Knowing I was forgiven, I shot back, "Be careful when you think that you have gotten a good deal. Check on your handsome rooster. Don't be surprised if he grows a set of teeth one day!"

"Go ahead and cartwheel on the back of a bull! I am a loyal admirer!"

"Yeah, the fox comes and cries at the chicken's funeral. Go away!"

CHAPTER 20

I wasn't sure whether it was my door or the neighbors' when I heard the knocking. The attic room where I lived was near the Shanghai waterfront, the Bund. At night I could hear porters at work and the sighing sound of passing ships. I tried to go back to sleep but the knocking grew louder. I realized that it was my door. I glanced at the clock. It was four in the morning.

"Willow!" came Dick's voice.

I went to open the door.

The expression on Dick's face scared me. His eyes were red and swollen, as if he'd been crying.

"What's wrong?" I asked.

Dick handed me a stack of newspapers.

I glanced at the headlines and staggered back in shock.

POET DIES IN PLANE CRASH!

HSU CHIH-MO'S PASSING AT 34 STUNS THE NATION!

POSTAL PLANE CRASHES NEAR NANKING, PILOT AND PASSENGER. NONE SURVIVE.

I recognized the words, but my mind refused to acknowledge their meanings. I kept flipping the newspapers back and forth. The date was correct, November 20, 1931. Hsu Chih-mo's face was on every front page. I looked at him, the handsome smiling face, the leaf-shaped gentle eyes and the silky black hair. The classic good looks of a northerner. I touched the image of his face with my fingers. My tears smeared the ink.

Dick held my shoulders and sobbed like a child. "Did you know about him taking free rides on postal airplanes?" he asked.

Of course I knew. Hsu Chih-mo had been in touch with me because Pearl had again been refusing to see him. Pearl wanted to end their affair. Hsu Chih-mo figured it was because he was still a married man. He returned to Shanghai and asked for a divorce from his wife. But his wife wouldn't release him without an impossible monetary settlement. To make money, Hsu Chih-mo accepted lecture invitations all over the country. He traveled every few days from city to city. He was also teaching part-time at both Shanghai University and Peking University. He was offered free airplane rides by a friend, a postal pilot. Hsu Chih-mo was grateful to save the money. The friend also flew Hsu Chih-mo to Nanking to meet Pearl in secrecy.

"Once bitten by a snake, forever in fear of ropes," Hsu Chih-mo once said about Pearl's anxiety about a new marriage.

"Isn't it enough that you are lovers?" I asked.

"No." His voice was soft but determined. "I'd like to spend the rest of my life with her."

The expression on Hsu Chih-mo's face was still vivid in my mind. He had sat on the chair in my attic. When he stood, his head touched the ceiling. He hunched to make himself fit. Behind him, beyond an open window, was a sea of Shanghai rooftops.

Pearl would learn the news in the next few hours. She would discover her lover's death at the breakfast table, perhaps. Carol wouldn't notice her mother's shock, and the servant wouldn't know where the mistress's tears sprang from.

I hadn't told Pearl about Hsu Chih-mo's last visit. He had been upset and angry at me for supporting Pearl's decision.

In the past, their separations had never lasted. It was like cutting water with a sword. They simply couldn't resist each other. Hsu Chih-mo took the free plane ride three times a week to be with her. I learned from Hsu Chih-mo that the pilot let him borrow his farmhouse near the airport. Pearl described to me her visits to the farmhouse.

"I was like an addict running toward opium," she said of her meetings with Hsu Chih-mo.

I kept finding out new details about the plane crash. On the day of the accident the weather was foggy. The pilot misjudged. The plane hit the mountaintop and crashed. One source said that the pilot often got absorbed in conversation with Hsu Chih-mo. They thought the accident might have taken place because the pilot was distracted.

The papers said that Hsu Chih-mo's wife was so heartbroken that she vowed to quit opium. She declared to the public that she would devote her life to publishing all Hsu Chih-mo's remaining work and letters.

Hsu Chih-mo's funeral was held in Nanking.

I asked Dick, "Why not Peking? Why not Shanghai?"

"It was Hsu Chih-mo's wish," Dick replied. "He wanted his ashes to be scattered over the Purple Mountain and the Yangtze River."

Had Hsu Chih-mo anticipated the possibility of his crash? I was astonished at the thought. Certainly the poet had had an active imagination. It wouldn't have been unthinkable for him to have entertained the idea of a dramatic exit.

I remembered Hsu Chih-mo's description of his last falling-out with Pearl. He visited me after days of drinking and sleepless nights. In fact, it was two days before he took the fatal flight.

"Will you give this to her?" he asked, holding out a package.

"She told you that this had to stop," I responded.

"It will be the last time that I impose on you."

"What is it?"

"My new book, a collection of poems."

I gave him a she-won't-read-it look.

"I don't care. She inspired it."

Mourners filled the streets of Nanking. White magnolias and jasmine were sold out. Dick and I had taken a train from Shanghai to Nanking.

We arrived in the afternoon. Dick had sent Pearl a message before we left but received no response.

The Nanking crematorium was covered with white flowers. A photo of Hsu Chih-mo on the wall greeted the visitors. A banner that ran the length of the hall read, PEOPLE'S POET RESTS IN PEACE. Beyond the flower wreath was the closed casket. Dick had seen his friend's body and said that Hsu Chih-mo would have wanted the lid closed.

No one in Pearl's house knew where she was. The maid said that her mistress had gone to the university. Eventually I thought of the pilot's farmhouse.

I only had Pearl's vague description of the place, but I told Dick that I would look for her. Once outside the city, I was lost. It was a peasant child who pointed me in the right direction. The child had seen an airplane landing and taking off at an abandoned World War I–era military airport near the house. The spot was cradled by the surrounding hills. Waist-tall weeds grew in patches across the cracked runway.

The farmhouse was covered with wild ivy. Frogs and crickets ceased their singing as I walked to the door. Grasshoppers jumped over my feet, and one almost got into my mouth. Giant mosquitoes buzzed around my head.

The door was ready to fall from its hinges. It leaned to one side and was open. I let myself in. Once inside, I smelled the incense.

She was in an ocean-blue Chinese dress, embroidered with white chrysanthemums, the symbol of grief. She was on her knees lighting incense. She had been performing the traditional Chinese soul-guarding ceremony for Hsu Chih-mo. She had set up an altar with flowers and water.

"Pearl," I called.

She rose and came to me and collapsed in my arms.

Softly, I told her that I had come to deliver Hsu Chih-mo's package. She nodded.

I passed her the package and said, "I'll be outside."

When she emerged from the farmhouse, she looked like an Oriental, her eyes were so swollen from crying.

She asked me to take a look at the first page of Hsu Chih-mo's book. The title was *Lonely Night*.

> *Across the screen the autumn moon*
> > *stares coldly from the sky*
> *With silken fan I sit and flick*
> > *the fireflies sailing by*
> *The night grows colder every hour*
> > *it chills the heart*
> *To watch the spinning Damsel*
> > *from the Herd Boy far apart*
> *A wilderness alone remains*
> > *all garden glories gone*
> *The river runs unheeded by*
> > *weeds grow unheeded on*
> *Dusk comes the east wind blows and birds*
> > *pipe forth a mournful sound*
> *Petals like nymphs from balconies*
> > *come tumbling to the ground*

I had known Pearl's loneliness since we were children. She had always searched for her "own kind." That didn't mean another Westerner. It meant another soul that experienced and understood both the Eastern and Western worlds.

It was in Hsu Chih-mo that Pearl had found what she was looking for. With him she had not been lonely. If she were the cresting wave's cheerful foam, Hsu Chih-mo would be the wrinkled sea sand beneath.

Ashes gathered at the bottom of the incense burner.

The sun set behind the hill and the room fell instantly dark.

In the future I would understand the connection between Pearl's accomplishments as a novelist and her love of Hsu Chih-mo. Over the eighty books she would create in her lifetime, she would carry on her affair with Hsu Chih-mo.

"Writing a novel is like chasing and catching spirits," Pearl Buck would say of her writing process. "The novelist gets invited into splendid dreams. The lucky one gets to live the dream once, and the luckiest over and over."

She was the luckiest one. She must have met with his spirit throughout the rest of her life. I will never forget the moment Pearl lit her last stick of incense. She composed a poem in Chinese bidding good-bye to Hsu Chih-mo.

Wild summer was in your gaze
Earth laughs in flowers
Lust in the chili of the grave
Wind's hand touches

Mind bent with the weight of sorrow.
Orchid boat I board alone
Spring rain blurs the lantern light
Deep green are my parting thoughts of you

I considered myself lucky too. Although Hsu Chih-mo didn't love me, he trusted me. It made our ordinary friendship extraordinary. There was commitment and devotion between us. Hsu Chih-mo had asked me to keep the original manuscripts of his poetry. His wife had threatened to burn them because in the pages she "smelled the scent of another woman."

I became the keeper of Hsu Chih-mo's secrets. I was so faithful that I didn't even share those manuscripts with Pearl. I'd like to think that Hsu Chih-mo loved me in a special way. The most important lesson he taught me was that there was no one singular perspective on things or emotions in the universe—no one way of comprehending truth.

Hsu Chih-mo, the man, the child, the poet who smiled at all that passed beyond his understanding, would remain in my life. I possessed, literally, his poetry, although I wished that I had won his heart. After Hsu Chih-mo's wife died, I began to release his poems one at a time. My intent was to make his legacy last. I created ambiguity and the public embraced it. "Let's allow mystery to pervade," I said to journalists.

Columnists speculated about what might have happened if Hsu Chih-mo had lived. The result was that the poems I released were printed in the newspapers. The public was hungry for Hsu Chih-mo. There were always new discoveries about his romantic life. He was more famous after death.

Over time, I became the collector of everything Hsu Chih-mo. In addition to his poems and letters, I sought copies of written materials about him, including the most frivolous gossip.

After Hsu Chih-mo's death I moved to Nanking to be closer to Pearl and to his memory.

In the name of the *Nanking Daily*, I organized the Hsu Chih-mo Conference. The event satisfied my desire to hear his name pronounced on the lips of the young. Female university students carried *The Collected Poems of Hsu Chih-mo* under their arms like fashionable handbags. They reminded me of myself, the way I once was in love, still was, and would forever be. I whispered Hsu Chih-mo's name in darkness and daylight, alone or with Pearl or without her.

People from every corner of China attended my conference. There were suspicions, rumors, and questions regarding the reason Hsu Chih-mo had chosen me to keep his papers. "We were best friends," I answered with ease.

I felt as if I were living in a fictional world when the list of Hsu Chih-mo's mistresses and love interests continued. The details were imaginative and vivid. Some did get close to the truth. Yet in the end none hit the target.

I enjoyed the colorful interpretations of Hsu Chih-mo's life while knowing that I alone held the truth.

Part Three

CHAPTER 21

Hsu Chih-mo's death reminded us how fragile life could be. Looking back, I realized that it was Dick's love for Hsu Chih-mo that bound us together. Dick had once been combative and imposing, and Hsu Chih-mo had changed him. Dick acknowledged, "If I am a giant today, it is because Hsu Chih-mo taught me the difference between physical and intellectual height."

I married Dick Lin after Hsu Chih-mo died. He worked in Shanghai and came to see me in Nanking once a month.

Pearl continued to teach at Nanking University but she no longer lingered on campus. Every time she saw the tree that Hsu Chih-mo used to sit under waiting for her, she would burst into tears. Hsu Chih-mo was more in her life than when he had been alive.

"Hsu Chih-mo was the only Chinese man I know who was true to himself," Pearl told me. "In his way, he was daring and almost impulsive. I couldn't help but love him. It was selfish of me. But I needed him. We needed each other."

One thing Pearl seemed unaware of was that Hsu Chih-mo had also been her challenge. I was never a challenge for Pearl, in contrast. She was attracted to challenges. When she lived in China, she never looked down on anyone, but she also never looked up to anyone until Hsu Chih-mo.

Without Pearl and Hsu Chih-mo in my life, I never would have been the person I am today. The three of us discussed Shakespeare, Rousseau, Dickens, and classic Chinese poets and novelists. Although I published and impressed others as a writer, it was never my air and rice, as it was for Pearl and Hsu Chih-mo.

Like Carie, Pearl worked obsessively for the church and offered her charity. She played Carie's piano, which was falling apart. The keys either didn't work or were out of tune. Pearl made the best of it. During Christmas season, we gathered. Pearl retranslated Absalom's lyrics into Chinese. We spent the evenings singing Carie's favorites, from "The God of Glory" to "Hail the Heaven-Born Prince of Peace"; from "Love Has Come" to "Hark the Herald Angels Sing."

Papa no longer worried about the church attendance—the members of the Chin-kiang congregation by now far outnumbered those of the local Buddhist temples. More and more people were choosing the Foreign God Jesus Christ.

Pearl's home became what Carie's once was, a shelter for the needy. Neighbors came by unannounced. People borrowed whatever they needed, from gingerroot and garlic to pots and pans, medicine and clothing. As they visited, they shared words with Pearl. They complained about bad weather, failed business deals, nasty mothers-in-law or troubled children. Pearl listened and comforted them. She believed that only when one understood suffering was one capable of happiness.

It was the house rule that no one mentioned Carol's condition to outsiders, but Pearl realized that people drew closer to her because of Carol. Pearl was better understood. Local children were taught to play with Carol as if she were normal.

I had a feeling that Pearl knew Dick's true identity, although she never asked. By 1933, Dick was the head of the Shanghai branch of the Communist Party. The party survived the Nationalists' brutal purge. Mao retreated to Shan-hsi province, a remote area in the northwest mountains. Dick was left alone to be in charge. He barely had time to travel to Nanking.

While the Nationalists fought the Communists, Japan penetrated into China. In early 1934 Japan launched a full-scale invasion and took Manchuria. The nation protested and forced the head of the Nationalists, Chiang Kai-shek, to unite with the Communists instead of hunting them down.

While the Nationalist troops turned around and marched toward Manchuria to fight the Japanese, Mao expanded his forces. Dick received secret orders from Mao to focus on key generals who served Chiang Kai-shek. Dick's goal was to inspire them to lead an uprising inside the Nationalist military.

"We will take the troops who rebel to Mao," Dick told me.

Although I was aware of the danger, I supported Dick. It was clear that he simply couldn't be stopped. What concerned me was his safety.

One day my fear turned into a reality: Dick's plan ran into trouble when sensitive information was leaked. By the time I heard the news, Dick was on the run. Overnight, he was on the government's most-wanted list. Dick was followed everywhere. Soon he ran out of places to hide in Shanghai. Whoever received him was followed and arrested.

I went to Pearl and asked if she could help by getting Dick a temporary job at Nanking University. "Dick must have a job in order to register with the city as a legal resident," I told Pearl. "Dick will take any job, even as a janitor or night guard. There would be no financial burden to the university because we'd give you money to pay his salary."

Pearl promised to try, but she warned me that the situation in Nanking was becoming uncertain.

"I would hire Dick as my house servant if it wouldn't be so suspicious," Pearl added. "I am watched because all foreigners are considered allies of Japan."

The moment Dick arrived in Nanking, he was arrested. He was thrown into the Nationalist military prison. Although his true identity was still undiscovered, he was tried as a Communist. He was asked to cooperate and produce the names of his comrades. When he refused, he was beaten and his jaw broken.

"Has he been allowed a doctor?" Absalom asked when I told Pearl the news.

"No," I replied.

"Nonsense!" Absalom said. "I don't think that we are helpless." He turned to Pearl. "There must be something we can do to help Dick."

"Father, we must be cautious. We are not the only ones at risk," Pearl said, reminding him of the other people in her house. "We are responsible for their lives as well."

Pearl's house was crowded. Besides Absalom and Carol, Pearl's sister, Grace, had moved in. Her family had also stayed in China, as missionaries. Pearl's new adopted daughter, Janice, was there too. She was a little older than Carol. The two were already close sisters.

Pearl insisted that I stay with her instead of going back to my own house.

When Nanking University turned down Pearl's proposal to hire Dick, the seventy-seven-year-old Absalom went to the Nanking government and claimed that Dick was his assistant working for the church.

"It was the first time in his life that Absalom chose to sin," Pearl later said, after Dick's release.

Absalom made it his duty to protect the members of his church. He had difficulty because Dick was not a Christian. It was Papa who convinced Absalom that by helping Dick he was helping our family.

"Dick needs to see God's work in action," Papa said to Absalom. "Because of your good deed, you may soon see his conversion."

Absalom knew that Chiang Kai-shek was a new Christian himself, although he'd converted only to satisfy his wife's marriage request. When Absalom heard this, he knew that he stood a chance.

"What if Dick refuses to convert afterward?" I asked. "We don't want to disappoint Absalom."

Papa replied, "Dick will remember that he was saved by a man of God."

Even covered with a beard, Dick's face was horribly misshapen. The right side of his jaw was swollen and much larger than the left. Pearl arranged for a doctor from the American Embassy to come. The doctor reset Dick's jaw and wired his mouth shut.

For days, Dick couldn't speak. This was perhaps fortunate, because he couldn't respond to Absalom's talk of God. If Dick had been able to speak, the two would have been in combat.

Laughing at the thought, Pearl said, "Dick would try to convert Absalom to Communism."

Eventually Dick had enough. He left without saying good-bye to Absalom.

Two weeks after Dick's release, an order arrived from Communist headquarters. He left the next day to join Mao at his base in Yenan. Dick told Pearl he was grateful for Absalom's rescue, but that he could never believe in God.

"Your father must learn that we Communists are fighting for a real cause," Dick said to Pearl. "China will one day be free of politics and religion. People will be their own gods."

Pearl told Dick that she and her father had disagreements on many things. "He is God's fighting angel. I don't understand him, but I love him."

Dick replied that it didn't make sense to him. "I could not love my father if he were my political enemy," he said.

Pearl smiled. "There is no enemy for me."

In retrospect, Dick's encounter with Pearl and Absalom helped him become a different kind of Communist. In a way, it was a perfect example of how God worked. Only the future would reveal the changes that had occurred in Dick. Without knowing it, his horizon had been expanded as God's light shone on him.

*   *   *

Before my husband left we spent the evening together. His jaw was still tender but I cooked him his favorite meal and we stayed up late into the night discussing our plans. Dick was excited by the journey he was about to take, although we both shed tears at the idea of parting. He promised to come back and fetch me as soon as he was settled. I knew that if I insisted, Dick would stay in Nanking. He would do it for me, even though his heart was already with Mao and his comrades. Dick left me with a quote from Madame Curie: *The weak one waits for opportunity while the strong one creates.* By *opportunity*, he meant his dream of a people's China.

When I sent my first letter to Dick two months later I had some news to share with my husband. On our last night together we had shared a bed and I had become pregnant. I was thrilled because years before, a doctor had told me after my miscarriage that I would not be able to bear children. I was forty-three years old and Dick forty-six. It was the happiest letter I've ever sent.

Pearl suggested that I start collecting medicine and packing it into bags. She had learned from an American journalist friend who had interviewed Mao that "medicine is the best currency in Yenan." And besides, I didn't want to be without medicine for my newborn.

CHAPTER 22

The day Papa abandoned his church in Chin-kiang and came to Nanking was the day Pearl sensed that the safety of foreigners in China was a thing of the past.

Papa told us that the church had been attacked. The Nationalist government was convinced that Communism was a foreign idea, thus the church must be a hiding place for Communists.

"Dick was fortunate to depart earlier," Papa said. "He could have been captured and murdered if he had stayed."

We learned that all the escape routes from Nanking to inland and coastal cities were now controlled by warlords who had become allies of the Nationalists.

The city of Nanking showed no sign of what was about to take place as we gathered on Sunday morning at the church. People believed that what had happened in Chin-kiang wouldn't happen here, because Nanking was a capital city and had a number of foreign embassies.

Absalom led the Bible reading. We studied chapter twenty-seven, Paul's voyage to Rome. I had difficulty concentrating. I worried about Dick and the safety of the baby inside me. Tracing the words with my finger, I followed Absalom. '*And when neither sun nor stars in many days appeared, and no small tempest lay on us, all hope that we should be saved was then taken away . . .*"

As Absalom strained to convince us that God would not let evil win, a young red-haired officer from the American Embassy ran in. He was breathless and drenched in sweat.

"Yes, sir?" Absalom was annoyed by the interruption. "How can I help you?"

The officer passed a letter to Absalom and said, "The consul general has ordered the immediate evacuation of all Americans in Nanking."

"*What* is going on?" Absalom put down the Bible.

"The Chinese government informed us that it has lost control over the spreading chaos." The officer spoke quickly. "There have been riots in the provinces of Shandong, Anhui, and Jiangsu. Mobs and soldiers have killed foreigners."

"We have seen none of this in Nanking," Absalom responded. "Are you sure our consul general is not making a storm out of a little breeze?"

"Sir, I must move on," the officer said and excused himself.

The church was silent.

All eyes were on Absalom.

Absalom gave an unconcerned expression as he picked up the Bible. He turned a page and began to read. His voice was calm, as if nothing had happened. "*And now I exhort you to be of good cheer: for there shall be no loss of any man's life among you, but of the ship. For there stood by me this night the angel of God, whose I am, and whom I serve . . .*"

Absalom asked the crowd to join him, and we followed. "*Saying, Fear not, Paul; thou must be brought before Caesar and God hath given thee all them that sail with thee, wherefore, sirs, be of good cheer, for I believe in God . . .*"

Papa was becoming nervous. Finally he couldn't contain himself. "Absalom," he called.

Absalom ignored him.

"Master Absalom." Papa's voice trembled.

"Yes, Mr. Yee?" Absalom was visibly disturbed. "You'd better have a good reason for interrupting like this."

With a note of panic in his voice, Papa cried, "Nanking will be the next Chin-kiang!"

"Calm down, Mr. Yee!"

"Time is short," Papa pleaded. "You and your family need to evacuate right away!"

"What are you talking about, Mr. Yee?" Absalom stared at him. "Where do you suggest that we go?"

"Home, Master Absalom!"

"We are home."

"No! I mean your home in America!" Papa began to stutter. "Sir, your life is in danger!"

"I'll be going nowhere." Absalom responded firmly. "My home is China."

Pearl watched the evacuation of all her Western friends. Laborers worked day and night carrying cases and bags toward the river, where steamboats waited. The last American family to depart was the embassy doctor's. When their boat pulled away, Pearl lost her composure.

"What if Carol gets sick?" she cried to Absalom. "What if you fall off your donkey and break a leg?"

Absalom replied, "Chinese people have survived thousands of years without Western medicine."

"What if surgery is needed?" Pearl asked.

"God will take care of us."

"Please, Father, this is a practical matter."

"I *am* talking about a practical matter." Absalom became impatient. "You must have faith in God."

"I have a sick child, Father, and I can't do without a doctor."

Absalom spoke without looking at Pearl. "God's work requires sacrifice."

"God's work?" Pearl became angry. "It's your work! It's Absalom's glory, Absalom's obsession! Why should the rest of us sacrifice for you?"

Grace joined Pearl, begging her father to reconsider.

"What's wrong with you all?" Absalom yelled. "By all means go ahead and evacuate! Get going before the steamboats are gone."

"We can't leave without you," both Pearl and Grace said. "You are an old man!"

"The Lord won't let anything happen to me." Absalom was confident. "He needs me to do his work."

The air smelled like it was burning. The streets of Nanking had turned ghostly. Businesses were closed. Nearly all foreigners had already fled. Pearl and Absalom hid inside their house. Although Pearl's servants were willing to stay on, Pearl insisted that they leave. She promised that she would hire them back once the danger was over. The servants departed. They knew that if they stayed, they could be killed for having served the foreigners.

Papa and I got busy trying to fill the water jars and stockpile food. Each day we checked on Pearl's family. Pearl told me that Absalom had become a problem. He refused to stay inside. He believed that what was happening was perfect for his work. "Desperate people turn to God," he said.

Pearl and Grace came to Papa for help. They begged him to find a way to stop Absalom.

Papa challenged Absalom on his Chinese translations of the Bible. The two men argued loudly.

"It's not an error," Papa insisted. "Some of the stories just don't make sense in Chinese."

Eventually, Absalom decided to sit down and work on his revisions.

In only a few days, the streets were filled with strangers. The boarded-up shops were broken into. People were running and others chasing. Screams and shouts could be heard day and night. I could hear the sound of distant gunshots.

I visited the university, wondering what had happened there. The campus was as quiet as a cemetery. I went to the science building and saw windows with bullet holes in them. Then I saw bloodstains on the sidewalk.

"Help!" I heard a voice.

To my horror, I found a foreigner hiding behind the bushes in a pool of blood. He had been shot in the chest. "Help!" the man cried, struggling to speak. "I am the dean of the school and I ... am an American missionary."

Before I could ask for his name, he passed out.

"Sir! Sir!" I knelt and shook him.

The man died in my arms. The sound of gunshots was so near now that I listened for the whistling of bullets. I set the dead man down and covered him with my blouse. I walked toward the town. The wind felt cool on my face. It was an otherwise perfect spring day with camellias blossoming.

There was a woman running toward me. Her arms were waving frantically in the air.

I recognized her. "Lilac!"

"The mobs have come!" Lilac yelled. "They are looking for foreigners! They have already killed one. I heard that he was the dean of the university."

"Lilac, that man died in my arms!"

Lilac saw the blood on my hands and clothes. The color drained from her face.

We took shortcuts through the hills toward Pearl's house. I regretted not insisting that Pearl and her family leave days ago. Panic began to overtake me as I pictured the mob. Lilac told me that she had witnessed the murders of Chinese Christians, our friends and neighbors.

Pearl felt fortunate that everyone in the family had survived so far. The house had been looted three times by soldiers and groups of angry men. Every valuable thing had been taken. The last group had left disappointed because nothing was left.

Absalom's forehead was bleeding. He had tried to stop the mob and had been knocked down. Even that hadn't stopped Absalom from continuing to reason with the intruders. He was determined to show God's grace. It had been Papa who had offered his last money to the looters so they would leave.

Pearl was devastated to learn that the dean of the university, a personal friend, had been killed.

"More soldiers will be coming to Nanking," Papa predicted.

Pearl and Grace held their children. Grace wept. The sisters wondered if it would be wise to separate the family.

Papa told Pearl that soldiers and mobs were everywhere and that it wasn't safe to be outside. "They will shoot the moment they see a foreigner."

Absalom talked again about faith in God.

Pearl turned away.

Absalom suggested that they all pray together. "Let us properly prepare to meet our fate."

No one responded.

Absalom went to his room and closed the door.

Pearl and Grace looked at each other. Their eyes were filled with tears. I was afraid. No one knew what to do.

Pearl took a pen and paper and began to write quickly.

"I'm going to the pier," she announced. "Perhaps a foreign ship might take pity on us. It won't hurt to try. I am writing down all our names."

"Let me do it," I volunteered. "You'd be a walking target with your blonde hair."

Pearl gave me the folded letter. "Give this to anyone whom you think could help us."

"Let me go," Papa offered. "The soldiers will rape Willow. Besides, she is pregnant."

"No, Papa," I said. "You are old . . ."

Before I could say more, Papa took the letter from Pearl and left the house. I had never seen him run so fast. His small frame bounded like a deer as he moved out of sight.

We dared not light candles. The children were asleep. Pearl and Grace stood behind the front door. They listened to every sound. I was exhausted from carrying water to the house and tried to sleep on a straw mat on the floor. I thought about Dick and Papa and prayed for their safety.

Hours later, a loud banging on the door woke me from a deep sleep. Thinking it was the mob, everyone jumped up.

"Who is it?" Pearl asked.

"Open the door, please! It's me, Soo-ching!"

"Do I know you?" asked Pearl.

"Yes, I delivered my son in your backyard!"

"What?"

"My name is Soo-ching, and my son's name is Confucius!"

"Oh, Confucius, yes, I remember!" Pearl opened the door.

A heavy manure stink came with her into the room.

"What has happened to you, Soo-ching?" Pearl asked.

"I poured a bucket of feces over myself for safety," she said.

"How can I help you?" Pearl asked.

"Help me? No, I'm here to help you! Because tomorrow you will be dead!"

"What do you mean, Soo-ching?"

"I was forced to cook for the soldiers. They are preparing a celebration banquet for tomorrow. I asked what for, and they said they were going to kill all the foreigners in Nanking, tomorrow!"

Pearl's face turned pale.

"I come to offer you a hiding place, Mrs. Pearl," Soo-ching said.

"How kind of you, Soo-ching!" Pearl cried.

"Buddha blesses you, Pearl. You offered me a drop of water when I was dying of thirst. Now it is my turn to offer you a flowing creek." Soo-ching turned to introduce her son. "Confucius, come and pay your respect."

Confucius, a stick-thin, cross-eyed boy, bowed to Pearl.

With tears in their eyes, Pearl's family, including Absalom, gathered. They followed Soo-ching and arrived at her thatched hut.

The moment Soo-ching opened the door, mosquitoes came swarming out like brown balls. They targeted our faces, arms, and legs. Their buzzing was like ten erhus playing at the same time.

"Everyone stays away because of the stink," Soo-ching said.

As soon as Pearl, Grace, Absalom, and the children had let themselves into the hut, Soo-ching moved bales of hay against the door to seal it shut and make it difficult to open. She brought buckets of donkey piss and slopped it on the hard-packed ground before the door.

Papa showed up exhausted. He hadn't been able to find any help. I asked what he'd done with Pearl's letter. He told me that he had given it to Carpenter Chan. "He'll find a boat if there is a boat to be found."

I was upset. "Pearl has been waiting for your return."

Papa said that it was time for us to think about our own survival. "Have you heard anything from your husband?" he asked. "I thought he would come to fetch you."

"Dick did send a message," I said. "But who is going to help Pearl and her family?"

"We have done our best," Papa replied.

"Why don't you go and find yourself a hiding place?" I was disappointed.

"I will."

I never anticipated what would happen next: Papa and I were kidnapped in broad daylight. Unable to resist a reward, an acquaintance sold Papa to the soldier mobs.

The informer pointed at Papa. "This man knows exactly where the foreigners are hiding."

Papa and I realized that we were dealing with professional soldiers whose leader was a warlord we used to know, Bumpkin Emperor.

It had been over twenty years since I had first met him. The man had gone from being a local warlord to becoming the commander of the Nationalist forces in our region. Bumpkin Emperor claimed that he had killed more foreigners than anyone else in the country. He was responsible for the dean's death.

The soldiers prepared to torture us. They wanted to know the hiding place of the foreigners. I clenched my teeth and prayed. The soldiers choked me with hot-pepper water until I passed out.

*　　*　　*

I woke to a clean room. Papa was sitting next to me.

I sensed his nervousness and asked, "Papa, where are we?" I saw that his fingertips were wrapped in cloth bandages.

"Have some water, Willow." He passed me the cup.

"No, Papa. Please, first explain what happened."

"I'm getting you out of here."

"Papa, what is going on?"

"I made a deal, and we are both going to be released."

"Deal?" I stared at him. "What kind of deal? What did you do?"

He avoided my eyes.

"Speak, Papa!" I tried not to let my imagination run wild.

"The important thing is that both of us are safe," he insisted. "Look at you, blood all over. You could have lost your baby."

The possibility of what he might have done hit me.

"Don't tell me, Papa, you didn't . . ." I stopped, realizing what must have happened.

Papa lowered his head.

"This can't be! No! Papa, it mustn't be . . ."

Papa began to cry like a guilty child.

I could feel my blood freeze in my veins.

"I have committed a terrible crime." Papa spoke in a small voice. "I deserve to go to hell."

I pulled at his arms and shook him. "No! You didn't do it!"

"They used sharpened bamboo splinters and shoved them under my fingernails." He raised his hands and pulled off the cloth, revealing bloody fingers. "They said that they were going to kill you if I refused to cooperate."

"You told them where Absalom and Pearl were hiding?"

Collapsing to his knees, Papa nodded.

CHAPTER 23

"There are no foreigners here!" Soo-ching and Confucius shouted as they tried to push the soldiers away from the hut.

A crowd gathered and watched in fear.

One soldier hit Soo-ching with the butt of his rifle. She stumbled back, dazed, and her nose started to bleed.

Confucius jumped on the soldier and bit him.

Other soldiers pulled Confucius off and kicked the boy in the stomach.

Standing hidden in the crowd, Papa and I were ashamed and scared.

"Let's burn the hut," one soldier suggested.

The other soldiers agreed. "Let's roast the foreigners!"

"No!" Soo-ching screamed.

The crowd moved forward. "There are no foreigners in the hut!" They began to push the soldiers.

The sharp crack of a gunshot came. A man in a high-collared military uniform with bars on his shoulders strode through the crowd. It was Bumpkin Emperor. A row of bright gold buttons ran down the center of his jacket. Medals were pinned across his chest. His hat looked like a lotus pad.

"Is there anyone here hungry for a bullet?" Bumpkin Emperor's fat cheeks quivered.

Soo-ching crawled to him and grabbed his legs. "Respected general," she cried. "Please spare my home!"

"Only if you produce the foreigners." Bumpkin Emperor waved his pistol.

"I know nothing of foreigners," Soo-ching cried.

"Mother of louses! How dare you lie to me?" Bumpkin Emperor slapped her face. He turned to his soldiers. "What are you idiots waiting for?"

"Please!" Soo-ching pulled at Bumpkin Emperor's arms.

"You stinking female hog!" He kicked her. "Get off me!"

The soldiers came. They removed the bales of hay from in front of the door.

Bumpkin Emperor walked to the door and kicked it open.

Soo-ching threw herself at Bumpkin Emperor's feet. "I will die first before you burn my home!"

Bumpkin Emperor walked away from Soo-ching and fired a shot at her.

"Mother!" Confucius screamed.

The soldiers pinned Soo-ching down, and she squirmed to be free.

"You are going to have a lingering death, crazy lady!" Waving his pistol, Bumpkin Emperor ordered, "Skin the rabbit and set fire to the hut!"

The soldiers started to tie Soo-ching with a rope.

Lit straws were thrown on top of the roof.

A voice came. "Stop in the name of God!"

Absalom filled the opening at the door of the hut.

Behind him stood Pearl, Grace, and the children.

"Tie the foreigners," Bumpkin Emperor ordered. "Line them up."

"Absalom!" Papa threw himself at Absalom's feet.

"Mr. Yee, my friend!" Absalom replied.

Papa slapped his cheeks with both hands. "I have betrayed you! I gave in to the torture! May God punish me."

Papa turned to Bumpkin Emperor and pleaded, "These foreigners have done China no wrong. They have been living with us all their lives. Look, this is Pearl. You remember her when she was a little girl? She was raised in Chin-kiang under your lordship . . ."

"Stay away or you will die with them!" Bumpkin Emperor yelled.

"Your lordship!" Papa cried.

The soldiers dragged Papa away.

Absalom, Pearl, Grace, and the children were lined up against the burning hut.

I no longer knew where I was. All I could think about was Dick's knife in a basket in my kitchen. My legs began to carry me home. I ran.

When I returned, a larger crowd had gathered. Many of the people were from surrounding towns and villages, having sought refuge in our city from the chaos. They outnumbered the city folks. Among them were many who believed foreigners were China's curse. They felt that the sooner we got rid of them, the better.

I pushed my way through the crowd, shoving people aside to reach Bumpkin Emperor. My intent was to stab him.

"You!" He saw me.

I held back, hiding Dick's knife under my shirt.

Bumpkin Emperor was standing near where Absalom, Pearl, Grace, and the children had been lined up. While I had been gone, their hands had been tied behind their backs.

I hoped I could reach Bumpkin Emperor before he shot me.

"I'll die first," Absalom said in a calm voice. He looked at his daughters and grandchildren. "We will be with God."

Terrified, the crowd watched in silence.

Absalom turned to face the crowd and started to sing.

> *The greatest gift the world has known*
> *When the God of Glory*
> *Who is full of mercy*
> *Sent His Son*

Pearl, Grace, and the children joined him.

Love has come
Hope has begun
Still a higher call
Had He, deliverance from our sins

"Master Absalom," the Chinese Christians called out as they dropped to their knees and joined in the singing.

For by the sin of man we fell
By the Son of God
He crushed the power of Hell
Death we fear no more

Absalom sang as if he were in his church.

"Prepare to shoot!" Bumpkin Emperor shouted.

I moved behind Bumpkin Emperor and took out the knife.

Hearing the noise, Bumpkin Emperor turned. I could clearly see his big frog eyes.

I have no memories after that. I only knew that I had lifted the knife and then everything went dark.

"You are an ant who tries to shake a pine!" was what I was told Bumpkin Emperor had said, after one of his soldiers had hit me in the back of the head.

When I opened my eyes I heard "Kill the rice Christians!" I discovered that my hands were tied behind my back and I was on the ground. The back of my head throbbed with pain.

"Have mercy!" I heard Pearl beg. "Willow is pregnant!"

"Pregnant?" Bumpkin Emperor laughed. "Good! I will save a bullet!"

The soldiers lifted me and placed me next to Absalom.

"Praise the Lord," Absalom said. "He will bless you with courage."

Papa threw himself to the ground and kowtowed to Bumpkin Emperor. "Let my daughter go!"

Soldiers beat Papa with their rifles until he was silent.

173

"Willow, we are going home," Absalom said to me.

I looked into Absalom's eyes. I saw no fear—only confidence and love.

"The angels are here," he murmured. "God is waiting for us."

I shut my eyes and leaned against Absalom. I didn't want to die.

The soldiers took up their positions and pointed their rifles at us.

Bumpkin Emperor shouted, "Get ready and . . . f—"

Before Bumpkin Emperor finished his sentence, the earth leaped beneath me. There was a flash followed by a loud roar.

I lost my balance and fell.

Clods of dirt rained down.

I choked as clouds of dust rolled across the ground.

"What is happening?" I heard Bumpkin Emperor yell.

"It must be the Christian God showing his anger!" Papa's voice said.

The soldiers ran like scattered monkeys.

When the dust cleared, I saw that hills near the city were burning and black smoke spiraled into the sky.

"The American fleet is here!" Carpenter Chan and Lilac shouted, running along the riverbank toward the crowd.

Another round of explosions came. The earth trembled again. There was more dust and smoke and flames.

My ears filled with a ringing sound. It was as if someone had stuffed them with cotton.

Bumpkin Emperor followed his soldiers and ran as fast as he could.

The crowd scattered, and soon we were alone in front of Soo-ching's burned-down hut.

Carpenter Chan untied Pearl's ropes. "Sorry it took so long for me to deliver your letter!"

"What letter?" Absalom asked.

"How did you do it, Chan?" Pearl's face was animated with excitement.

"I thought I was never going to find any help, but I was lucky," Carpenter Chan replied. "I found the American fleet near the mouth of the Yangtze and managed to get your note to their leader. He sent one warship."

"God has heard our prayers," Absalom said in his loud preacher's voice.

Pearl stared at the river. She then turned to Lilac, who was tending to Carpenter Chan's blistered feet.

The warship steamed along the shore. Flames burst from the muzzles of the cannons and there were more explosions in the hills. The ground kept shaking. I watched Pearl's lips as she said, "Thank you, America."

CHAPTER 24

Twenty-four hours was all she had to say good-bye. She would be uprooted and transplanted to America, a country she called home but barely knew. Later in her life, this last day in China would haunt her. It never stopped haunting her as long as she lived. It was useless to tell herself, "My roots in China must die."

Life simply caught her. The American captain wouldn't wait. His ship was literally the last boat leaving China. Pearl had only a few hours to pack up forty years of her life.

I convinced myself that our separation would be temporary. Since we had been children, it had happened before. She had gone to Shanghai and then America, but always she had returned. I had no doubts that we would see each other again.

Pearl said that she didn't feel at home when she was anywhere else, even when she was in America, her birthplace. When she talked of home, she meant China.

"How could I go someplace else when my mother's grave is here?" she once said.

Pearl was used to accepting reality. She knew that Bumpkin Emperor and his kind would return and murder again. "There is a positive side to moving to America," she reasoned. "Carol will receive better medical care there."

"What about Lossing?" I asked.

"I haven't heard from him," Pearl said. "He hasn't bothered to send one word or to try to find out how his daughter is."

The American captain insisted that Pearl and Grace leave all their belongings behind. Pearl wanted to take Carie's piano, but she had to give that up. Instead she took Carie's sewing machine.

Absalom gathered his congregation at the church and announced that Carpenter Chan would take his place. Carpenter Chan was to head the Nanking church while Papa continued to head the Chinkiang church.

But Carpenter Chan had no confidence in himself. With tears filling his eyes, he pleaded, "Old Teacher, I am not capable of doing as good a job as you."

"God has let me know that you're the one to carry on in my place."

Absalom told Carpenter Chan that if he ran into difficulty, Papa would be there to help.

Papa was touched—he couldn't believe that Absalom's feelings hadn't changed after he had betrayed him.

While the children's choir sang, Absalom delivered his final sermon. It was the first time Lilac's youngest son, Triple Luck Solomon, led the singing. The young man had inherited his mother's beauty. Carie would have loved his sweet voice. We all wished Pearl's family a safe journey to America.

I told Pearl that I would take care of her garden. "I'll bring fresh flowers to Carie's grave in the spring."

"I'll return soon," Pearl promised.

If I had known that this was the last time we would see each other, I would have held her longer and closer. I would have made an effort to remember how she looked, the clothes she wore and the expression on her face. I would have perhaps tried to talk her out of leaving.

But I didn't know. In fact, we wanted to get the pain of saying good-bye over with as quickly as possible. The sooner the parting was over, the sooner we could start working our way back together. Pearl was not usually one to dwell on sadness. It was Carie's training to press back and swallow your bitter tears. Always look forward and be hopeful.

We all started for the river. Lilac came with her children and Soo-ching brought her son, Confucius.

We carried the family's luggage to the smaller boat waiting to take them out to the warship in the middle of the river.

The large ship excited the children. They called it a big floating temple.

Carpenter Chan followed Absalom. He had been weeping and begging. "I can't do without you, Old Teacher!"

Papa echoed, "Absalom, without you as our compass we will lose our direction on the sea."

"Have faith in God" was Absalom's reply.

"But there are qualities needed in a pastor I don't possess," Carpenter Chan insisted. "People won't follow me the way they follow you! Monkeys will flee when the big tree is down. I am afraid the church will fall apart."

"Carpenter Chan is right," Papa agreed. "No matter how hard we work, people see God's spirit in you, Absalom—not in us."

Wang Ah-ma, Carie's former servant and Pearl and Grace's nanny, arrived to say good-bye. The seventy-year-old woman surprised everyone. After Carie died, Wang Ah-ma had moved back to the provincial village where she had grown up. After hearing the news of foreigners being murdered in Chin-kiang and Nanking, she had come to check on Absalom, Pearl, and Grace. Wang Ah-ma hadn't known that she was reaching Nanking just in time for the family's final departure.

"Wang Ah-ma!" Pearl and Grace cried, getting down on their knees to kowtow.

"My sweet girls!" Wang Ah-ma touched Pearl and Grace all over with her trembling hands. She said that her sight was failing and that she could barely see.

"You shouldn't travel so far." Pearl wiped her tears.

"When will you return to China?" Wang Ah-ma wanted to know. "Before the New Year or after?"

"What's the difference?" everyone asked.

"The fortune-teller predicted that I will expire soon after the New Year," Wang Ah-ma replied.

"Grace and I would like to prove that you wasted your money on the fortune-teller," Pearl said.

Wang Ah-ma smiled, cupping Pearl's face with her hands. "My child, promise that you will come back as soon as you can."

"I promise." Pearl gently kissed Wang Ah-ma's cheeks.

"On board now or never!" the captain of the American warship yelled through a loudspeaker.

Wang Ah-ma let go of Pearl and Grace as she broke down.

The family got on the smaller boat that would take them to the warship. Absalom went to stand in the bow with his back to shore. Looking out across the water, he seemed frozen.

The horn blasted.

The Chinese Christians moaned, "Old Teacher, Absalom!"

Carpenter Chan and Papa sobbed like two abandoned children.

"May the wind blow in your favor!" the crowd chanted.

Absalom was no longer at the spot where he had been standing. It was as if he had suddenly vanished.

"Father!" Pearl and Grace called.

Papa was stunned. "Oh, dear God, Old Teacher has changed his mind!"

Running along the gunwale, Absalom moved quickly. Like a mountain goat, he jumped into the water and began to swim toward the shore.

"Old Teacher!" the crowd cheered. "Old Teacher!"

"Absalom has decided to stay with us!" Papa cried.

Carpenter Chan waded into the water and swam toward Absalom.

"Captain, help!" Grace cried. "Please, stop my father!"

The crowd received Absalom with happy tears.

A few minutes later the American captain arrived from the warship on another small boat. He talked with Pearl.

I could guess exactly what Pearl said to the American captain. She would have said, "Let the fighting angel be."

When Pearl, Grace, and the children went aboard the ship, Absalom smiled. He waved good-bye to his daughters and grandchildren. His long arms rose like flagpoles in the air.

Pearl waved back. I sensed that she knew that she had made the right choice in letting go of her father.

What Pearl did not know was that she would never see her father again. Absalom would continue to do what he loved all the way to the end. One day Absalom would deliver his sermon. Afterward he would tell Carpenter Chan that he would take a break. Minutes later Carpenter Chan would find him in his room, lying on his bed as if sleeping. But he would be dead. Before that moment, Absalom had lived his dreams. With the help of Papa and Carpenter Chan, Absalom had built the largest Christian community in southern China.

Part Four

CHAPTER 25

I felt lonely and alone after Pearl left. Living in Nanking became difficult. In order to rid the country of the Japanese and the Communists, the Nationalist government increased taxes. To buy a bag of rice, one had to bring three bags of paper money to the store. Dick wrote repeatedly from the Red Base in Yenan, urging me to join him. Finally I made my decision. I let him know that I was ready to be a "bandit's wife." Dick was elated. He prepared me for the hostile, unfertile land and the hardship in Yenan.

"Try to look on the bright side," Dick encouraged. "After all, the first emperor of China was born here two thousand years ago."

I told Papa that I would worry about him. He told me not to. Before my departure he went back to Chin-kiang. Even Absalom agreed that Papa was a changed man. To redeem himself, Papa had become absorbed in church work. His devotion enabled Absalom to take longer trips inland. During Absalom's absence, Papa asked Carpenter Chan to build a stained-glass window featuring Jesus Christ for his church. When the work was completed, it delighted everyone. Every morning the sun shone through the glass. Christ looked as though he was floating on top of clouds.

The stained glass boosted attendance. People loved the "Moving Foreign God." Sunday-morning service became Papa's showtime. People told Papa that they liked and felt closer to the image of this particular Jesus Christ. Papa was pleased. He had slightly altered Christ's features. The stained-glass version of Christ had slanting eyes, a flatter nose, and full lips. The Christ also had large earlobes and browner skin.

"This goes to show you that ideas spring fastest from a well-furnished mind!" Papa said proudly.

My daughter was born in a Yenan cave on a snowy day. I tried to find a good name for her but nothing satisfied me. Dick was filled with joy when he held the baby for the first time. "What a beauty!" he exclaimed. "Instead of my lizard eyes and crooked nose, she has her mother's features: a Chinese princess's bright almond eyes, a delicate, straight nose, and fine pink lips! What good fortune!"

Dick had been working with Mao's inner circle. Mao called Dick his secret weapon. Because of Dick, Mao's image had slowly changed from that of a guerrilla leader to that of a national hero. Through his propaganda, Dick had convinced the masses that Mao, not Chiang Kai-shek, had been fighting the Japanese.

In 1937, Dick's agents successfully infiltrated Chiang Kai-shek's organization. Dick was able to persuade several generals of the Nationalist army to join Mao. One general even arrested Chiang Kai-shek. In history this came to be called the Xian Incident.

Mao's name began to appear regularly in the headlines. Chiang Kai-shek was pressured to invite Mao to talk peace. Dick turned the occasion into a publicity opportunity. The stories he created about Mao made him into a myth.

Dick worked through the night. He composed Mao's speeches and set up interviews. He often stayed inside a bomb shelter printing leaflets till dawn. Dick put my English to good use. I translated Mao's articles and mailed them to outside news agencies. These attracted the attention of Western journalists, who came to Yenan seeking private interviews with Mao.

The town of Yenan was no longer a spot on the map no one could find. Yenan was now the headquarters of the nation's war against Japan. Mao had become an equal to Chiang Kai-shek.

Mao was so pleased that he wrote a poem and dedicated it to Dick. In Chinese tradition, this was the highest honor. Mao's poem was titled

"In Contrast to Poet Lu You." As all know, Lu You, born in 1172, wrote the famous lines *"With a mountain-high aim, but an old mortal frame."*

> *Lake Tongting*
> *Lake Green Grass*
>
> *Near the mid-autumn night*
> *Unruffled no winds pass*
>
> *Thirty thousand acres of jade light*
> *Dotted with the leaflike boat of mine*
> *The sky with pure moonbeam overflow*
> *The water surface paved with moonshine*
> *Drinking wine from the River West*
> *Using Dipper as our wine cup*
> *Felicity to share with you my friend*
> *No more talk of the bitter Poet Lu You*
>
> *Brightness above*
> *Brightness below*

While life meant hardship for most people in Yenan, Dick and I lived like royalty. We were given one of the best caves for our home. It had two rooms and faced south and was warmed by the sun. We had meat once a week, while the rest ate yam leaves mixed with millet. At first I enjoyed the luxury and Dick's new status. People came to him at all hours for instructions. But soon I began to resent the intrusions. Sleep was difficult with so much coming and going. I also had trouble reading and writing by candlelight. Dick's eyesight was so bad he had to wear thick glasses, which enlarged his pupils to the size of mung beans. When Dick took off his glasses at night, his eyes looked like pigeon eggs bulging from their sockets.

Dick didn't care about his eyes. He wanted me to be more conscientious about his comrades' political sensibilities. He asked me to hide my bourgeois habits. My desire for privacy, for instance.

"It is ridiculous to call privacy or basic hygiene and love of nature bourgeois habits," I protested.

The real fight began with naming our daughter. I preferred Little Pearl, but Dick had another idea. He wanted our daughter to be called New Art. By *new* Dick meant the proletarian art. To create proletarian art was his job for Mao.

Dick decided to take our argument to Mao, who lived three caves down the slope.

Mao was in the middle of studying the French Revolution, but he received us warmly. When asked his opinion regarding our daughter's name, Mao thought that neither of our choices was good. He took a brush pen and wrote down his choice in red ink.

Thus Rouge Lin was created. It became our daughter's official name.

I didn't like the name. Peace and tranquillity were what I had in mind. In Chinese, *Rouge* meant revolution. The name was associated with violence and blood.

"That's what we are fighting with, our blood!" Dick quoted Mao. "All the parents living in Yenan give their children revolutionary names: Red Base, Yenan, Bright Future, and Soldier of Mao. Our next generation must carry on the red flag and Communism until . . ."

"What?"

"Until the world is rouge—in revolution!"

I could take Yenan's hardship but not the brainwashing. I resented the fact that I was not allowed to even mention the word *God*. Dick did everything he could to hide the fact that I was a Christian.

"It could cost my job—worse, my life—if you are not careful," he warned. He asked me to promise to never mention that I knew any foreigners like Pearl and her family. "In Yenan, who one *was* is more important than who one is," Dick said. "You must be pure in order to be trusted."

My daughter was called Comrade Rouge Lin in kindergarten. Like every other toddler, she had to wear the gray, poorly tailored cotton uniform. After she grew out of it, she passed it on to a younger child.

Rouge was taught combat skills the moment she learned to walk. Her first spoken line was "I am a brave soldier." By the time Rouge was two, she could sing "My Red Army Brother Is Coming Back." She had no interest in learning "Silent Night." She thought that I was strange and was closer to her father. When she was four, she won a competition reciting Karl Marx's famous phrase "Capitalism is a greedy monster."

Although I told Rouge how I grew up and she knew that Pearl Buck was my best friend, she didn't know any foreigners and never saw anyone dressed differently from herself. Even the way people cut their hair at the Red Base was the same. Everyone was focused on the revolution and nothing else. Rouge's world was red and white. One was either a comrade or an enemy. By the time she was eight years old, she was clear about who she was and what she wanted to do with her life. She worshipped Mao and wanted to liberate the poor.

It bothered me when Dick told our ten-year-old daughter that Communists and Christians were enemies.

"Not all Christians believe that China is evil until it accepts God," I argued. "Pearl Buck, for instance. She is a Christian and she criticizes Christianity's worst practices." To prove my point, I read an essay Pearl had published in *Southeast Asia Missionary Magazine* a few years earlier. In this essay, Pearl pointed out that she had seen missionaries lacking in sympathy for the local people: *"So scornful of any civilization except their own, so harsh in their judgments upon one another, so coarse and insensitive among a sensitive and cultivated people that my heart has fairly bled with shame."*

Dick was surprised. "Absalom's daughter wrote that?"

I nodded.

"That's unexpected," he admitted.

"If only Mao could be more open-minded . . ."

Dick interrupted me and whispered, "My darling wife, you are not in Shanghai or Nanking. Remember, I have rivals. Jealous hearts do murder. Remember your Shakespeare?"

Dick believed that Mao would be more relaxed and allow more freedom when he became sure of his power.

"For now we must unite as one to survive." Dick turned to Rouge. "No more criticism of the Communist Party, because it will be considered disloyal and a betrayal."

Rouge's eyes widened. She nodded seriously. "Baba is right and Mama is wrong," she said.

"What about your name, *Dick*?" I challenged. "It definitely doesn't sound proletarian!"

"My comrades know that Dick is my work name." My husband smiled.

"What do you mean, work name? Do you have another name?"

"Yes."

I laughed. "Why don't I know it? After all, I am your wife."

"Such is the life of a Communist." Dick extended his arms and rocked his head from side to side, stretching his neck.

"What is your real name, Baba?" Rouge asked curiously.

"Well, we call it the work name or the current name."

"So, what is your current name?" I asked.

"Well, it is Xinhua."

"Xinhua? *New China*?" I laughed. "I think *Old China* would fit you better. You come from a background of scholars, landowners, and Capitalists! You studied Shakespeare and Confucius in college! Old China is in your blood! You have Western friends and you speak English!"

"No comment." Dick was embarrassed.

From the few letters that reached me, I learned that Pearl had settled into a life of sorts in America. Although the United States was in a financial depression, she published and her books sold well. In 1932, she had won the Pulitzer Prize for *The Good Earth* while still among us. In 1938, she won the Nobel Prize for literature. In her letters, she mentioned her new awards casually. Her tone was no different than when she told me how she admired the American plumbing system, and she never explained how important the awards were. It wasn't until many years later that I discovered that Pearl had become an international celebrity. The subject Pearl asked about most was Rouge. She wanted to know what my daughter's life was like and if she had friends. She said that she had never realized how fortunate we had been to have each other as childhood playmates.

I wanted so badly to talk to Pearl about my daughter, but I didn't want to remind her of what she didn't have with Carol. Instead, I asked Pearl about her writing methods. She replied that her trick was to think like a Chinese farmer. "Before planting, the farmer already knew what, where, and how much to grow, the budget for seeds, fertilizer, animals, and field hands," she wrote. "In other words, I try to make the best use of my material."

About her daughter, Pearl reported that American doctors confirmed Carol's early diagnosis that she would never have a chance to lead a normal life. There was nothing new in this news, but Pearl still sounded devastated. "The conclusion took away any happiness I would have felt in my accomplishments," she wrote.

She did gain some comfort knowing that the income from her writing enabled her to provide permanent care for Carol. "Since Carol loves music, I made sure that the cottage, which my money helped build, was equipped with a phonograph and a collection of records," she continued.

She talked about the farmhouse she had bought in Pennsylvania. "It is gigantic by Chinese standards!" she wrote. "I have been renovating the place so that I can adopt more children."

Pearl and I still talked about Hsu Chih-mo. She let me know that she had finally been able to grieve and move on. "A new man has appeared on the horizon of my lonely love life," she reported. "But I can't do anything until my divorce with Lossing is finalized."

The new man was her editor and publisher, Richard Walsh. Pearl was proud of the fact that they were best friends before they were lovers.

I was so happy for her and wrote to congratulate her. In my letter, I complained about Dick and the Red Base.

To my shock, the letter was intercepted by Communist intelligence agents. It got Dick in trouble.

"I have warned you!" Dick hissed at me. "We Communists don't trust the Americans! Our enemy is supported by the Americans! Why is it so difficult for you to remember that? Yenan's security is about Mao's survival!"

In the past Dick had discouraged me from writing to Pearl. Now I was ordered to stop.

I refused to sign the Communist membership application Dick put in front of me. No matter how many times Dick explained the benefits and the necessity, I wouldn't pick up the pen.

Finally, after months of struggle, I agreed to sign. I did so out of loyalty to my husband. Without my being a member of the Communist Party, Dick would never gain Mao's full trust.

My biggest problem was following the Communist Party's rules. I seemed to always say the wrong thing at the wrong time. I would praise the wrong people and criticize the right ones. For example, I remarked that I felt sorry for high-ranking heroes because they had achieved their rank only by killing a great number of people. I also said that all war was wrong. Because of these mistakes, I was ordered to criticize myself in public.

Dick was demoted as a result. His temper was no longer containable. Instead of fighting with me, Dick exploded at work. He applied for a transfer to be nearer the fighting. He was eager to join the battles. He wanted to be the first to engage the enemy and the last to retreat. The irony was that it turned out to be good for his career. He earned medals and promotions. His courage earned him the respect of the Communist leadership. He was restored to his former job. Mao welcomed Dick back and praised him as "the Red Prince."

"Does that mean that Mao is the Red Emperor?" I joked the moment Dick entered the cave.

Dick didn't find my comment funny, and warned me not to say such things again.

My life, as a fortune-teller had once predicted, was about the constant turning of feng shui, meaning that my fortunes were always changing. My future as a Communist would soon prove the fortune-teller's wisdom. I had never imagined that there would be a benefit to claiming my background as a beggar. For the family background section in the party's membership application, I truthfully wrote "Beggars." This qualified Papa as a proletarian, and that included Rouge and me. If my grandfather hadn't lost all his money, my father would have inherited his land and become the enemy of the Communists. I would have been denounced and perhaps shot as a spy.

The strain between Dick and me had much to do with the innocent souls Mao murdered at the Red Base. It happened before my eyes. People were arrested in broad daylight, sent away, and disappeared for good. These were young people, former college students. They were independent thinkers—people whom Dick had personally recruited. They had joined Mao to fight the Japanese. Overnight they were labeled as enemies, arrested, denounced, and murdered.

Dick said that my Christian values had ruined me. I told him that he was ruined, not me. Dick refused to see Mao's flaws and the fact that he had become a bully. Mao had learned from Stalin, a man who murdered whoever disagreed with him. Half of Dick's friends were detained and questioned and one third executed as traitors.

"How can you sleep at night?" I asked my husband.

Dick encouraged me to make friends with Madame Mao. "She is a better choice than Pearl Buck," he insisted.

I tried, but I couldn't get Madame Mao to like me. She was the opposite of Pearl, judgmental and opinionated. Blessed with good looks, she was also flashy, pretentious, and egotistical. As a former actress, she knew her craft. She called herself "Chairman Mao's humble student" and was proud to be his trophy. She was not shy about her "capital." Her skin didn't turn potato brown as the rest of ours did in the desert sun and harsh wind. Her eyebrows were as thin as a shrimp's feelers. She and Mao made a perfect couple. They both wanted power and fame. Madame Mao loved to say that she was a peacock among hens. By hens, she meant the women of Yenan, and that included me.

My biggest disappointment was that Mao didn't turn out to be the hero I had expected. Under the guise of a scholar, Mao sold confidence to people. He made the peasant soldiers hear their own voices when he spoke to them.

When I listened to Mao, I watched his eyes. They appeared to be smiling even when he uttered the most violent phrases. Mao had a broad forehead, a rice-patty-shaped face, and a feminine mouth. He never looked people in the eyes when he talked with them. Mao let people observe him. Never once did I hear him answer a question in a straightforward manner, although he encouraged others to do so. Mao was a master when it came to the art of beating around the bush. He even said himself that he enjoyed catching his enemy by surprise, whether in conversation or on the battlefield.

Dick made the best conversational partner for Mao in the inner circle. He and Mao often talked deep into the night. "We simply enjoy each other's minds," Dick told me. Yet Dick failed to learn one important lesson, which was that Mao hated to lose.

Dick had yet to find out that Mao wanted absolute power, though he appeared to desire the opposite. Mao repeated the same phrase over and over again to foreign journalists: "My dream is to become a classroom teacher." He would open his conversation with a Chinese poem and close by reciting Marx or Lenin. People were easily charmed by Mao. His broad knowledge and sharp wit disarmed. Once, Dick helped Mao issue a telegram to the war front. He was shocked that Mao insisted on ending the communiqué with a line from a poem. "*Only flies are afraid of winter, so let them freeze and die.*"

Dick told me later that when Mao had trouble giving direction during battles or was unsure of his next move, he would telegram poems to his generals. The confused generals would have no choice but to make up their own minds about whether to charge or retreat.

"Such is Mao's brilliance," Dick said admiringly.

*   *   *

Dick brought Madame Mao the local singer who wrote the song "Red in the East." Dick never guessed that one day the tune would become China's unofficial national anthem.

I went to listen to "Red in the East" being performed at a weekend party for high-ranking officials. Madame Mao introduced the singer, whose name was Li You-yuan. Li was a peasant dressed in rags with a dirty towel wrapped around his forehead. He was in his forties and had three missing front teeth. Dick did a background check and found that Li was not one hundred percent proletarian, because his family owned a half acre of land.

When Dick reported this to Madame Mao, she said, "If I say Li is a peasant, he will be a peasant."

The song "Red in the East" was Madame Mao's birthday gift to her husband.

When the peasant opened his mouth, the listeners' jaws dropped. Li's voice was like a goat's cry.

Mao remained seated, because he had the good sense to trust his wife's magic-making abilities.

After Li exited the stage, Madame Mao presented her version of "Red in the East." The singing was performed by the Yenan repertory group conducted by Madame Mao herself.

> Red in the East
> Rises the sun
> China has brought forth Mao Tse-tung
> Creating happiness for the people
> He is our greatest savior

Li You-yuan didn't write more than the first line of "Red in the East." The peasant had no knowledge of the Red Base or its leader, Mao. He hummed the tune to pass the time when he plowed his field. Dick happened to cross his path and heard him singing. Dick foresaw the usefulness of the tune and brought Li to Madame Mao's attention.

To demonstrate his modesty, Mao rejected Madame Mao's proposal to list "Red in the East" as a "must-learn song" for the troops.

Madame Mao insisted that it was the people's wish that Mao be regarded as the rising sun of China.

Madame Mao asked Dick to send me a message. She criticized me as arrogant. I tried to hide my disgust for the sake of Dick.

Madame Mao was unaware that I had some knowledge of her past. Before coming to Yenan, she had been a third-rate movie actress in Shanghai. She had had an affair with a newspaper reporter who happened to be Dick's friend. At the Red Base, Madame Mao's past was a stain on an immaculate embroidery. Desperate to get rid of the stain, she behaved like a passionate revolutionary. She invited me to watch her perform a newly learned skill—making yarn out of raw cotton.

I was instructed by Madame Mao to follow her making yarn instead of spending time with my daughter. Sitting next to Madame Mao, I was miserable. She recited her husband's phrases as she rolled the wheel. "*We will never understand peasants if we don't soak our hands in manure, make yarn out of raw cotton, and sweat in the fields. We won't be qualified to be a member of the proletarian class until we smell like manure and garlic instead of perfume.*"

I did something behind Dick's back. I bribed the base's special postman who traveled between Yenan and Shanghai as a merchant. The man smuggled my letters out to Shanghai and then mailed them to Pearl in America using a secret address. In my letters, I reported that I had begun telling Christian stories to Rouge. I told Pearl that my day was brightened when Rouge started to fall in love with "Amazing Grace."

Like raindrops in the middle of a drought, I received a letter from Pearl. It comforted me and soothed my anxiety, for I had been friendless. Pearl told me that she had been traveling the world and had spent a great deal of time in India, Southeast Asia, and Japan. The line that filled my eyes with tears of happiness was that she was "dying to return to China."

CHAPTER 26

When Mao defied Stalin and crossed the Yangtze River in pursuit of Chiang Kai-shek in 1948, Dick told me that the Communists would win China. By May 1949 it was a reality. The people had suffered for twelve years: eight years fighting Japan and then four years of civil war. It was hard to believe that the wars were over. Russian and American advisers on both sides had to admit that they had been wrong. Mao believed that there ought to be only one lion on the mountain. He would never share power with Chiang Kai-shek.

The day his capital, Nanking, fell, Chiang Kai-shek fled to Taiwan. Mao would have continued the chase until he captured Chiang Kai-shek if it hadn't been for the American military forces on the island. Mao was cautious. He didn't want to be stretched too thin, so he claimed a nation and named it the People's Republic of China.

I was ordered to pack immediately and move north. Rouge was excited. The fifteen-year-old had never stepped outside of Yenan. She had joined the Communist Youth League the previous year and had been working as a frontier journalist for the *Yenan Daily*. Several times Rouge had received awards as an Outstanding Comrade and had been given a Mao Medal. Her favorite songs were Soviet anthems and she favored a Lenin jacket.

We were to meet Dick in Peking. Mao had decided to make the city his new capital, and he had its name changed from Peking to Beijing. Also seeing a change were troops from the Eighth and Fourth Army Divisions. Previously under the command of Chiang Kai-shek, they now fell behind Mao and were incorporated into the People's Liberation Army.

Dick drove an American jeep to pick us up. Although he was dark brown and thin from the stomach ulcers he had developed, he was happy. He told us that the car's former owner had been Madame Chiang Kai-shek.

The People's Liberation Army was received joyously by the city residents. Dick's American jeep was part of the parade when we entered Beijing. The cheering crowd beat drums. Children threw flowers. "Long live Chairman Mao!" they shouted. "Long live the Communist Party of China!"

October 1, 1949, was the day of celebration for the nation. Standing on top of the Gate of Tiananmen, Mao proclaimed China's independence to the world. He promised freedom and human rights. From that moment on, Mao was regarded as the wisest ruler heaven had ever bestowed on China. Few knew that it was Dick who had negotiated the peaceful transition.

Dick had been secretly working with General Chu, who had guarded Peking for Chiang Kai-shek. Dick had talked General Chu into surrendering. He convinced the man that Chiang Kai-shek had abandoned him. In Dick's view, further fighting would mean a bloodbath from which Chu would emerge the loser no matter how hard he fought. In Mao's name, Dick promised General Chu a high-ranking position in the People's Liberation Army. Dick signed his name on this secret agreement for Mao. The moment General Chu raised the white flag, he would be called the People's Hero.

I couldn't believe my eyes when Dick took us to see our new home. It was inside the Forbidden City. We were to occupy one of the palaces. Dick told me that Mao and his wife, along with his vice chairman, his ministers, and their families, had already moved into the Forbidden City.

It took me days to convince myself that my life had really changed. At last, I didn't have to live in a cave. I no longer had to endure air raids. Food would never again be a problem. I looked at myself in the mirror and saw a face I hardly recognized as my own. At age fifty-nine, I was finally able to settle down.

Instead of calling the palaces by their former Imperial names, the Communist housing authority gave them numbers. Our residence used to be called the Palace of Tranquillity; now it was called Building number 19.

I walked around my new home admiring the splendor of the Imperial architecture. The palace was a living work of art. Like a true beauty, she changed her face according to the light. Tremendous arching beams and brick columns reminded me of opera stage sets. Rouge was impressed by the huge wooden gate. She ran from room to room cheering and singing. We had four spacious main rooms and seven utility rooms. There was a roofed hallway to the garden with evergreen trees, luxurious bushes, and wonderfully scented flowers.

"How can we afford to live here?" I asked.

Dick smiled. "It's free."

"What do you mean free?"

"I didn't choose this place," Dick said. "It was Chairman Mao's decision." Looking at my expression, Dick explained, "It's for Mao's convenience. He wants me to be near for the sake of business." He paused, looking at me attentively. "I thought this arrangement would make you happy. How many people in China get to live in a palace like this?"

I would have chosen a place where we could be private. I understood that Dick had no choice. Rouge was to join other children of high-ranking officials attending a private school where she would be taught more Russian than Chinese. The school's goal was to prepare its graduates for the University of Moscow.

I felt a growing distance from my daughter after she started school. She no longer wanted to pray with me. She threw away the little picture of Jesus I kept in my bathroom. She told me that she had been selected captain of her class. Instead of a hug and a good-bye in the morning, she would raise her right hand to her temple and say, "Salute, comrades!"

One day I found a portrait of Mao in my bedroom, replacing my favorite lotus painting. When I protested, Rouge said, "It is for your own good, Mother. You don't seem to understand what is going on outside our family."

I was not used to my new role as a revolutionary's housewife. For security reasons, I was not allowed to share my address with anyone, including Papa. I complained to Dick and said that I missed my father. A month later, Papa was dropped at my door like a package. Although robust in health and glad to see me, Papa described his journey as being "kidnapped." Mao's secret agents plucked him from Chin-kiang and brought him to Beijing. Papa was not told where he was going or whom he was going to see. During his stay in the Forbidden City, Papa was reprimanded for trying to exit the gates without permission. He fought with the guards and said that he didn't want to be a prisoner. Finally Papa begged me to buy him a ticket so that he could return to Chin-kiang. I bought him a ticket and was sad when he didn't turn his head as he boarded the train. We barely had time to talk and catch up about our lives. I didn't even get a chance to ask Papa how everyone was doing in Chin-kiang.

I tried to find a way to let Pearl know about my move to Beijing. I assumed that she would know about Mao's victory. I wondered what she thought about Chiang Kai-shek's defeat. In a way, Pearl had predicted the outcome during our earlier correspondences. So many had been impressed by Madame Chiang Kai-shek, who had campaigned in America for her husband and succeeded in rallying the public behind her. But Pearl did not believe her claims. Pearl had often said in the past that the Chiangs were in power for themselves. She believed that there was a divide between the Chiangs and the peasants of China. She had said long ago that Mao's power came from his understanding of the peasants.

Pearl never trusted the Communists. She enjoyed her friendship with Dick and supported my marriage to him because she saw that he loved me. On the other hand, Pearl didn't like my being brainwashed by Dick.

When I mentioned Dick's worship of Karl Marx in a letter, Pearl wrote back and asked, "Do you know who Karl Marx is? He is this strange little man, long dead, who lived his narrow little life, and somehow managed by the power of his wayward brain to lay hold upon millions of human lives!"

This made sense to me, although nothing I said changed Dick's mind. With Mao's victory, Dick had gone further on what I would call a journey of no return.

A party commemorating national independence was next on Mao's agenda. Dick was put in charge of arranging it. He was grateful that Mao trusted him with the job. He was finally doing what he loved—bringing talented people together. I rarely got to see Dick in daylight. I told myself that I was lucky my husband had not died in battle, and that I should be satisfied our lives were taken care of by the Communist Party. We were given chefs, drivers, doctors, dressmakers, bodyguards, and house cleaners.

I wrote to Pearl the first chance I got. Beijing was a huge city where I could easily melt into the crowd when visiting a post office. I told Pearl that while Dick became an ever more devoted Communist, I remained an independent bourgeois liberal, and worse, I continued to be a Christian. "The changing China excites me and scares me at the same time," I confessed. "Mao has made himself into a god to the people. I feel like I am losing my husband and daughter to this man. The irony is: I am the person they think mad."

For the sake of my daughter, I stopped trying to seek out churches in Beijing in which to worship. But even if I wanted to, I could never give up my faith in God. I prayed in the dark. I was on my knees when Dick and Rouge were asleep. I was also determined to keep up my correspondence with Pearl as long as I could.

Dick's stomach pain worsened and finally he needed surgery. Two thirds of his stomach was removed. He continued to work from his hospital bed. He met with some of the day's most influential people, from Chiang Kai-shek's former ministers to famous artists. Dick's goal was to secure domestic and international legitimacy for Mao. "Chairman Mao must make more friends. At any time, America could use Taiwan as its military base to launch an attack on China," Dick told Rouge.

As China's new minister of the Bureau of Culture, Science, and Art, Dick encouraged overseas Chinese to return to their homeland. For the next ten years Dick would write hundreds of letters telling his friends all over the world that "Mao is a wise and merciful leader who recognizes and appreciates talent."

Among those who returned were intellectuals, scientists, architects, playwrights, novelists, and artists. In the name of the Communist Party, Dick guaranteed their salaries and offered privileged lifestyles and freedom of expression. Dick appointed them as heads of national theaters and universities. Every morning, Dick drove his jeep to pick up the new arrivals. Every evening, he hosted a gay welcoming party.

At one welcoming party, Dick drank too much. The next morning, with puffy, bloodshot eyes, he said, "If Hsu Chih-mo hadn't died, I would have invited him. He would have enjoyed himself."

"Hsu Chih-mo would not hide himself like I do," I responded. "He would have criticized Mao. He would have told Mao to his face that he was an amateur poet."

"Who are you trying to challenge?" Dick was irritated. "Why are you so cynical all the time?"

"I just question how true China's freedom of expression is," I said. "Are you sure that you can keep the promises you have made to so many?"

Dick understood my concern. He could not answer my question, because deep down he knew that "Mao's will" would be the "nation's will."

"You might end up carrying the stone that will eventually smash your own toes," I said, afraid.

Dick put his arm around my shoulders and said that he agreed with me. "But I must have faith in what I do."

I rubbed my face against his hand and told him that I understood.

"I must trust that others share my values," Dick said in a gentle voice.

"You are being naïve."

"I know, I know," he cut me off. "Your worries are legitimate but unnecessary."

"I can see it coming."

"Willow, you have a wild imagination. Don't let it drive you crazy."

"I won't say this again. Listen, I am your wife, and I know you enough to know that you and Mao are different people."

"We complement each other."

"That is not what I mean."

"I know what you mean, darling."

"Let me finish, will you?" I was upset. "To get his way, Mao will not hesitate to persecute or—dare I say the word?—murder. He's done it before."

Dick stood and put some distance between us. "Mao doesn't own the party," he said in a firm voice. "Communism is about justice and democracy."

Dick led me to his room and opened the top drawer in his desk. He took out an envelope. I could tell that the Chinese writing on the envelope was Pearl's. The stamps showed that the letter had arrived two months ago, and the letter had already been opened. The envelope was empty.

"My privacy has been invaded," I protested.

"Mao's internal security agents opened it."

"Where is the letter?"

"The central bureau has it. They notified me that it was to be confiscated."

"Why didn't you speak up for me?"

"You would not be here now if I hadn't!" Dick almost yelled.

I knew Dick had done his best.

"Look." Dick pulled more documents from his drawer. "Here is more evidence. I have fought for you not once but repeatedly."

I had had no idea that I was in so much trouble.

"You are being watched by internal security," Dick continued. "You are one step from becoming known as an enemy sympathizer. Your friendship with Pearl Buck is seen as a threat to national security. Pearl's status in America and her public criticism of Mao and the Communist Party have categorized her as an enemy of China."

"Am I a suspect?"

"What do you think? You were caught passing her information."

I remembered that in my letters I had shared with Pearl my doubts about Dick's efforts to recruit people to the Communist cause. I had confided to her that I could never forget what had happened in Yenan in the thirties. Several Shanghai youths Dick had recruited had been arrested as spies and shot. All these years later, their families still wrote to Dick asking for information about their loved ones. Dick put on a mask when talking to them. He had no answers for them. He felt responsible and couldn't forgive himself no matter how many times he told himself that the murders had been caused by the war with Japan.

I didn't mean to mail Pearl another letter. I knew it was too dangerous. The political atmosphere had begun to change after Mao's experiment called the Great Leap Forward. It began in the year 1958 and lasted three years before utterly failing. It forced the entire nation to adopt a communal lifestyle. The result was millions of deaths and a starving nation. By the end of 1962, respect for Mao had faded. There were voices calling for a "competent leader."

Feeling that his power was threatened, Mao suppressed the growing criticism. Madame Mao opened a national media conference to "clear away the confusion." Dick was to draft a "battle plan." The first thing Dick was ordered to do was close China's door to the outside. He had to personally apologize to foreign journalists and diplomats for canceling their entry visas. "It is temporary," Dick assured them. "China will be open for business again sooner than you know."

But when Dick came home he told me that he had little confidence in what he had promised his friends. Mao had no intention of reopening China's door. It led me to think that mailing the letter would be my last chance to contact Pearl. It would be now or never.

Acting like an undercover agent, I disguised myself as a peasant and dropped my letter in a post office outside Beijing. It was a warm day in April. The sunshine filtered through the clouds. The trees were light green with new leaves. Children wearing red scarves on their necks were singing cheerful songs. I made sure to cover my tracks by taking different buses. On my way back I couldn't help wiping my tears. I sensed that I might never again hear from Pearl.

Hard as I tried, I could no longer put on a smiling face and maintain a positive attitude. As far as the party was concerned, this meant being politically correct at all times. It grew harder every day. I would attack Dick at home and my anger would spill over.

"Mao robs the lives of innocent people!" I would yell and throw my chopsticks at the wall. "It's brutality!"

"Sacrifice would be a better word." My husband hushed me and went to shut the windows.

"Speak to me without your mask, Dick! Tell me, in your heart have you questions, reservations, doubts?"

Dick went silent.

"How can you bear the thought that you have murdered for Mao? You are struggling to justify yourself."

"Enough, Willow. This is 1963, not 1936! The proletarians rule today. Our Chairman is following in Stalin's footsteps. One wrong word and you can lose your tongue, if not your head."

"You haven't answered my questions."

"I am tired."

We sat facing each other for a long time. Our dinner was on the table, but we had no appetite.

"When Mao panics, he gets carried away," Dick said, taking a deep breath. "He needed to purge the anti-Communist bug."

"Did he do the right thing ordering the murders of those young people you recruited?"

"At the time, yes. But now, no. The tragedy was the party's loss. It benefited no one but our enemies."

"Dick Lin, I have been watching you running around trading on your reputation to get people to return to China. What if Mao changes his mind? What if those people say and do things that end up displeasing and offending Mao? Are you going to be the executioner?"

"It won't happen."

"I thought by now that you knew Mao."

"I do."

"Then you are evil to follow him."

"I am riding on the back of a tiger. I will die if I try to get off."

"What a selfish statement!"

Dick turned away and went to sit in a chair. He cupped his face with his hands. "You have never approved of what I do anyway."

"You refuse to acknowledge the truth."

"What truth?"

"There is no Communism but what Mao wants!"

"Comrade Willow." Dick stood up. "I have never insulted your God, so please stop insulting mine."

CHAPTER 27

I was arrested at home while washing the dishes. I never expected a postal officer to turn me in. I was denounced and accused of being an American spy. Without a trial, I was thrown in prison. I had seen this happen to others, but I was shocked when it happened to me.

Dick pulled strings. But no one dared to help. My crime was my friendship with Pearl Buck. Dick said that it wasn't Pearl Buck's literary success that made her China's enemy, but her refusal to be the Maos' friend.

Since taking over China, the Maos had wished that Pearl would give her support to the regime. But Pearl kept her distance. Agents from China repeatedly contacted her hoping that she could do what the American journalists Edgar Snow and Anna Louise Strong had done for China. Although Pearl was friendly with both journalists, she held her own political views. In the late 1950s, when millions of Chinese starved to death during the Great Leap Forward, Pearl criticized Mao. She pointed out a crucial fact that others had ignored: "Mao allowed his people to die of starvation and disease while he helped the North Koreans fight a war against the Americans."

"Is Pearl Buck a friend or an enemy?" Dick told me Mao had once asked him.

Dick answered truthfully that Pearl Buck loved the Chinese people, but she didn't believe in Communism.

Mao instructed Dick to work on Pearl Buck. Mao wanted Dick to repeat the success he had achieved when he had talked General Chu into switching sides in 1949. Mao made Pearl Dick's next challenge. Mao's order to Dick was clear: "I'd love to gain a Nobel Prize winner as a comrade."

Behind my back, Dick wrote to Pearl. She didn't respond, and she didn't mention Dick's efforts in any of the letters she wrote to me.

Frustrated, Dick asked Mao why he had to have Pearl Buck.

"There is no comparison between Pearl Buck and Edgar Snow," Mao replied. "Pearl Buck is read in every country on the world map. Her books have been translated into over a hundred languages! If Edgar Snow is a tank, Pearl Buck is a nuclear bomb."

Dick failed in his mission because Pearl was too knowledgeable about China to be fooled. Pearl judged Mao by his actions, not by his fancy slogans. "Serve the people with heart and soul" meant nothing to her. Like her father, Absalom, Pearl refused to be bought. The novels she wrote during the 1960s depicted the tragic lives being led under Mao, although she wrote them from across the sea and was only guessing. It seemed that her senses were growing sharper as she aged.

Dick never shared with Mao his opinion that Pearl Buck was the only Westerner with the ability to write about China's reality with both humanity and accuracy. Dick never mentioned that he admired Pearl, but I knew he did.

Dick didn't have the courage to challenge Madame Mao when she declared Pearl's newest novels attacks on Communism. Madame Mao believed that Pearl was part of the American conspiracy against China. Dick was ordered to encourage China's propagandists to mount a counterattack. Pearl Buck was labeled a "cultural imperialist."

Madame Mao set Pearl Buck up as a negative example. She was getting ready to help her husband launch the Great Proletarian Cultural Revolution. The goal was to secure Mao's power in China and beyond.

Making his personal passion for destroying his enemies the nation's obsession was Mao's greatest talent. Dick said that I was better off in prison. When Rouge visited me in May of 1965, she told me that the outside world had turned upside down. Teenage mobs calling themselves

Mao's Red Guard chanted, "Whatever our enemy embraces, we reject, and whatever our enemy rejects, we embrace." They sang Mao's slogans as they attacked people they suspected were anti-Mao.

Rouge was worried about my declining health and the fact that I was not allowed to see a doctor. She prayed with me for the first time in many years. She told me she wanted to learn more about God, but I feared that she had been brainwashed too thoroughly and one day might turn on me. I felt the best way to influence her was through my own example.

Early one morning, I was dragged from my cell. I was told that the Red Guard had taken over the prisons. I was to be beaten to death unless I denounced Pearl Buck.

Thin, rancid rice porridge was all I was fed and there was never enough. Hunger gnawed at my insides. There was no electricity or water. My cell was a dark concrete box without windows. I lost all sense of time. I knew many people had been driven mad that way.

To preserve my sanity, I began singing Christian songs to myself. When I was ordered to stop singing by the prison guards, I changed my methods. I practiced finger calligraphy, recalling sentences from the Bible. Since there was no water available, I wet my index finger in the urine bucket and wrote the words on the concrete surface of the floor as if it were rice paper. I moved from left to right. By the time I reached the lower corner, the top corner was dry and ready for me to write on again.

Time passed without measurement. There was no mirror, so I didn't know how I looked. One day I noticed strands of my own hair on the floor and realized that my hair had turned white.

Eventually, a prison guard came and led me to another room, where there was a table, chair, and sink. I was given a comb and a toothbrush and was told to make myself presentable.

"You have an assignment," the guard told me. I was to meet a high-ranking party official.

After I had cleaned up, two men in soldiers' uniforms escorted me to a car. One of them tied a cloth blindfold over my eyes.

It was a long ride over bumpy roads.

When the blindfold was removed from my eyes, I discovered that we had arrived in front of a military complex. We passed through a narrow entrance. I smelled food cooking. The soldiers led me to a large room where there was a stained carpet, red sofas, and deep-green curtains. There was a basket of bananas on the table.

"Help yourself," a female attendant said in perfect Mandarin.

I would not have touched anything if I hadn't been dying of hunger. Like a monkey, I grabbed a banana. Quickly peeling off the skin, I stuffed the banana into my mouth. I was so absorbed in chewing that I didn't pay attention to anything else. When I reached out for another banana, I noticed a person sitting on the sofa. At first I thought it was a man because she was dressed in a man's army uniform. She was wearing the green cap with a red star in the front.

"Take your time," she said.

I froze. I couldn't believe my eyes.

"Old friend, have you already forgotten me?" She smiled.

I stared, recognizing the long, bony fingers. "Madame Mao, is that you?"

"Yes, it's been a long time." She smiled. "See, I didn't forget you."

She offered to shake my hand.

I refused, explaining apologetically that my fingers smelled of urine.

Madame Mao withdrew her hand. "The Chairman sends his greetings. As you can imagine, he's been very busy. I'd like to work with you toward a solution that will please him."

"How could I possibly be useful to you?" I said.

"Comrade Willow Yee, I am offering you a great opportunity. You can change your life by proving your loyalty to the Chairman."

It was hard to figure out the meaning of her words. She looked changed since the first time I had met her in Yenan. Still imposing, the Madame Mao in front of me today had dyed her hair ink black. Her eyes said, "I am powerful." She kept herself in shape physically, but she was no longer a beauty. Although her eyebrows were still as thin as a shrimp's feelers, the dark-framed glasses took away her femininity.

"I see that you are hungry," she said, showing her bright white teeth. "Would you like to start lunch?"

Before I could answer, she clapped her hands.

A door on the far side of the room opened.

"A private banquet has been waiting for you," Madame Mao said cheerfully, as if we were at a party.

The servants came and lined themselves up against the wall.

Stretching out her arms, Madame Mao took up my hands. "Let's have a heart-to-heart chat, just the two of us."

"We are fighting a cultural war with the Western countries led by America," Madame Mao said dramatically. Her thin lips quivered. She reached out and grabbed my hands again and squeezed them. "We will defeat the American cultural imperialists. We will chase them to the end of the universe. They will have no time to catch their breath!" She shivered as if she was cold.

"Excuse me . . ." I didn't know what to say.

She put a hand up in a let-me-finish gesture and continued. "When we succeed, we will take over the Capitalists' propaganda machine. We will have our voice heard and views printed in the newspapers of the world. Imagine—the *New York Times*, the *London Times*. It will be the victory of the proletarians of the world! The Chairman will be so proud of your efforts!"

"I am not quite following you, madame . . ."

"You eat, eat." Madame Mao placed a dish of roast duck in front of me.

"I'd like to know my assignment if I may," I requested.

"Relax, dear comrade." Madame Mao smiled gleefully. "Believe me, I would not assign you a task that you would be incapable of accomplishing."

"What is it exactly, then?"

"The assignment is easy: Write two articles. One will be titled 'The Good Earth Is a Poisonous Plant' and the other 'Exploitation: Pearl Buck's Forty Years of Evildoings in China.' The subtitle will be 'Crime Exposed by a Childhood Friend.'"

Although I had no idea what exactly was going on, I sensed that Pearl had done something that had offended Madame Mao personally, over and above her refusal to endorse Mao's policies for China. Many years later, I would learn that Madame Mao had dreamed of having Pearl Buck write her biography. With *The Good Earth* being made into a Hollywood movie, Madame Mao had imagined that she could be the next subject for the Nobel Prize–winning novelist. With characteristic confidence, Madame Mao had her agents approach Pearl Buck. The book's title would be *The Red Queen* and the character of Madame Mao would have the style and flavor of Scarlett O'Hara from *Gone with the Wind*.

Pearl's rejection had come quickly. Madame Mao had been in the middle of watching *Gone with the Wind* for the fourteenth time. She had imagined Vivien Leigh playing her.

Seeds of revenge had sprouted. Madame Mao vowed destruction.

"Besides attacking Chairman Mao through her writings, Pearl Buck has been discovered helping Chinese dissidents escape to America," Madame Mao told me.

I asked if I could just "digest" her words first.

"I am not asking whether or not you're willing to do it," Madame Mao said, raising her chin toward the ceiling. "I am asking for the date you will deliver the weapon."

I was reunited with my husband and daughter. We were provided with a room in the complex. My punishment if I did not cooperate had been spelled out. Saying no to Madame Mao meant saying yes to the continuing prison sentence and perhaps death. My age had never bothered me before but it did now. My body was tired and sick. I was over seventy and the idea of dying in a cold cell terrified me.

"You should not consider this an act of betrayal," Dick tried to convince me. "You won't hurt Pearl if you denounce her. She will understand. She is not in China. It is very likely that you two will never see each other again. Pearl won't even know that you wrote the criticism."

"But God will know," I cried.

"Consider the circumstance," Dick said. "We must protect our public from Pearl Buck's influence. Her books have damaged the Communist Party's reputation worldwide. Pearl is no longer the friend you used to know."

"Unfortunately, I have read *The Good Earth*," I replied. "I read it when it was a handwritten manuscript thirty years ago. Pearl Buck didn't insult Chinese peasants, as Madame Mao claims. On the contrary, she showed what we were truly like."

"You are letting your personal feelings get in the way of your political judgment," Dick warned.

"To hell with my political judgment!"

Rouge came. She sided with me.

Dick was upset. "Nobody says no to Madame Mao."

"I can't do it," I said.

"Make up stories," Dick suggested. "Lie!"

"I can't tell the world how evil Pearl and her family were!"

"You have to do it to survive, Willow. You can tell Pearl that you didn't mean it later."

I looked at my husband and was overwhelmed by unspeakable sadness. Telling lies had become Dick's way of life. I wished that I could bend with the wind the way he had.

"I don't want to teach my daughter a lesson of betrayal by my own example," I concluded.

Dick pleaded, "Because of you, Rouge is having a hard time finding a man who will marry her, and she's already passed her thirtieth year!"

The words stabbed me like a knife. I blamed myself for ruining Rouge's life. So many times my daughter had suffered a broken heart. Young men fell in love with Rouge at first sight, but as soon as they found out that her mother was a people's enemy, they avoided her like a virus. To pursue Rouge would mean a lifetime of hardship and persecution.

My prison sentence was increased to ten more years and then reduced to five more because I was Dick's wife. I was sent to a labor prison in a remote province near Tibet. I spent my days working in the fields planting wheat and cotton and my nights scavenging for food and fighting cold, heat, and vermin. Our family was spread out over hundreds of miles. Dick was in the north, Rouge in the south, and I in the southwest. Dick and Rouge took turns visiting me once every three months and during New Year's. Rouge never complained about the hardship, but the pain was written on her face. She had become a quiet woman, more mature than her peers. After graduating from Beijing University with a degree in medicine, she was not allowed to practice. She worked at a textile factory as a laborer. Dick wouldn't tell me his punishment, but I learned what it was anyway. He was demoted and sent to an obscure post in the provinces. After a year, Mao called him back. Dick worked hard to regain Mao's trust.

Rouge and I tried to keep our perspective. We saw that ours was not the only family that suffered. Millions of others shared the same fate. By the end of 1969, the Cultural Revolution was showing itself to be one of the most destructive episodes in China's long history.

After serving five years in the labor prison I was ordered to go back to where I came from, Chin-kiang. It was considered a continuing punishment. I was ordered to reform through physical labor as long as I lived. I was nearly eighty years old.

Rouge was given the option to stay where she was or come with me. She chose the latter and quit her job. She said that she had barely been earning enough to eat anyway.

We went home on a slow train. My skin was sun-beaten and my back was in constant pain. I couldn't walk straight. I had injuries to my joints, spinal cord, and legs. But my spirit had not been crushed. I was proud of myself for paying the price for decency—I could honestly say that I had never betrayed God, and that God had never abandoned me.

Dick was given no option but to remain at Mao's side in Beijing. For fifteen years Dick had been China's chief propaganda director. He was the ghostwriter for both Mao's and Madame Mao's speeches and articles. When he begged for my release so I could join him, Madame Mao answered, quoting her husband's poem, "*Enjoy the beauty of snow while feeling no pity for the flies that freeze.*"

I thought Dick had suffered from my absence and had been waiting for me. But I was wrong. One year after I was sent to the labor prison, the party provided him with a young woman one third his age to be his secretary and nurse. In the beginning, Dick was unaware of the trap that had been set for him. By the time he figured it out, he had fallen in love.

CHAPTER 28

Summer in Chin-kiang was hot and humid, like living in a steam bath. Papa came to pick us up at the Chin-kiang station. We hadn't seen each other for many years. It was amazing that Papa was still alive. He had shrunk in size and was bald and stooped. Our tears fell when we embraced. Rouge was excited to see her grandfather, although she barely knew him.

"I have lost track of your age, Grandpa," Rouge said. "How old are you exactly?"

"Twenty-nine!" Papa said.

"You must mean ninety-two," Rouge said.

"You got the joke! Yes, but actually I'm even older," Papa said, straightening his back to look taller.

"But you do look like twenty-nine!" Rouge said.

"I do?" Papa was pleased. "I feel like twenty-nine, too."

"I don't remember your being this short," I said. "Four feet?"

"I used to be double the height," replied Papa.

"What made you shrink?" Rouge asked.

"My body knew how to conserve when times were hard."

Rouge laughed. "I can't imagine myself shrinking like you."

"*Thirty years in the river east, and then the next thirty years in the river west,*" Papa said, reciting Confucius.

"What does that mean?" Rouge asked.

"In the concept of feng shui, it means that there are equal opportunities in the circle of life."

"What is the secret of your longevity, Grandpa?" Rouge asked.

Papa smiled and whispered, "Having faith."

"In Buddha?" Rouge teased.

"How dare you forget who I am?" Papa pretended to be upset, but not very convincingly.

"What will our living arrangements be, Papa?" I changed the subject. "Where are we to stay?"

"In the church," Papa said.

"The Chin-kiang church?"

"Yes, Absalom's Chin-kiang church."

"But the Chin-kiang church was not built for people to live in ..." I immediately realized the silliness of my statement. Living conditions in China had deteriorated so much that people had turned animal barns into living quarters.

"To many people, it is no longer a church," Papa explained. "It was the headquarters of the Nationalist troops during the war against Japan. When the Japanese took over, it became a barracks. After the 1949 Liberation, the Communists repossessed it. It has been put into different uses ever since. First it was a military headquarters, and then a utility storage for the new government. During Mao's People's Commune movement, it was a public cafeteria. After the communes failed, it was turned into a shelter for the homeless. At the beginning of the Cultural Revolution, Red Guards from outside the province took over. They broke my stained-glass windows and painted Mao's picture over every image of Jesus on every wall. They climbed the roof and knocked down the cross."

"Are there families living inside now?" I asked.

Papa nodded.

"How many?"

Papa stuck up two of his fingers.

"Two?" Rouge guessed.

"Twenty."

"Twenty families?"

"Yes, twenty families, one hundred and nine people."

"How can anybody manage?"

"Oh, we manage, like caged pigeons."

Memories of Absalom and Carie rushed up at the sight of the Chinkiang church. I had to stop for a moment to collect myself. The gray structure had faded, but the building looked sound. The stone steps at the entrance were so worn they looked polished.

Although Papa had warned me about the crowded space, I was still shocked when I stepped into the church. I was prepared to see a pigeon cage, but what was in front of me looked like a beehive. There were no windows except those high up near the ceiling where the stained glass had been. These were the only light source for the entire interior. From floor to ceiling, the walls of the church had been divided into wooden, man-sized boxes, like giant wall-to-wall bookshelves, for people to sleep in. One could only lie down inside. To get into the boxes, people used a tangle of rope ladders. Young people and children occupied the top levels, while the old lived on the lower levels. Every inch of space was put to good use. The washing area was dominated by a large sink made from a water pipe about twenty feet long and split open at the top. Ten faucets poured weak streams of water. Below the sink was a slanted open gutter covered by a metal grate. Plumbing pipes and a dragonlike aluminum chimney were suspended in the air by wires. A loft had been built right under the ceiling as a shared storage space. Where the rows of church benches used to be was now a communal dining area. A large wooden table was surrounded by crooked benches. The raised stage where the altar had been was now a kitchen. There was split firewood piled high against the back wall. Baskets of coal spilled their contents. Wooden frames held buckets, pans, and woks. The podium where Absalom had preached now housed a stove. Behind the stage there was a room in which chamber pots were divided by curtains.

"What do you think?" Papa asked.

"Well, what ingenuity!" Rouge remarked.

Trying to ignore the terrible odor from the chamber pot area, I told Papa that I was impressed.

"No windows and it is so hot!" Rouge wiped sweat off her face. Her shirt was drenched.

"Welcome home," Papa said.

Rouge and I were given one of the larger sleeping boxes. Rouge tried to slide into the narrow space and bumped her head.

Before we had a chance to unpack, the sound of knocking erupted. Papa went to open the door. A group of people rushed in. The men were bare-chested and the women wore thin shirts. They all had wooden slippers on their feet. They called my name excitedly.

"Don't tell me that you don't remember me!" said a wrinkled, hunchbacked old lady who grabbed me by the shoulders.

"Lilac?"

"Yes, I am. Are you Willow?" she cried. "How you have aged! Your hair is gray and white! Is this really you? Where have you been? Where is Pearl?"

At the mention of Pearl, I broke down.

"I can't believe that I have lasted to see you return!" Lilac said. "Here, come meet your aunt Willow!" She turned to her sons. I didn't recognize the men in front of me, although I knew they must have been Double Luck David and John and their younger brother, Triple Luck Solomon.

"Where is Carpenter Chan?" I asked.

"Oh, he is long dead," said a toothless man.

"Dead?" I asked, then instantly recognized Carpenter Chan himself.

"Don't expect an elephant's ivory teeth to grow in a dog's mouth." Lilac slapped her husband's back. "Since Absalom's death, Chan is good for nothing."

"When did Absalom leave?" I asked. "And how were his last days?"

"Old Teacher had a good ending," Carpenter Chan said.

"Absalom didn't suffer?"

"No, he didn't. I was with him until the end. Old Teacher delivered his last sermon and went to lie down. Shortly after, I found him sleeping on his bed, and he was with God."

A white-haired woman squeezed through the crowd and jumped on me. She scrunched her eyelids together and then stretched them as if trying to open her eyes, but couldn't. "Guess who I am?" She drew her face so close that I could smell her rotten breath.

I shook my head and said that I couldn't recognize her.

"I am Soo-ching, the beggar lady!"

"The beggar lady, yes! How are you? What's wrong with your eyes?"

"I can only see a shadow of you, Willow. I am blind. But I remember your face before you left us."

"How have you been?"

"I am a believer in Jesus Christ," Soo-ching said. "How is Pearl? Is she here with you? I am upset that you two no longer visit."

"Where is Confucius, your son?" I asked.

"You remember him? Good!"

"How could I not? He has such a unique name!"

"He is no longer Confucius," Soo-ching said. "He changed his name to Vanguard."

"Vanguard? Why?"

"Confucius is no longer a beggar lady's boy," Lilac whispered in my ear. "He has become somebody important."

"That's right," Papa confirmed. "Vanguard was the first person in Chin-kiang to join the Communist Party. He is the town's boss today."

"Donkey shit!" Soo-ching coughed up phlegm and shot it at the ground. "I regret naming him Confucius. He doesn't deserve it. Willow, you'll see him soon enough."

"How is your husband, Dick?" everyone asked me.

I hesitated, because I didn't know how to answer.

"Oh, my father is well," Rouge answered for me. "He is busy working in Beijing."

Papa sat down and told me how the town of Chin-kiang had changed over the years. "It is a place of exile," he began. "The government dumps people back in their hometowns once they can no longer be of benefit."

Carpenter Chan explained further. "The government seems to think that undesirables should fall back on their native regions and relatives to survive."

"It saves prison costs," Papa said. "We had to build all this ourselves." He waved an arm indicating the inside of the church.

Carpenter Chan smiled. "I am still building it."

"We are truly under God's roof now," Papa said.

"Chan never learned his lesson," Lilac said. "We could have stayed in Nanking if he had denounced Absalom. I told him that Absalom wouldn't mind because he was dead. My stubborn husband wouldn't do it. So we were sent back to Chin-kiang. What can I complain about? The old rule for a woman has always been: *Marry a dog, follow the dog; marry a rooster, follow the rooster*. But our children's future was ruined. In Nanking they would have had opportunities, better schools and better jobs. Here in Chin-kiang, my twins work as coolies, and my youngest son is a field hand ... They see no brightness in their future." Lilac began to weep.

"Who is making that racket?" a man's voice came from above.

I raised my eyes and saw three figures crawling out of the sleeping boxes.

A dark, bearded old man came down a rope. He was followed by two other men. "Damn lousy bones, they won't stop protesting! This rotten body is falling apart."

The voice was familiar, but I couldn't place the speaker.

The bearded man approached me. He smiled, mocking. "I bet you'd never guess who we are."

The other two men echoed, "But we know you and your friend well."

I searched the corners of memory but could find nothing that would match the images in front of me.

The bearded man sighed. "Twenty years in the national prison must have changed my appearance ... Willow, look hard at me. I am Bumpkin

Emperor." He turned around and pointed at the men behind him. "They are my sworn brothers."

"Bumpkin Emperor? General Lobster and General Crab?"

"Yes, that's us!" the men cried in unison.

Papa came and put his arm around the men's shoulders. "They are with us now."

"What do you mean by 'with us'?" I asked. "Bumpkin Emperor almost killed Absalom, Pearl, Grace, and their children! Absalom would have sent him to hell!"

"On the contrary, my child, on the contrary." Papa shook his head. "In fact, it was Absalom's wish. He made sure that everyone in his church forgave Bumpkin Emperor and his sworn brothers. After all, Christ died for our sins and his Father forgives us."

"I don't believe it, Papa."

"Ask Carpenter Chan."

"Is it true?" I asked.

"Yes." Carpenter Chan nodded. "It was indeed Absalom's wish."

"To forgive Bumpkin Emperor for what he did?"

"Yes."

"God is good, God is fair, and God is kind," Bumpkin Emperor murmured with tears in his eyes.

"Absalom is happy with me in heaven!" Papa sang his words. "I converted the three of them."

The sound of Sunday service woke me. It took a moment to realize that I was not dreaming. I was inside my sleeping box. I rolled over onto my stomach and stuck my head out to see what was going on. I saw Papa performing a sermon in front of the kitchen stove, which was covered with a white cloth. Papa was dressed in his old minister's robe, so washed and worn that it looked like a rag, the color no longer black. Papa's expression was solemn and calm. As he continued speaking, I could hear Absalom in his voice.

I glanced at the door in fear, and I noticed that it was closed and secured with a thick wooden bar.

The hundred and nine residents of the old church listened to Papa quietly. They were either sitting on the benches or on the floor or inside their sleeping boxes.

When Papa finished, people began to sing "Amazing Grace." Memories of sitting with Carie at her piano rushed back to me. I had never understood the lyrics until now

> 'Twas Grace that taught my heart to fear,
> And Grace my fears relieved;
> How precious did that Grace appear,
> The hour I first believed.
>
> Through many dangers, toils, and snares,
> I have already come;
> 'Tis Grace that brought me safe thus far,
> And Grace will lead me home.

I slid back into my sleeping box. I hadn't cried when Dick had told me that he had fallen in love with his secretary and had decided to end our marriage. But now I was hit by an emotion that felt like the ocean's high tide.

Rouge rolled over and hugged me as I sobbed.

"You are home, Mama." She gently wiped my tears. "We are home."

CHAPTER 29

The person in charge of my reform was Chin-kiang's Communist Party boss, Vanguard, formerly known as Confucius, the son of the beggar lady Soo-ching. Vanguard had grown into a squirrel-faced, cross-eyed, middle-aged man with a fat belly. He enjoyed denouncing me so much that he ordered others to do the same.

Vanguard pretended that he did not know me. He spoke Mandarin with a heavy Chin-kiang accent, and he was proud of being an illiterate. Since becoming the party boss, he had banned the worship of God and made it a crime to mention the names of Absalom, Carie, and Pearl.

When Vanguard learned that Pearl had won the Nobel Prize, he saw an opportunity to advance his political career. He invited Mao's favorite journalists to Chin-kiang to tour the hometown of the notorious American cultural imperialist. The event caught Madame Mao's attention. Vanguard was summoned to the Forbidden City to be honored as "Chairman Mao's great foot soldier." Madame Mao awarded Vanguard with a work of her calligraphy that read, "*The hope of launching a cultural atomic bomb on the world's Capitalism rests on your shoulders.*"

Vanguard called me "the evil twin sister of Pearl Buck" and "Chin-kiang's shame." He encouraged children to call me scum. He ordered me to clean out the town's sewage drains and public restrooms daily. Every Friday afternoon I reported to Vanguard to confess my crimes. Depending on my response, Vanguard would either pass or fail me. If he was displeased, he would add more to my workload. He might order me to clean his office, which was the former British Embassy. If he felt

I needed further humiliation, he would order me to walk through the town banging a chime with a stick. I was instructed to shout, "Come and see the American running dog!"; "Down with Willow Yee!"; and "Long live the proletarian dictatorship!" Vanguard hated it when I protested by staring at him in silence.

"I can have you tortured, you know," he threatened constantly.

Vanguard expected me to tell him the details of my relationship with Pearl Buck.

"I want you to trace back all the way to your childhood," he ordered.

Papa taught me to forget about preserving my dignity. "Speak the wolf's language!" If he were me, Papa said, he would toy with Vanguard.

I tried, but it didn't work. Vanguard was determined to please Madame Mao. He didn't buy my abstractions and empty words. "How dare you try to fool the Communist Party!" he yelled at me.

To pressure me further, Vanguard organized rallies. They took place in the town's square. The crowd repeated after Vanguard as he shouted, "Confess or be tortured to death!"

While Vanguard pulled my hair back to show the public my "evil features," I imagined the opera *The Butterfly Lovers*. I remembered every detail of Pearl and me going to see the performance together with NaiNai. When Vanguard used a whip to beat me, I saw the birds, bees, and dragonflies flying into Absalom's church. When the blood came and pain burned inside my body, I heard Carie singing her favorite Christmas song, "What Child Is This?"

In my dreams, I visited Pearl in her American home. The furniture I imagined for Pearl was made of red sandalwood in the style of the Chinese Ming dynasty. I saw the pictures on her walls, beautiful Chinese brush paintings and ink calligraphy. Also, I dreamed of Pearl sculpting. It was something she had said that she would love to learn. We used to watch Chin-kiang's craftsmen making cookie figures out of sugared flour. For three pennies, we bought our favorite colored animals and opera figures. At our playground behind the hills, Pearl once sculpted a mud head using me as a model, and I did one of her. To emphasize our individual characteristics, I made her nose high and she slanted my eyes. Both faces were smiling because we couldn't help laughing while making them.

I dreamed of Pearl's play stove, a real one built by Carie's gardener. It was located behind the hillside. It was there that we cooked real food. Wang Ah-ma taught us to bake yams and roast soybeans and peanuts. I could still hear the sound of Pearl and me chewing beans as if our teeth were made of steel.

Since moving back to Chin-kiang, I had been praying with Papa. Vanguard had no power over my spiritual being. My resistance against the Communists grew stronger. I decided to try to bore the crowd with my confessions, filling and padding them out with Mao quotations, slogans, and self-name-calling. My typical first sentence would be "I was a cat that lost her way before I was guided back home by Chairman Mao's teaching." My second sentence would be "Although I have never read a word of *The Good Earth*, my desire to read the book is absolutely reactionary and criminal."

After Vanguard's lectures and criticisms, it was my task to lead the crowd in shouting, "Burn, fire, fry, and roast Willow if she doesn't surrender!" To amuse myself, I created variations. "Down with Willow Yee" became "Down with the American running dog Willow Yee!" and then "Down with the big liar, big traitor, big bourgeoisie, big snake, and big rotten, assless, slummy, and poisonous spider Willow Yee!" I began to play with the crowd's breath. I dragged the sentences out as long as I could. I invented slogans to shout as breathing exercises. My favorite only a few could follow: "Long live our great leader, great teacher, great helmsman, great leader Chairman Mao's great, glorious, and forever correct revolutionary line!"

In the winter, Vanguard conducted a political rally in the former British Embassy's ballroom. The crowd was ordered to sit on the floor for hours on end. As I confessed, men smoked cigarettes and played cards, while women sewed their clothes and knitted. Old people napped and babies screamed. Vanguard insisted that my confessions were not heartfelt. He concluded that I purposely resisted reform and ought to be further punished.

I was put to work as the town's slave.

To those who were sympathetic toward me, Vanguard warned, "The word *mercy* doesn't exist in our proletarian dictionary!"

When Vanguard decided to lead Chin-kiang to "enter Communism overnight," he eliminated the use of chamber pots. Everyone was to use the public restrooms, but because restrooms didn't belong to anyone, no one cleaned them. They became a breeding ground for maggots, flies, and mosquitoes. It became my responsibility to clean them.

I labored day and night. Rouge helped when she could. Her old job as a textile worker had been given to a relative of her boss, and now she worked as a concrete mixer for a construction company. Close to the Chinese New Year in 1970, Rouge was ordered to work both the night and day shifts. I made my rounds of the public restrooms alone. As my tired hands scrubbed the walls of the feces-filled pits, I felt helpless and exhausted. I asked myself, "What is the point of going on?"

I had to restrain myself from crying or I would wake everyone. Papa was asleep. Rouge was working. The shadow of Dick's secretary-nurse would not leave me alone. I had finally learned her name, Daisy. My mind's eye saw that she had a full-moon face, big eyes, and a cheery mouth. She and Dick were embracing in the bed that used to be mine.

"Papa," I called.

No answer.

I got up, climbed down, and landed on the floor. Papa was not in his sleeping box.

I went searching for him. I checked the washing area and the dining area. Passing the stacked firewood and coal buckets, I arrived in the kitchen. I heard a noise over my head. It came from the storage area behind the kitchen. Standing still, I listened carefully. It was the sound of a radio—someone was tuning through the channels.

Like an old monkey, I climbed the rope ladder. My legs were shaking and I was out of breath. I lost my balance and my shoulder hit the storage door.

The radio stopped.

After a long moment of silence, the door opened.

Holding a candle, Bumpkin Emperor stuck his head out. "What are you doing here?"

"I am looking for Papa."

"He is not here."

"I heard the sound of a radio. What's going on?"

"Nothing."

"Can I come in?"

"No, you can't."

"Don't make me wake up everyone," I threatened.

"I said no."

"Let me in, please."

"No."

"You are hiding something, aren't you?"

"It's none of your business . . ."

"Let me in!"

"Don't make me push you . . ."

"Willow!" Papa's voice came from inside.

Bumpkin Emperor pivoted his body, and I entered.

Papa's face was lit by candlelight. He was holding a brick-sized box. It was a radio of a fancy make, better than the one Dick had owned. Papa turned the radio dial. Static filled the shadowy room. The scene reminded me of a propaganda film in which criminals gathered in conspiracy. Papa was in his pajamas. He was calm and focused. I had never seen him concentrating like this. He tilted his head to the side as he searched for a signal and listened. I looked around and saw more faces. Besides Bumpkin Emperor and his sworn brothers, there were Carpenter Chan, his sons, and a few others. They all looked nervous but excited.

"What are you listening to?" I asked.

"Sh-sh!" Bumpkin Emperor pushed my head down.

Papa kept adjusting the dial. Finally there was a human voice. Papa was ecstatic. "I got it, I got it!" The signal didn't last. It turned to static again. Papa kept trying while the others waited patiently. After a long while the signal returned. A voice speaking foreign-accented Mandarin came on. "This is Voice of America broadcasting from the United States."

Chapter 30

The radio had belonged to Bumpkin Emperor. It had been a gift from Chiang Kai-shek when Bumpkin Emperor was at the peak of his power as a warlord. The two men had joined forces against Mao. What made the radio valuable was that it had been made in America for military use. Bumpkin Emperor had donated the radio to the church after Papa had converted him.

Papa no longer felt isolated since he'd mastered the radio. He was obsessed with it. Papa shared the latest world news with carefully selected church members. Life became more bearable, although not better. The Cultural Revolution continued and Mao worship intensified. Food shortages became the worst they'd been since the Great Leap Forward. Vanguard loosened his grip on me in order to catch people who were selling vegetables they grew in their backyards.

One day, a stranger visited me. His name was Chu. Although I didn't recognize him, I remembered the name. He was the Beijing general Dick had talked into surrendering in 1949. Dick had been proud when he saved the Imperial city and avoided a bloody battle in the streets of Beijing. Dick had negotiated with General Chu. Mao had promised Chu a high-ranking position in the People's Liberation Army.

The man who stood in front of me was sick and thin. He had wax-yellow skin and sunken eyes. He spoke in a whisper and his words confused me. He said that he had been Dick's cellmate in prison. He then explained that he was on a medical release from the national prison. I told him that Dick was working for Mao. He said that it was no longer the case.

"What do you mean by 'cellmate'?" I asked. I hadn't talked to Dick for two years. I knew nothing about his life.

General Chu produced a wadded paper on which ink letters the size of ants were written.

Dear Willow,

This letter gives me a chance to explain everything, which I consider a blessing.

I am writing from the Southwest Labor Prison near Tibet. You might wonder what I did to offend Mao. Well, again, the story has to do with Pearl Buck. But truly my own ambition is to blame.

Mao summoned me on the evening of May 30, 1969. Madame Mao was there and unusually friendly toward me. Mao didn't seem to be aware that it was the middle of the night. He was dressed in a white bathrobe. His hair was wet and he was barefoot.

Once I was seated he simply said, "Pearl Buck wants to come to China. Premier Chou En-lai thinks we should make an exception and open the door for her. What do you think?"

Out of the corner of my eye I was aware of Madame Mao's wooden expression. A slight smile quivered on her lips.

Given all my personal history with Pearl Buck, I marveled at Mao's audacity. Had he forgotten that you, my wife, had gone to prison because of your refusal to denounce your friend? But I also knew that Mao's desire for international recognition had only grown stronger over the years. No matter how strong he was at home, his reputation had not kept up abroad. He would do anything to gain the prestige that had eluded him. I saw at once that he was willing to rewrite history if it would fulfill his ends. I wasn't so sure about his wife.

I sat there sweating in my chair as Mao went on. He asked me to cultivate Pearl Buck and convince her to change her mind about China. "Tell her we now rule a quarter of the human race on earth," Mao said.

Mao revealed that his intelligence agency had recently reported that Pearl Buck had been a consultant to President John Kennedy. Mao believed that she had the potential to be his bridge to America.

Looking back, my fate was set. Madame Mao was jealous of any female Mao was interested in. She had made secret arrests, tortured, and murdered in order to gain Mao's affection back.

Unfortunately, my own ambition made me willfully blind. Connecting Mao and Pearl Buck would be the best thing I could do to advance my career. Going down in history tempted me so much that I played with fire. The wind was in my favor, I thought, and I'd be a fool not to ride it. I planned on making a case to back up Chou En-lai's position.

I translated Pearl's recent articles on China and carefully edited out her negative comments. But before I submitted the material to Mao, the wind changed its direction. Madame Mao got ahead of me.

As evidence against Pearl, Madame Mao presented parts of her latest novel, Three Daughters of Madame Liang, in which Pearl depicted senseless murders taking place during the Cultural Revolution as if she had witnessed it. The novel amazingly mirrored the truth.

From that moment on, Mao lost interest in Pearl Buck. But Madame Mao was not finished with me. She saw Pearl Buck as a personal threat and was determined to punish anyone with a connection to her. Accusing me of deceiving Mao, Madame Mao had me arrested.

I expected Mao to offer his protection, but he didn't.

I met General Chu in prison. What a twist of fate! On one hand, I felt guilty because Mao never honored his promises—the terms I negotiated. Once Chu surrendered, he became useless to Mao and was abandoned. Although Chu was granted the title of commanding general of the People's Liberation Army, it was a paper title only. Chu ended up without the army or his freedom. I felt that I had let the man down. Ending my life in prison almost makes me feel better, because it separates me from Mao.

The Tibetan weather is harsh and the air is thin. We live like rodents in underground holes, which we dug ourselves—talk about digging one's own grave. However, the dead do not get buried here. The prison doesn't have enough prisoners to dig the holes to bury them all. Instead, the dead are dragged away and left in the open about a half mile from where we live. When the wind is strong, we can smell the rotten stench. Eventually, Tibetan wolves and buzzards eat what is left.

I live on leaves, earthworms, and mice. Before summer ends, the leaves and earthworms will be gone. We have stripped the trees of bark and eaten the rough fiber. Now those trees have died. We don't have enough energy to catch mice. I have begun eating "suicide seeds." This is a kind of grass seed that one slowly dies from. At least it cures the hunger. I've been constipated for weeks. My belly hurts so much that I pass out from time to time. You would never imagine the scene: cellmates helping each other scoop the shit from each other's rear ends with bare fingers. It is a bloody business.

Chu was my partner. He hadn't shit for nine days. I used a chopstick and tried to break the stool and scoop it out with a spoon. But his stool was as hard as a rock. He was in terrible pain. His stomach swelled like a big balloon. Another cellmate was from Shanghai, a doctor. Yesterday he died of constipation. He was only thirty-seven years old.

People here don't count on waking up when they go to sleep. Strangely, most people die quietly in their sleep. Like the end of a burning candle, the flame flickers and is swallowed by eternal darkness. Each night I think of you. I regret deserting you for Daisy. She reported my complaining to Madame Mao. My foolish pillow talk! Near the end, before I went to prison, she admitted that she was Madame Mao's spy. I knew Daisy kept a diary, but I didn't know it would be used as a weapon against me. I thought I was on top of the world when I said to her, "Human beings make mistakes. Mao is a human being. He makes mistakes." Daisy received a promotion for reporting my comment. Before my arrest, Mao invited me to accompany him to Russia. He made me believe that I was his most trusted man.

There was never a hint that I was to be punished. Then all of a sudden, Madame Mao told me that Mao was upset with me. Next I was stripped of my Party membership. I was to go to prison because I was no longer a comrade but a reactionary. Mao wouldn't answer my calls or letters.

I know I have hurt you by my disloyalty. I have stayed away as you wished. I am writing this letter because I believe that I won't last much *longer. My belly is larger than a pregnant woman's. I am chewed up by remorse and shame. I deserve Hell. I don't expect myself to live beyond the New Year. There is no mail and almost no one gets out alive. In case Chu succeeds in getting out and this letter reaches you, I want you to know that I still love you and have always loved you, even when I was a foolish man.*

 Dick

My only thought was to see Dick before it was too late. I didn't bother asking Vanguard for permission to leave because I knew he wouldn't agree. Rouge bought the ticket, and I left Chin-kiang by train the next day. It was a standing-only ticket because I didn't have enough money to buy a seat. For the next seventy-two hours, I stood during the day and managed to rest at night, curled up next to urine-soaked newspapers.

After the train, I traveled on foot. It took me two weeks to reach the prison camp. Then they made me wait for days before I was told the truth, that Dick had already died. He had been punished for stealing food. The story was that Dick hadn't reported the death of another prisoner so that he could claim the dead man's share of food. Dick slept with the corpse until the stink of rotting flesh gave him away. After that, the prison guards starved Dick and he died.

I wept imagining Dick sleeping with a corpse. I asked that I be allowed to identify Dick's remains, but I was refused. I went to the prison headquarters and put on a hunger strike. After a week, I was taken to the open graveyard Dick had described in his letter.

As Dick had written, none were buried. Bodies and bones were everywhere. The smell was horrible. I stumbled from body to body looking for my husband. It was almost impossible to recognize any of the dead. I refused to give up. Hours later, I found him. Dick was naked. I recognized him by a scar I remembered. The flesh on his body had been torn by vultures and chewed on by wild dogs.

I fainted. When I woke up, I struggled to remember Dick's face as I had known him. I did not want to remember him like this. I went and found a local peasant who owned a donkey. I paid him to bring me a bucket of gasoline and some firewood. I borrowed a rusty old shovel and dug a ditch. I dragged what was left of my husband to the ditch and piled the wood on him and poured the gasoline over that. I set this on fire. Afterward, I collected Dick's bones, but they were too big to fit inside my bag. I had to abandon most of them. I never imagined Dick would end like this.

After I returned to Chin-kiang, Papa performed a memorial for Dick. We invited only the people we trusted who had known Dick. I meant to invite General Chu, but he was nowhere to be found. He had gone into hiding. Papa said that prison life must have made Chu cautious and distrustful. "Let's remember him as a loyal friend to Dick."

"What's important is that Chu risked his life to deliver Father's letter," Rouge said.

"God must have guided General Chu," Papa agreed.

I remembered Chu's words. He felt blessed to be the messenger because he believed that he would soon join Dick. He believed that finding me would be the best gift he could offer to his friend.

I burned Dick's writing, which I had saved over the years. Dick would have liked me to do that. He had worshipped Mao and Communism with all his heart. It was what Dick had believed.

I saved Dick's last letter for Pearl, although I had no idea if we would ever see each other again. A reunion with my friend was becoming harder and harder to imagine. Today's Chinese children knew Americans only as enemies, and things seemed to be getting worse. I wondered whether Pearl would be amused or horrified at the fact that Mao had considered converting her into a proletarian.

Chapter 31

Papa was a master when it came to tricking the authorities. "Mao fought guerrilla style and won China," Papa said to his congregation. "We stand the same chance to save souls for God if we follow his example."

I warned Papa that he was asking for trouble.

"I have an advantage over Mao," Papa replied with confidence. "I have the radio."

I was worried. "You will end up in prison."

"That already happened before you came home." Papa stuck up three fingers. "Three times I was in and out of that filthy place. What more can the authorities do to a century-old man?"

Papa reminded me more and more of Absalom. He attended births, marriages, and funerals. He fooled the government spies with the language he used. He commenced each ceremony the traditional way and then turned it into a Christian event without anyone being the wiser—even when an agent was in the crowd. Papa started each sermon with Mao's Quotation Book in his hand. He would begin with *We are people from all walks of life* and conclude by reciting from the Bible, *"He that had gathered much had nothing over; and he that had gathered little had no lack."*

Papa developed a language only his Christian congregation understood. He referred to God as "the Cloud-walker," punishment in hell as being "handpicked by Karl Marx," the Bible as "the Quotation Book," and salvation as "the revolutionary mission."

During the celebration on China's twenty-second National Independence Day, Papa was arrested for the fourth time for spreading poisonous thoughts. Papa confessed quickly to avoid torture. He denounced himself and made promises to the authorities, but he had no intention of keeping them.

He came home quoting a Chinese saying: *"A hero is someone who doesn't swim against the current."*

Papa forgave himself in God's name. He called his lies strategies to avoid unnecessary sacrifices. Using himself as an example, he taught his congregation how to deal with the authorities. Once, Papa pretended to have a nervous breakdown. He claimed that he suffered flashbacks from the time when he was "poisoned" by Absalom. At public rallies Papa pointed at himself and shouted, "Down with Absalom's number-one running dog!" This caused stifled laughter to ripple through the crowd.

When ordered to criticize himself, Papa said, "My hands would be busy picking your pockets if Absalom hadn't introduced me to Jesus Christ."

Vanguard tried to stop Papa. "How dare you praise that American cultural imperialist!" he yelled.

"Down with Absalom!" Papa shouted back as he punched his fists into the air. "I salute Comrade Vanguard!" Turning toward Mao's portrait on the wall, he bowed deeply. "I'll confess more to you, Chairman Mao!"

"More confessions!" the crowd cheered. "More confessions!"

Papa carried on. "Chairman Mao teaches us that 'we must educate the masses by exposing what our enemy has done.' Now, let me tell you what Jesus Christ has done."

I learned from Papa not to "swim against the current." I still felt hurt when children called me evil, but I no longer felt guilty. My true healing started when I began to help Papa with his guerrilla church.

To his amazement, Papa started to receive shocking confessions. Although he did not share them with me at first, eventually he did. I learned that Carpenter Chan had confessed that he had been a secret member of the Communist Party and Vanguard had been his leader. Carpenter Chan joined the party in 1949 believing that Mao and the Communists represented the poor. Carpenter Chan's assigned task was to report on Papa. However, Chan became troubled when he realized how flawed and power-hungry Vanguard was. As the years went by, Carpenter Chan became convinced that Vanguard was a false prophet and Mao a false God.

My childhood memories were like splendid Imperial Palaces where I wandered and lingered. Often I imagined that Pearl and I were reunited. That scene was my favorite daydream. I felt closest to God when thinking about Pearl. I considered such moments like opening gifts from heaven.

Unlike me, my daughter, Rouge, was a realist, especially after her father's death. Memories weren't the same to her as they were to me. She chose to forget over remembering.

I would live with Rouge until she was in her forties and finally married. My son-in-law was a hardware-factory technician who had lost his wife to illness. The man struggled to raise his two young daughters. I was pleased when Rouge married him and adopted both girls. A year later Rouge gave birth to her own baby girl. My favorite activity was taking my granddaughters to visit the places where Pearl and I used to play hide-and-seek. I enjoyed the sunshine and the gentle rolling scenery, especially when the wind blew softly, brushing against my face. During such moments, I forgot how old I was. I felt like a girl again until one of my granddaughters started singing Carie's favorite song and I realized that she wasn't Pearl. That's when I wondered if Pearl was still alive.

The day before Chinese New Year's Eve in 1971, Papa came with a surprise.

"Pearl Buck will speak on Voice of America!" Papa could barely contain his excitement.

So, she was alive! I got down on my knees and thanked God. It had been thirty-seven years since I had last seen her. I was white-haired and imagined her to be the same.

It was no use when Papa advised people not to come.

"It's an enemy radio station," Papa warned. "You will be considered a traitor if caught listening. You will be arrested and sent to prison."

The day was carefully planned. The secret gathering would be disguised as a Chinese New Year's banquet.

I was surprised when Vanguard and his assistant, nicknamed Catfish, walked into the church moments before the broadcast.

"Secretary Vanguard, welcome, and please join us," Papa greeted the two with a smile.

I pulled Papa aside and whispered in his ear, "Have you lost your mind?"

Papa ignored me. He took out his radio and began to set it up.

"Bring out the best wine for our boss," Papa said.

People started to crawl out of their sleeping boxes and climb down the ropes. Carpenter Chan and Lilac came to stand near Papa. Behind them were Bumpkin Emperor and his sworn brothers.

The hallway and the dining area soon became crowded.

Papa poured wine and made sure that Vanguard and Catfish had the largest share. He poured an inch into the other glasses, but filled theirs to the top. Papa made a toast. "Let's drink to demonstrate our loyalty to Chairman Mao!"

Vanguard had to drink all of his wine. Papa waited until Vanguard's glass was empty before he refilled it and toasted to Mao's health. Glasses were emptied and refilled again. Papa's third toast was to the victory of the Cultural Revolution. The fourth full glass and toast were for Vanguard's continued success in leading Chin-kiang into Communism.

When Vanguard slipped from the chair onto the floor, his face was the color of a rooster's comb. Catfish was still awake, but Papa ignored him and changed the radio's channel. The church filled with the sound of Voice of America.

We listened intently.

In Mandarin the host introduced Pearl S. Buck.

I stopped breathing when I heard a female voice say in Chin-kiang-accented Mandarin, "Happy Chinese New Year! I am Pearl Sydenstricker Buck."

The first reaction was that no one could believe their ears. We all thought that it was our imagination.

As the conversation continued, the reality sank in.

"It's her! It's our Pearl!" Jumping for joy, we screamed and hugged each other.

"Happy New Year to you too, Pearl!" Papa said. He was smiling, but tears streamed down his cheeks.

It was as if she had never left China. Her accent hadn't changed. Her tone was gentle and clear. She began to tell us about her life. We had little understanding of the events she was talking about, such as the Great Depression and the Vietnam War. But it didn't matter. We were gathered to hear her voice. The fact that she was alive filled me with happiness.

Pearl talked about her books, including her translation of *All Men Are Brothers*. She mentioned that *The Good Earth* had been made into an American movie. "Although it's a wonderful movie," she said, "I am afraid that you wouldn't like it, because all the Chinese characters are played by Western actors. They all have high noses and speak English." She said that she lived in Pennsylvania and had adopted eight children, most of them of Asian descent.

We wept when Pearl said that she wanted to visit China.

"The details of my youth have become more and more clear to me as I have aged." We could hear that Pearl's voice was full of emotion. "When I close my eyes, I see Chin-kiang's hills and fields at dawn and dusk, in sunshine and in moonlight, in summer green and winter snow." She said she missed the Chinese New Year's celebration the most. "I would be having a banquet with my friends right now if I were among them. As we all know, to be Chinese means one lives to eat."

The host asked Pearl to describe a typical scene in Chin-kiang for the world's listeners.

She paused for a moment and then replied, "A typical scene would be the mist over the big pond under the weeping willows. There would be frail clouds in the sky, and the water would shine silver. Against this background, I would see a great white heron standing on one stalk of a leg."

I let my tears flow as I imagined the smile on my friend's face.

Pearl went on. "My American friends often praise Chinese artists for their vivid imaginations, but no, let me tell you, the artist only puts down what he sees. I grew up and spent forty years of my life enjoying such scenery. It is the China I know and the China I continue to live in within my mind."

Catfish grew terrified as he listened. He was not drunk and was aware of the consequences. He slapped Vanguard's face and splashed water over him. "Boss! Wake up! We must go!"

Like a pile of wet mud, Vanguard did not move.

"We are trapped!" Catfish became hysterical. He turned to Papa and threatened, "I'm going to report this!"

"Go ahead!" Papa said. "Don't forget to mention that Vanguard supported us and that is why he was here with us. He was so excited to listen to Voice of America and Pearl Buck that he got drunk to celebrate. Everyone in this building saw him do it."

CHAPTER 32

Although Vanguard confiscated Papa's radio, he lost his position. He was replaced by Carpenter Chan, who was appointed the new Communist Party secretary of Chin-kiang. Carpenter Chan didn't want the job, but Papa convinced him to accept the position. Papa believed that God's work needed information and intelligence. "I'd appreciate it if you could get me the monthly Communist Party newsletter, the *Internal Reference*."

Papa's wisdom paid off. The *Internal Reference* forecast the changes in China's political weather. Papa devoured every issue. He analyzed and looked for traces of change, especially in Mao's attitude toward the United States.

In July 1971, Papa noticed a stamp-sized announcement that Mao was to receive a special guest from America, a man named Henry Kissinger.

"Mao's pot is cooking!" Papa said to Carpenter Chan.

Three months later Papa learned that China had been accepted as a member of the United Nations.

"A deal is in the works," Papa predicted.

Papa and Chan became the first in town to figure out that America's President Nixon was about to visit China. Through the *Internal Reference*, Papa and Carpenter Chan also learned that there were two powerful factions within China's Communist Party. One was called the Wife Party, Madame Mao's faction, which Mao trusted to carry on his Cultural Revolution. The other was the Premier Party, led by Premier

Chou En-lai, which Mao trusted to manage the country. Both factions competed for Mao's favor.

The battle between the two intensified when Nixon's visit was announced publicly. A group of investigators came to Chin-kiang. We had no idea that it had to do with the fact that Nixon had selected Pearl Buck to accompany him to China. It was only later that we learned the momentous news.

By candlelight Papa conducted discussions with his guerrilla-church members. "The world's attention will be focused on Nixon when he comes," Papa said, his eyes glowing and every wrinkle dancing. "Imagine, our Pearl introducing Nixon to Mao in perfect Mandarin and Mao to Nixon in American English!"

The question seemed to be: Would Madame Mao let it happen? Would she stand for another woman taking over the role she believed she was entitled to?

"Hundreds of cameras will be clicking and flashing," Papa continued. "Madame Mao will be jealous of Pearl standing between Mao and Nixon."

"There is another possibility," Carpenter Chan said. "Mao might show interest in Pearl, like he did with the wife of Philippine president Marcos. I saw the documentary in which Mao kissed the lady's hand."

I wouldn't be surprised if Mao was charmed by the blue-eyed Pearl. I imagined Pearl dressed up. She would look like Carie, beautiful and elegant. Mao would ask questions in his native Hunanese, and Pearl would answer in the same tune. As far as I knew, Pearl was fluent in many Chinese dialects besides Mandarin. It would only be natural for Mao to extend an invitation to Pearl to visit him in private, as he had with so many famous Chinese actresses, poets, and novelists.

"Perhaps Mao will offer Pearl a personal tour of the Forbidden City," Papa imagined. "I can see the two strolling together down the Imperial Long Corridor, where the Last Empress, Tsu Hsi, walked every day after dinner. Mao would share his knowledge of Chinese history."

"Mao might suggest visiting the Great Wall," Carpenter Chan added. "He and Pearl would be carried by the palanquin bearers."

Lilac nodded. "Certainly Mao would propose dinner at the Imperial Summer Palace."

"Yes," Papa agreed. "The dishes would be given names after Mao's poems. Crabs with ginger and wine would be called Taking Down the Capital Nanking. Roasted duck with wheat pancakes would be called Autumn Uprising Triumph."

"Hot red pepper with fried frog legs would be called The Birth of the People's Republic." Bumpkin Emperor and his sworn brothers drooled.

The pictures continued to scroll through my mind. Pearl might win Mao's heart if she presented to him her translation of *All Men Are Brothers*, a favorite of Mao's. He would assume that Pearl shared his passion for the peasant heroes.

I could hear Mao call Pearl "My comrade!" Mao would forget his age, his toothaches, his sore eyes and stiff joints. He would take Pearl's hand and tell her that it was *All Men Are Brothers* that had inspired him to become a revolutionary. To earn her affection, he would want Pearl to know how he became the modern emperor of China. He would expect her to share the story with Nixon.

"*People, only the people, are the creators of history.*" Carpenter Chan mimicked Mao's famous quotation. "Pearl would be flattered."

"I don't think so," Lilac disagreed. "Pearl wouldn't like Mao at all."

"Pearl is lucky that Mao still hasn't read *The Good Earth*," I said. "If he had, he would know that Pearl will never be his comrade. Nothing Mao says or does will change Pearl's view. And I believe that Pearl would disappoint Mao as well. Mao would discover that although Pearl spoke his language and knew his culture, she could never worship him like the rest of China. Pearl would see his flaws. She could be Mao's nightmare."

"We'll see," Papa said. "Wine might bring alive the poet in Mao. He could pick up a brush pen and write Pearl a calligraphy couplet as a gift. Pearl might demonstrate her appreciation by recognizing the rhythm in which Mao composed, and she would sound out the phrases in ancient Chinese."

"Mao would ask Pearl to stay for late-night tea," said Bumpkin Emperor, nodding.

"Pearl would refuse," Rouge said. "And she would say, 'President Nixon is waiting for me.'"

"The rejection would be worse than Nixon dropping a nuclear bomb on China," everyone agreed.

The town of Chin-kiang was to be given a task of national importance. As the party boss, Carpenter Chan started to receive messages from his superiors. The first was from Premier Chou En-lai, instructing him to prepare for Pearl Buck's homecoming.

"Get ready to show the town to America's President Nixon," the message read.

The second message contradicted the first. It ordered the town to cooperate with Madame Mao's investigators. "It is time to reveal Pearl Buck and her parents' crimes against China and the Chinese people," that message read.

Believing that it would be an opportunity to get back on top, Vanguard exposed the underground Christian church. "Absalom's ghost is not only alive but active in turning people against Mao and Communism," he claimed.

The Communist newspaper, the *People's Daily*, published an article titled "The Nobel Prize Winner Makes Her Living Insulting China." Carpenter Chan told us that Madame Mao had barred Chin-kiang from receiving the American guests.

Secretly, Carpenter Chan took back the confiscated radio. He and Papa tuned in to Voice of America for the latest news. Between the lines, they learned that Nixon's delegation would depart from the United States for China in a week, and that the Chinese authorities had refused Pearl Buck entrance.

Carpenter Chan composed a petition signed by everyone in town and sent it to Premier Chou En-lai.

"Pearl Buck grew up in Chin-kiang," the petition pleaded. *"It is her right to visit her mother's grave and our duty as her neighbors and friends to see her wish granted."*

Never before had the entire town been united in one common goal. It was not Pearl Buck's visit that we were fighting for, but our own lives and our children's future. Since the beginning of the Cultural Revolution, those whose paths had crossed Absalom's and Carie's had been denounced and made to suffer. The major events had happened years ago, but our memories were still fresh. Some people had been affected more directly than others, but all had stories to tell. I remembered that the teenage mob that called itself Mao's Red Guard had even come to Beijing to "clear Pearl Buck's evil influence." They knew that I had delivered letters to Pearl from Hsu Chih-mo. They took me out of the prison to attend a public rally, where the teens hung a wooden board around my neck that read, PIMP. The crowd demanded that I confess Hsu Chih-mo and Pearl Buck's relationship. Pearl's former students were terrorized. They were forced to inform on me. One pointed out to the crowd that I was Pearl's best friend and Carie's adopted daughter. Other students recalled that I was the one who had tried to steal Hsu Chih-mo from Pearl Buck.

The Red Guard located Absalom's grave near Chin-kiang and vandalized it. They smashed the stone-carving tablet honoring Absalom's lifelong service to God. The Red Guard also sought Carie's grave. It was Lilac who removed the tombstone to a different location. The grave the Red Guard destroyed was not Carie's.

Lilac's sons were ordered to change names. Double Luck David and John were now Down with Christ and War on God. Triple Luck Solomon's new name was Mao's Loyalist.

When the Red Guard ordered Bumpkin Emperor and his sworn brothers to smash a ceramic figure of Christ, the former warlords exploded. They took the anti-Christ boards off their necks and smashed them instead. When they were locked up, they escaped into the mountains.

Papa took the risk of protecting Absalom's hand-drawn pictures of Jesus Christ. He hid them behind the wall-sized portrait of Mao. When Carpenter Chan and his workmen learned that the Red Guard had decided to burn the church, they transformed the church into an "Education Museum" in which Mao's head was painted on every surface. The sculptures of Christ and the saints were boxed and caged and captioned "The Negative Teachers." The boxes were put on display for criticism. To prevent the sculptures from being defiled, the workmen wrapped them in red ribbons with slogans like "Long Live Chairman Mao!" and "Salute to Madame Mao!" written on them.

What pained Papa the most was when members withdrew from the congregation. Although Papa understood that people did it under pressure and out of fear, he couldn't help feeling defeated. He threatened people with "going to hell," although he was appalled by their response: "Hell will be a better place than where we are."

For years Chin-kiang was considered an area severely infected by a "Christian plague." It was decided that the town needed a deep cleaning. Although Vanguard set himself as an example for denouncing Christianity, few followed him. People called Vanguard "the Chin-kiang Judas." The police discovered that Bibles were hidden inside the covers of Mao's books and clay figures of Christ were hidden inside rice bags. Christmas songs were heard during the Chinese New Year, and flowers by Carie's grave never failed to blossom in spring. Children who woke up in the middle of the night to relieve themselves would find themselves tripping over their parents, on their knees praying in the dark. Despite his age, Papa made his rounds rain or shine when there was no place safe to worship God.

Age finally took its toll on Papa. He collapsed one day as he went from house to house, visiting members of his congregation. Rouge and I rushed to his side. When he woke up, he told me that he had met Absalom.

"Old Teacher still rode his donkey," Papa said.

"Did you ask him if he was pleased with your work?" I asked, teasing.

"I did."

"What was the reply?" Rouge was curious.

Papa took a few deep breaths before he answered, "Absalom cried, which was rather out of character. It was about Pearl."

"Pearl?"

"Absalom regretted that he never got the time to be a good father to Pearl."

"What was your response?" both Rouge and I asked.

"I told him that he should be proud, because she carried on his work—that we all heard her on Voice of America."

A week later, Papa stopped breathing. Like a ripe melon, Papa hung happily on his vine before dropping to the ground. He went to sit under the tree outside the converted church building and looked like he had just fallen asleep with his chin on his chest.

PART FIVE

CHAPTER 33

Overnight, the "Down with American Imperialists" slogans were replaced with "Welcome American President Nixon." Mannequins dressed in U.S. Army uniforms for military bayonet practice at schools nationwide were removed. Children were instructed to learn the English phrases "Welcome" and "How do you do?"

The day Nixon arrived in China, children filled the streets from the airport to the hotel where the president would stay. Each child was given paper flowers and instructed to smile with their teeth showing.

Carpenter Chan received an urgent dispatch that Nixon was to visit Chin-kiang, and that Pearl Buck was with him.

The town vibrated with anticipation.

I so wished that Papa could have lived to see this day. It would have thrilled him to greet the American president—but even more, the daughter of his beloved Absalom.

The guerrilla-church members counted the hours and then the minutes. In the morning, state police came to secure the town. Everyone was ordered to stay inside until called. While the men exchanged news and information, the women began to prepare Pearl's favorite foods. Every family contributed. We soaked rice and soybeans, steamed bread and yams, and brought out all the pickled radishes and dried meats, which were usually saved for New Year's. The sound of chopping vegetables lasted all day, and the smell of roasting garlic peanuts filled the air. "Pearl will smell our cooking miles away when she arrives," Lilac said.

When I heard the sound of drums and the music of China's national anthem, I knew the American guests were here. I rinsed my hands, combed my hair, and slipped on my blue Mao jacket. Rouge wanted to join me but her boss wouldn't give her permission. As Dick's daughter, she was ill-treated.

I was nervous and tense. My doubts had grown when my friend's face had failed to appear in newspapers. There were photos of Mao and Nixon shaking hands. And Madame Mao, her big, wide mouth smiling like a white sailboat. But no Pearl. Was I foolish to believe that she would be allowed to come?

"Is Pearl with Nixon or isn't she?" I kept asking Carpenter Chan.

"I don't know" was Chan's reply.

I had been more than living for this moment. To me, it was as if my life depended on it. Now I was afraid. I imagined what Madame Mao might have done to keep Pearl out of China. Dick's fate reminded me not to underestimate her power.

Yet I couldn't stop hoping. I rose before dawn to climb the rolling hills. When I reached the top of a favorite hill where Pearl and I used to play, I lay on the grass and closed my eyes. The scent of jasmine drifted from below and brought back memories. I could see my friend's clear blue eyes. She looked at me without speaking.

My tears welled up at the thought that we would be like two strangers. She might not even recognize me. Maybe she had simply forgotten me. But no, another voice spoke inside my head. "You will always be able to recognize each other." We would pick up where we had left off. I would satisfy her every curiosity about China.

"Tell me how you followed Dick and what happened," my friend would say. She knew that Dick had been Mao's right-hand man.

Or maybe Pearl would not ask. She was not the kind to presume. She would have heard about Mao's persecutions and would have wondered about Dick's fate. In comparison to Hsu Chih-mo, Dick was hot in temper and strong in character. Although he had tried to ride the tiger, he was too honest for Mao. He didn't even know when he had offended Mao. The people of Chin-kiang thought that Dick deserved his tragic ending because he had followed Mao. Papa and Carpenter Chan had never understood Dick. His rejection of Christianity made him suspect to both men. But Dick was against all religions. Like Mao, Dick claimed himself godless. But he had ended up doing exactly what he hated, worshipping Mao.

Pearl was the only one who understood both Dick and me, the same way she understood China. Perhaps this was why Nixon had picked her to accompany him.

Pearl would not have forgotten Hsu Chih-mo. I was sure of that. But I would tell her that Hsu Chih-mo was a lucky man. By that, I meant that he was better off dead. Hsu Chih-mo would have suffered horribly if he had lived to see the Cultural Revolution. He would have ended up worse than Dick.

We were falling asleep waiting inside when we heard Carpenter Chan's voice.

"They are gone!" He came through the door, gasping.

"Who's gone?"

"The Americans."

"Was Nixon here?" Rouge asked.

Carpenter Chan nodded, trying to recover his breath.

"We saw the foreigners," Double Luck David said, "but the authorities took them away as fast as they came."

"Where is Pearl?" I asked.

Carpenter Chan shook his head. "I am afraid that she didn't come."

I tried not to let the disappointment get to me. I composed myself and asked again, "Do you mean Pearl didn't come to China, or do you mean she didn't come to Chin-kiang?"

"Take a look at this." Carpenter Chan produced a paper from his pocket. "It has Madame Mao's signature on it."

Miss Pearl Buck:
Your application for a visa was duly received. In light of the fact that for
a long time you have in your works taken an attitude of distortion, smear,

and vilification toward the people of New China and its leaders, I am
authorized to inform you that we cannot accept your request for a visit to
China.

In the past, families chose different couplets to decorate their door frames for the Chinese New Year. The most popular couplets focused on luck, health, and fortune. But this year, every family in Chin-kiang wanted the lines I tacked to my door.

The right side read: *Mountains stay erect forever.*
The left side read: *No worry for getting firewood.*
The horizontal top read: *As long as it takes.*

It was the town's silent protest. It expressed our feelings for our friend in exile.

The next morning an unexpected message came: The American guests had requested another tour of Pearl Buck's hometown. Carpenter Chan was instructed to order the people to tear down all the couplets as soon as possible.

But people were slow to act. By the time the Americans appeared, the families were still on their ladders trying to take down the couplets.

I forgot rules, warnings, and the possibility of imprisonment as I moved toward the center of the town.

The crowd followed me.

We didn't see Pearl. We saw a big-nosed foreign man surrounded by guards. He must be Nixon, we figured. Nixon was talking to people, perhaps asking what they were doing. People had stunned looks on their faces. With his big smile, Nixon asked the Chinese translator, a young woman, what the couplets said.

The translator looked frightened. She avoided explaining the meaning behind the couplets.

Nixon was confused and said that he had a lot to learn about Chinese culture.

Followed by the Chinese authorities, the police, and his American Secret Service agents, Nixon moved on.

We followed quietly at a distance. Rouge joined me. The crowd grew larger.

Nixon was led to his car. Before entering, he stopped as if he'd changed his mind. He turned to the translator and asked, "Do you by any chance know Pearl Buck?"

"No, I don't," the young woman replied quickly.

"Would you ask the crowd if anyone knew Pearl Buck?"

"I am sorry. I don't think so." The translator shook her head.

"Would you ask, for me?" Nixon pressed gently.

The translator grabbed the tail of her braided hair and sank her teeth into it. Her fear was obvious.

Nixon repeated the question.

The translator burst into tears. She stared into her notebook and forced out the words "It is beyond my duty."

"Pearl Buck is a personal friend of mine," Nixon said. "She grew up right here in Chin-kiang. She asked me to say hello to her friends. She wanted so much to come back . . ."

I could hear every word even from where I stood, a few yards away. My heart felt like it was bursting inside its chamber.

Receiving no response from the translator, Nixon turned to the crowd and asked, "Do any of you know Pearl Buck?"

A dead silence was the response.

The government's shadow hung like a thick black cloud over our heads.

"I am sorry," Nixon said, nodding. He stepped back and turned again toward his car.

"Wait a moment, Mr. President," Rouge called out. "My mother does."

"Your mother?" Nixon was delighted.

"Yes, my mother. She knew Pearl Buck, and she is right here." Rouge pushed me toward Nixon.

Nixon stepped between the Chinese guards and stopped in front of me before anyone could react. The guards looked confused. It was obvious they didn't know how to respond, how to stop him. Nixon's Secret Service agents stayed close to their president, so the Chinese agents couldn't get near him.

"So you know Pearl Buck?" Nixon asked.

"So does everyone here," I said in English. "Not only did we know Pearl, but we knew her father, Absalom, and her mother, Carie . . . Pearl and I grew up together." I stopped, trying desperately to press back my tears.

"How wonderful that you speak English!" Nixon's face lit up. "What is your name?"

"My mother's name is Willow Yee," Rouge spoke.

"Richard Nixon." The American president offered his hand. "Nice to meet you, Willow Yee."

The moment I touched his hand, my tears poured. The reality that I might never see Pearl again caught up with me.

"What is the meaning of the couplets?" Nixon asked. "And why are they being taken down?"

"*Mountains stay erect forever* means that our hearts continue to pray for Pearl's return," I answered. "*No worry for getting firewood* means that we don't worry because opportunities will come our way again. *As long as it takes* means we have faith in God."

"Good couplets!" Nixon nodded. "Now everything makes sense to me."

"Mr. President, why isn't Pearl with you?" voices in the crowd asked. "Why didn't she come?"

"Well, folks," Nixon said, smiling, "all I can tell you is that Pearl really wanted to come. Trust me, she did everything she could. Absolutely everything!"

"Please help make her visit happen, President Nixon," I pleaded. "For Pearl and for all of us."

"Please try, Mr. American President," the crowd echoed.

"I will," Nixon said, and we heard the sincerity in his voice.

Knowing exactly what might await me once Nixon was gone, I spoke my last words. "President Nixon, would you tell Pearl that her friend Willow misses her and the entire town of Chin-kiang misses her?"

"You have my word." Nixon bit his lower lip and made the promise.

The moment Nixon and his guards moved on, the government agents arrested me.

"Madame Mao has authorized me to take charge of this case," Vanguard said. "Your days are numbered!"

I was charged with four crimes. First, for insulting Madame Mao. Second, for exposing national secrets to Nixon. Third, for degrading China with couplets. Fourth, and the worst, for being a "planted agent" of Pearl Buck's.

I did not feel defeated. Instead, I luxuriated in the memory of my encounter with Nixon. I imagined him returning home and meeting with Pearl. I imagined him describing his experience. Pearl would be pleased. She would say, "Willow. Of course I know her. She was my best friend."

The prison was called Donkey's Crotch by the inmates. The area was desolate and rocky and covered with snow year-round. The inmates were forced to do hard labor before their execution. Because of my age, I was given a job making straw mats for the other prisoners. The mats were used to wrap the dead. Since they didn't have to make coffins, it saved wood. The mats were in short supply, so I was ordered to work long hours. I had to make ten a day or starve. It was impossible to complete the task, so I starved. The prison also limited the inmates' water usage. Each inmate was allowed a half cup a day for drinking. There was no water for washing.

I had no idea how Nixon found out about my imprisonment. Pearl must have insisted that he check on me. She knew how cruel Madame Mao could be and must have sensed that I might be in trouble. Pearl must have convinced Nixon not to trust any information provided by the Chinese government regarding my safety. Nixon's aides must have inquired about me. They must have eventually learned about my imprisonment from Rouge. Premier Chou En-lai must have gone to Mao with Nixon's request regarding my release. He must have received Mao's permission to let me go. If Madame Mao might have ignored Premier Chou En-lai's request, she wouldn't disobey Mao. What counted was that Mao needed Nixon to be on his side in order to keep Russia from starting a war with China.

After nine months in prison, I was free to go home.

CHAPTER 34

Cameras followed her as she moved like a famous actress. In her sixties, Madame Mao shined like a superstar. She was in a crisply pressed green army uniform with two mini red flags on both of her lapels. The matching green cap held in all her hair. Standing between her husband and Nixon, she smiled broadly. Her head turned left and right as she laughed and nodded. Viewers of this documentary film would get the impression that it was not Mao but Madame Mao who had invited Nixon to China. The climax of the film came when Madame Mao led the Americans to the grand national theater. There, she presented her propaganda ballet *The Women of the Red Detachment*. The crowd roared her name.

For the next four years, the people of Chin-kiang were forced to watch this film as part of the punishment called "mind reform." Chin-kiang was cut off from the outside world. I had no idea that history was about to change.

In January 1976, Premier Chou En-lai died. Rumor said that the man had spent his last days pleading for Mao to end the Cultural Revolution. He tried to convince Mao that to save the economy was to save the public's respect for the Communist Party. Chou En-lai suggested that his replacement be the former vice premier Deng Xiaoping, who had been in exile for years. Mao didn't listen. He insisted on carrying on the revolution. Nobody was aware that Mao himself was reaching the end of his life. Madame Mao, on the other hand, figured that her time had finally come, and she positioned herself to take power after her husband.

Like everyone else, I was forced to attend the self-criticism meetings. I was eighty-six years old. I followed the crowd and shouted slogans. Inside my mind, I continued to cherish my dreams. I did not desire longevity. It was just a way of life for me to indulge in my past. I had no idea that Pearl had quietly passed away in 1973, less than a year after her request for a visa to China had been rejected.

One morning in October, Bumpkin Emperor went about the town striking his gong and shouting, "Down with Madame Mao and her gang!"

We all thought that he had gone mad.

What was unusual was that Vanguard didn't come out to arrest Bumpkin Emperor.

"Madame Mao has been overthrown!" Bumpkin Emperor continued. "Deng Xiaoping has taken power!" Bumpkin Emperor tried to convince the people that he was not crazy, but nobody believed him.

A week later an official announcement came from Beijing. What Bumpkin Emperor had told us was true. Madame Mao and her gang had indeed been arrested and were in prison. All her victims, including the people of Chin-kiang, were liberated.

Vanguard was tossed aside as if he were Madame Mao's trash. My daughter, Rouge, was appointed by the new regime to replace him. Rouge was offered an instant membership in the Communist Party. The decision came from the top. It was the Communist Party's way to compensate our family for the loss of Dick. Rouge's only condition was that she be allowed to keep her Christian faith. Papa would have been proud of his granddaughter.

The excitement produced an unexpected tragedy. Carpenter Chan had a stroke after getting drunk during the celebration. He was laughing when it happened. The smile froze on his face. His grandchildren thought he was playing dead with them. They kept pinching his nose. By the time the doctor arrived, it was too late.

The first thing Rouge did as the town's new boss was hold Carpenter Chan's funeral. The ceremony took place in the same church he had built for Absalom half a century ago. In his will, Carpenter Chan named Bumpkin Emperor as the next pastor for the Chin-kiang Christian Church.

I sat behind the rows of benches and watched the wide-eyed children. Although their parents had been members of Papa's guerrilla church for years, this was the first time they had been able to worship openly as a Christian family. Also, it was the first time the church had officially opened its doors in decades. Curious people poured in just to look.

Over the years, we had lost Carie's piano. But Carie's songs had survived and been passed on through generations. The children were fascinated by the modern tape player. It played Christmas melodies Lilac had bought from a Hong Kong tourist. "Amazing Grace" remained the all-time favorite.

I closed my eyes as I followed along with the lyrics. I could feel the spirits of Carie, Absalom, and Pearl. I smiled when I remembered how the wood beams had sprouted and how Pearl and I had watched the butterflies coming in and out of the windows while Absalom preached.

Bumpkin Emperor was not a natural when it came to preaching. He tried hard to imitate Papa. "I can't find words to describe my happiness in serving the Lord," he said. "That I read from the Bible translated by the founding father of this church, Mr. Absalom Sydenstricker, is a great honor."

The new regime sought to open the doors to the outside world. Overnight, Chin-kiang became the focus of the media because of its connection to Pearl Buck.

In 1981, the government granted funds to restore the Pearl Buck Residence in Chin-kiang, although Pearl's family had lived in it for only a short time. The original bungalow, at the lower end of the town, where Pearl had grown up, was long gone. During the seventies, concrete Russian-style buildings had filled the landscape where it once stood. Though many opposed her, Rouge fought to honor Absalom and Carie as the original founders of the Chin-kiang middle school and the Chin-kiang hospital.

My life changed dramatically. I was protected by the government as "living history." I was respected and preserved as a "national treasure" and was given many privileges as if I were a baby panda. I moved to a senior home reserved for high-ranking party officials. Doctors were available for me around the clock. To further please me, the government ordered Pearl Buck's books directly from America. I was given a pair of new glasses plus a magnifier to help me with reading. I sobbed through *The Good Earth*, *The Exile*, and *Fighting Angel*. I felt Pearl's affection for China on every page. I imagined her frustration and loneliness when she cried, "My Chinese roots must die!" She had more money than she could spend, but she couldn't buy one ounce of Madame Mao's mercy.

"Mother," Rouge said, "my position in the party allows me to see that you get one last wish before your life ends. Name it, and I will see that it is done."

I already knew the answer. "I would like to visit Pearl Buck's grave in America."

Rouge smiled. "I thought you would say that."

Rouge had inherited her grandfather's sense of practicality. Although she was not moved by power, she was aware of what power could do. Rouge outlined a proposal regarding my wish to visit America. She made it sound like my visit would benefit the Communist Party.

I worried about rejection when I applied for the passport. Like everyone in China, I understood that when the government spoke about an open-door policy, it didn't mean that common people were allowed to travel abroad freely, especially to America. The shadow of persecution for having any contact with foreigners still weighed heavily on my mind.

However, Rouge was confident. She wrote letters to important people and made personal visits to the governor's office, the police bureau, and the passport agency. She didn't hesitate to play the role of the Communist Party boss that she was.

"Willow Yee's trip to America will build a bridge between China and America," Rouge insisted. "Chin-kiang strives to be a model town when carrying out Deng Xiaoping's new foreign policy. Willow Yee is a loyal citizen whose only motive is to serve her country. As the party leader, I suggest that we make use of her before she expires."

I went to Carie's grave and collected a bag of dirt before my departure for America. I packed the bag next to my medicines in my suitcase. Although I suffered only age-related stiffness, the doctors were worried. They didn't trust that I was fit to travel long distances.

I knew I would make the trip easily. I had been living my life to see Pearl one last time. Rouge was concerned that the American consulate wouldn't grant me a visa due to my age. She was right. The consul requested proof of health insurance. We didn't understand what "insurance" meant and had never heard of it. The consul suggested that we purchase a temporary policy for traveling in America. When Rouge received the estimated cost, she was stunned. "The cost of a three-month insurance policy is more than a Chinese person earns in ten years!"

Like Papa, Rouge felt no guilt about taking risks. She redoubled her efforts and pulled strings. She located Dick's former prisonmate, General Chu, who not only was the new head of the national congress but also knew the American consul general himself. My visa was instantly granted. While Rouge confirmed the last details of my trip, I walked the hills, with the help of my grandchildren, where Pearl and I had once played. My legs were shaky, but I was happy.

I didn't have to imagine Pearl's American home, because Rouge showed me the photos sent by the Sino-American Friendship Association. It was beautiful. The place was a complex of houses against green rolling hills and blue sky. I couldn't wait to see the interior. I imagined the rooms filled with tasteful furniture and decorated with Western art. Pearl would have a library, for she had always been a lover of books. I also imagined that she would have a garden. She had inherited Carie's passion for nature. The garden would be filled with plants whose names I wouldn't know, but it would be beautiful.

Where would she lie? I wondered. Growing up in Chin-kiang, she was familiar with the concept of feng shui. But would she apply the concept to her own resting place? After all, she had lived in America as long as she had in China. I wondered what her grave would look like. What would she surround herself with? Would she have a tombstone? Would there be carvings on the stone?

I intended to conduct a little ceremony after I arrived. I would light incense handmade by her friends in Chin-kiang. I would then spread the soil collected from her mother's grave on her grave. I wanted to see the spirits of Carie and Pearl reunited. It would make me happy if I could accomplish only that.

CHAPTER 35

In Washington, D.C., the Chinese consul, a handsome young man dressed in a Western suit, was upset with me. He had a television crew waiting to document my journey, but I insisted on going alone.

It took a few days for the consul to accept my terms. He bought me a train ticket to Philadelphia. He told me that he had also made a reservation for me at a local inn. I was excited and nervous. I could barely sit still after I got on the train. The landscape passing my window fascinated me. Springtime in America seemed to carry a more masculine yang element than southern China's feminine yin. America's mountains and trees were in contrast to Chin-kiang's rolling bamboo-covered hills and swaying willows. If I were to describe the landscape using a Chinese brush, I would paint America with big strokes and splashes of ink, and I would paint China with hair-thin lines in elaborate detail.

I kept thinking of the time Pearl told me about her first trip to America. She was shocked that not everyone had black hair. She was fascinated at the different-colored people. She had never considered that she was not Chinese until that moment.

I wondered what it had been like for her to return to America and to be with her own people. Except for her face and the color of her hair, she was a complete foreigner. Beneath her skin, she was Chinese. I wondered how she had changed from the Pearl I had known and what she had looked like after she had grown old.

The old lady sitting opposite me had a petite figure. She was fair-skinned with blonde hair. Had Pearl looked like her when she was

263

older? What did my friend have to change about her Chinese self to fit in to American society? It was possible for her to change her tone of voice, but what about her tastes and views that she had formed in China as a child, a teen, and an adult? Pearl once said that she felt enriched, like she owned more than one world. I liked that idea and envied her.

The moment I checked in to the inn, I received a phone call from the Chinese consul. He wanted to make sure that everything was going well. He suggested that I rest and visit the Pearl Buck House the next morning. I thanked him and said that I couldn't wait. He then suggested that I leave my luggage at the inn. Over the phone, the consul admitted that he was a fan of Pearl Buck, and that he believed that Pearl had honored the Chinese people. He felt terrible about Madame Mao using her influence to have Pearl's request for a Chinese visa rejected. "Madame Mao was a mad dog," he concluded.

The consul told me that he had learned from American books and newspapers that Pearl had been wearing a brightly colored, embroidered Chinese robe prior to her death.

"It was said that for weeks Pearl sat in a large chair facing east staring out her window," he said. "I wonder if what she was looking at is still there. I am curious about the final image she was seeing."

What had she been thinking? I wanted to know too. Would it be thoughts of her childhood? Would I be in them? To survive, I had been escaping into my past for decades. I often recalled the popcorn man, the way Pearl pushed and pulled the bellows while I rotated the cannon. It was easy to close my eyes and see a vivid image of the popcorn man putting his dirt-colored cotton bag over the cannon while Pearl and I covered our ears. The big bang was always real and loud to my ears. I could even imagine the smell of the delicious popped corn and see Pearl's smile as we stuffed handfuls into our mouths.

*　　*　　*

It was late afternoon when I first stepped inside the Pearl Buck House. I stopped just inside the door and examined the space. The room was exactly as I had imagined it. Friendly Caucasian women greeted me. They seemed to be accustomed to receiving non-English-speaking visitors. They suggested that I join the last house tour of the day. I was led to what was called the "Chinese view."

I held my breath, afraid that it would vanish.

I could no longer hear what the guide was saying. It sounded faraway. I was in shock. The view on the other side of the glass looked like Chin-kiang. I felt like I had stepped into one of my dreams.

There was a gemlike pond cradled by rolling hills. White clouds drifted across the blue sky. Oriental maple trees stood by the pond like giant brown mushrooms. Mandarin ducks waddled about. Baby ducks followed their mothers and played in the water.

Like Carie, who had created an American garden in the middle of Chin-kiang, Pearl had created a Chinese garden around her American home. I remembered Carie's struggle in growing American roses and dogwood. She helped the plants adapt to the southern Chinese climate and had to fight fungus and diseases. Carie's roses would produce buds but no flowers. She used soap water and vinegar to kill the bugs and she composted her own soil with wood chips. She held a garden show when her roses finally bloomed.

To what lengths did Pearl go to surround herself with the memories of China? Traces of her effort were everywhere. The rocks laid and plants arranged were according to classic Chinese paintings. I imagined Pearl explaining Chinese aesthetics to her gardeners. I smiled thinking that she might have ended up confusing them.

The tour moved to Pearl's greenhouse, which was filled with camellia trees. Although it was a large greenhouse, the camellias were crowded. It looked more like a garden nursery. The tour guide said that Pearl Buck was determined to see camellias blossom in the middle of Pennsylvania's winter. She insisted that it could be done because she had seen camellia trees blossom in the winters in China.

Indeed, camellias thrived during the winter season in southern China. Their blooming branches could be seen on country hills and city streets. Chinese families loved camellias in their living rooms as ornaments. Camellias were among the most popular subjects for Chinese artists.

"The gardener suggested replacing the dying camellias with American winter plants, but Pearl refused," the tour guide continued. "Pearl insisted on her Chinese camellias. They inspired her to write."

I learned that Pearl had tried to grow Chinese tea trees, lotus, and water lilies, but they had all failed to survive. Who would understand that this was Pearl's way of going back to her home in China?

Pearl's surviving camellias were mature trees now. There were eighteen of them in the greenhouse. They were cramped. They were only two feet apart when it should have been ten. The camellias had run out of space to grow. The view amused me, because I could tell that my friend had been truly desperate. Like a Chinese, she was so in love with camellias that she acquired every variety and color and filled the greenhouse with them. Judging by the size of their trunks, the trees were more than twenty years old. I imagined my friend watering them in the morning. I could see her running around trying to clear weeds, loosen the soil, and spread fertilizers. She loved to use her hands. Her fingernails would look like Chinese peasants', filled with earth.

The tour showed the visitors that Pearl Buck constantly remodeled her house. In order to create a Chinese-style kitchen, she tore down walls and rearranged studs and beams. She had a large wooden table made, with long benches on each side.

"The kitchen used to be four bedrooms," the guide said, pointing to where the walls used to be. "Pearl changed things around because she wanted a spacious kitchen." When she was a child, the kitchen was Pearl's playground. It was where she spent time listening to stories told by Wang Ah-ma and other servants. It was also where she played hide-and-seek with me.

I was impressed by the door design. It was carved with Chinese characters that said Precious Gem, which was the Chinese translation of Pearl's name. I didn't see American arts and crafts. I also didn't see pictures of Jesus Christ. Instead there was Chinese art and other objects throughout the house. Beautiful indigo carpets, Chinese glass bottles painted with cloud-patterned symbols of luck. Chinese brush-and-ink paintings and calligraphy hung on the walls. Under a single-stemmed lotus was a line from a classic Chinese poem: "*Rise out of dirt she remains pure and noble.*" The tour guide pointed at the roofed hallway that connected the main house to the cottage and said, "Pearl told her workmen that the Dowager Empress of China had a roofed walkway in the Summer Palace."

I wondered how Pearl felt when she received the set of Chinese nest boxes—a gift from President Nixon after he returned from China. Pearl must have been pleased and heartbroken at the same time. Did the gift give her hope? Did she still believe that she would one day return to the land of her dreams? Or did the gift make her think that there would never be another opportunity?

My eyes caught the shelf where Pearl's books lay. Among them was the Dickens novel Pearl had held under her arm when we first met. I would have pulled the book out and kissed its cover if there hadn't been a DO NOT TOUCH sign.

In the bedroom I saw Carie's sewing box laid on the table. I was so impacted by the sight of it that my entire being was thrown back in time.

"The soil is prepared and you don't plant!" I could hear Absalom yelling at Carie. He wanted her to help convert people when they came to thank her for healing their children with Western medicine. Absalom couldn't get anyone to listen to him because he was seen as a crazy man. He blamed Carie and Pearl for not making their best efforts. "Christians are not Christ!" he told them constantly. Sewing was Carie's way to escape Absalom. She sewed quietly while Absalom exploded.

Although Pearl defended her father in public, she told me that Absalom deserved his defeats. Pearl couldn't bear her mother's sadness, especially when she saw Carie's tears soaking the cloth she was sewing. "Absalom's flaw is too big for him to overcome," she said. "Mother and I are afraid of helping him."

CHAPTER 36

If it hadn't been for the heavy bag I was carrying, I wouldn't have believed that I was walking on American soil. It was early evening. The tour was over and the other visitors were gone. The air was brisk and the sky was turning dark. The trees and earth were blending into one gray color like shadows. It was clear that Pearl had bought this house and the land around it because the place had reminded her of Chin-kiang. For the rest of her life, this was the China she lived with.

How many times had she walked the path where I stood?

Darkness had almost settled in when I exited the house. I went on looking for Pearl's grave, but it was getting hard to see. I moved like a ghost following the barely visible path. The side road led me back to the inn where I was staying.

The innkeeper, a middle-aged lady, asked if I'd had a pleasant visit.

"I missed seeing Pearl's grave," I told her.

"You must have walked right by it," she said. "It's easy to miss."

"There wasn't a sign, or did I miss that too?" Since arriving in the United States, I had learned that Americans were good with signs.

"Well, it was the way Pearl Buck wanted it." The lady took out her keys and led me to my room. "Would you like me to book you a cab for tomorrow morning? What time is your train or flight?"

"I won't leave until I see Pearl's grave," I said.

The lady looked at me and I could see the questions in her eyes.

"I have some business at the grave," I tried to explain, hoping that my English would make sense to her.

"What kind of business?" She sounded cautious, a little suspicious.

I unzipped my backpack and took out the incense and the bag of dirt. I made a gesture of sprinkling dirt and put my palms together under my chin.

She didn't seem to understand but said, "Here, let me draw you a map."

I had been awake for a long time waiting for the dawn. At first light, I got up. I followed the inn lady's map carefully. After turning off the main road, I went down a small dirt path.

The sun outlined the mountains and trees and coated the leaves gold. The view was unfamiliar yet I felt I had been here before. I could hear the sound of my feet moving through the sandy dirt. After a while, I thought I heard the sound of running water. Was it my imagination, because Chin-kiang was known for its creeks? I didn't expect myself to be missing home, not yet. But no, I wasn't imagining the sound of water. Here it was, in front of me, under my feet, a running creek.

I decided to inspect the creek and then continue my search for the grave.

The sunlight played across the water's surface. I followed a path along the creek as it curled into the hills. On the far side of the creek were giant pine trees.

A view opened up. In front of me was a stand of bamboo—the same kind of golden bamboo we had in Chin-kiang.

Then I saw it, my friend's grave, hidden among the bamboo.

My strength fled me. I dropped to my knees.

There was no English. The grave had three Chinese characters carved in the stone. 賽珍珠, meaning Pearl Sydenstricker.

My eyes filled with tears of happiness, and this time I did not fight them. I understood Pearl's intent. Her roots in China hadn't died. China was the final thing on her mind. China was what she took with her to eternity. It was impossible for her to remove her love, for she, in her own words, "had known the fullness of such love, which was absolute in height and depth." A Westerner wouldn't understand the meaning of these Chinese characters, but Pearl didn't care. No wonder the innkeeper had said that the grave was easy to miss.

I felt as if Pearl were greeting me. I could hear her voice. "How was your journey?"

The three Chinese characters were Pearl's signature stamp, given to her by her Chinese tutor, Mr. Kung. Pearl once explained her name to me when we were young. The first letter was pronounced *Sy*, as in Sydenstricker. Out of many same-tone-sounding characters, Mr. Kung chose the one with a "mansion, which has a grand roof," and a "baby" playing underneath.

"My last name in Chinese means 'a darling doll in the mansion.' " Pearl was proud as she explained. "Do you like it?"

"I do," I remembered replying, although I couldn't read. I tried to hide this by examining the shape of the first character, 賽. "Look," I said. "This is not an ordinary mansion. It is the symbol of money."

"That's not money," my friend laughed. "That's the people shape."

"Four of them under the roof!"

"Four workers. My father said that we are all the Lord's workers."

"The baby is big-bellied," I cried.

"She loves food!" Pearl laughed.

The second Chinese character, 珍, was the picture of an oyster, but when combined with the third character, 珠, the meaning changed into *Pearl*.

My friend had chosen her final resting place beside the creek on purpose. The grave faced east, demonstrating that she had followed the rule of feng shui. The surrounding garden was walled in by pines and cypresses. Besides the bamboo, there were maples, evergreen bushes, and flowers. Wild lilies were scattered alongside the creek. There was a seemingly dead old tree that looked as if it had fallen across the creek. Its trunk was about two feet in diameter and it was rotten and hollow inside. What amazed me was that the tree had a lush green canopy. In the center of the rotten trunk, a young branch was healthy and robust. Pearl must have liked this tree. It fit a line from a Chinese poem, "*Spring shows its power in rotten wood and dying trees.*"

I touched the cold stone and rested my cheek against it.

* * *

Dear Pearl,

Since you couldn't go to China, I have brought China to you.

It is not the reunion I wished for for so long, but I feel blessed to have the opportunity. Because my memory is failing, and because I didn't want to forget a thing, I have written six notes to be burned with the incense at your grave.

The first note regards the end of Madame Mao. When she denied you a visa, she was sure of her power. She believed that she would rule China after her husband. But she didn't last. After Mao died, she was arrested and sentenced to death. It was less than four years after Nixon's visit.

The second note regards your mother's grave. It almost didn't survive during the Cultural Revolution. Mao's teenage mobs came to destroy the grave. Lilac removed the stone tablet and fooled them. In other words, what the Red Guard destroyed was not your mother's grave. Today the town of Chin-kiang has reclaimed Carie's status. She is officially titled the founder of the Chin-kiang middle school. Her spirit is celebrated and honored at each Spring Memorial.

The third note regards you. The mansion where your mother last lived has been turned into the Pearl Buck Residence. I can hear you say, "But that wasn't my house!" True, however, it is important that the residence in your name be presentable. You should understand that to a Chinese, the place that houses your spirit has to be a temple. Copies of your photos, letters, and books are on permanent display. I was not happy about the display of your calligraphy, because the strokes were not yours. Your writing was touched up by a professor from Beijing College of Art and Calligraphy. It was part of the act of transforming you into a goddess so that people could worship you. I didn't bother to fight, because I thought that it was better than calling you an American Cultural Imperialist.

The fourth note regards the people who knew you, who, as long as they lived, wondered how you did in America. I'd like to begin with Dick because he knew you well and had the worst luck. He was too close to Mao and died a horrible death. Please forgive me for being unable to report more about him. Dick knew that Hsu Chih-mo loved you. Dick wanted to congratulate you in person when he learned that you won the Nobel Prize. We were not allowed to send a telegram to America. Dick said that Hsu Chih-mo would have been so proud. He would have danced on his head. You will be pleased to know that today Hsu Chih-mo's poems are extremely popular. Young people worship him as a poet whose voice speaks to their own generation. Newspapers continue to print stories of his affairs as if they took place yesterday, and, of course, they continue to miss the real target.

Papa kept the church going until he died. He became a fighting angel like Absalom except he fought guerrilla style. I am sure you missed Carpenter Chan and Lilac. You knew that Carpenter Chan became a Christian, converted by Absalom, but you might not have known that he joined the Communists after Mao took power. Later he went back to God and worked for Papa. I don't think Americans are able to comprehend such a life, but you would. You lived in China and knew how things can be.

Lilac missed you so much that she could never stop talking about you. She is the town's longevity star and is in her nineties. Her three sons inherited their father's trade. It was a pity that you couldn't see how they rebuilt Absalom's church, which is called the Chin-kiang Christian Church. Lilac still fights with Vanguard, the beggar lady Soo-ching's son, whose name used to be Confucius. This was the mother and son you found in your garden so long ago. He betrayed everyone to please Madame Mao. Soo-ching wanted to disown her son, but Papa convinced her that she'd better forgive or she wouldn't go to heaven.

You don't know my daughter, Rouge, but she knows everything about you. She is currently the mayor of Chin-kiang and is in charge of the Pearl Buck Scholarship and the Hsu Chih-mo Scholarship. She gave birth to one girl and adopted two girls from her husband's previous marriage. All my granddaughters share the same middle name, Pearl. They are Pearl Delight, Pearl Bright, and Pearl Flight.

Remember Bumpkin Emperor, the warlord? He became an ardent Christian and the pastor of our church. You will be shocked. Who wouldn't be? Like your father, Bumpkin Emperor was obsessed with converting people. He tried to save them the way your father saved him. Bumpkin Emperor remembered you as the mean, straw-haired girl. He never got tired of telling people the story of how you fooled him with that bucket of ink. The People's Publishing House approached him with the idea of publishing a children's comic book based on the story.

My fifth note regards the dirt I brought here. It is from your mother's grave. I'll sprinkle it around. In the meantime, if I may, I will dig some soil here, a little, just enough to fill the bag. I'll carry it to your mother's grave as soon as I return and mix the soils. It pleases me to join your spirits.

The last note regards my own wish. If you don't mind, I'll collect some seeds from your trees here. I have no idea of the names of all the trees except that they are American trees. According to the shapes of the nuts, they are flowering trees. The importance of the trees is that they are from where you are buried. I wouldn't be surprised if you planted them yourself. I imagine you would have. You understood that spirits gather through nature. I hear your voice speaking through the creek, the pines, maples, bamboo, birds, and bees. I will plant the seeds where I will be buried when my time comes. We should then accompany each other forever. I have brought your favorite Tang dynasty poem, "The Tune of Posaman." "Yangtze River" ought to be changed to "Pacific Ocean," but I leave it the way it is. I know you always preferred the original.

> I live by the Yangtze River near its source,
> While you reside farthest down its course.
> You and I drink water out of the same stream,
> I haven't seen you though daily of you I dream.
>
> When will this river water cease to run?
> When shall I not love you, the way I do?
> I only wish our two hearts would beat as one,
> And you wouldn't disappoint me in my love for you.

Joy, gratitude, and sense of peace are what this moment means to me. I thank God for the fortune of having known you.

The creek is singing a happy song. The wind whispers like our old *conversations through trembling leaves. The air is pure and the sun warm. Once again, I see you running toward me with sunshine in your face. You look like a jumping cloud in your indigo floral Chinese dress, your golden hair bouncing.*

"Willow," I hear you call, "hurry up, the popcorn man is here!"

THE END

Author's Note

I was ordered to denounce Pearl Buck in China. The year was 1971. I was a teenager attending the Shanghai 51 Middle School. Trying to gain international support for rejecting Buck's China entry visa (to accompany President Nixon on his visit), Madame Mao organized a national campaign to criticize Buck as an "American cultural imperialist."

I followed the order and never questioned whether Madame Mao was being truthful. I was brainwashed at that time, although I do remember having difficulty composing the criticisms. I wished that I had been given a chance to read *The Good Earth*. We were told that the book was so "toxic" that it was dangerous to even translate it. I was told to copy lines from the newspapers: "Pearl Buck insulted Chinese peasants therefore China." "She hates us therefore is our enemy." I was proud to be able to defend my country and people.

Pearl Buck's name didn't cross my path again until I immigrated to America. It was 1996 and I was giving a reading at a Chicago bookstore for my memoir, *Red Azalea*. Afterward, a lady came to me and asked if I knew Pearl Buck. Before I could reply, she said—very emotionally and to my surprise—that Buck had taught her to love the Chinese people. She placed a paperback in my hands and said that it was a gift. It was *The Good Earth*.

I finished reading *The Good Earth* on the airplane from Chicago to Los Angeles. I broke down and sobbed. I couldn't stop myself because I remembered how I had denounced the author. I remembered how Madame Mao had convinced the entire nation to hate Pearl Buck. How wrong we had been! I had never encountered any author, including the most respected Chinese authors, who wrote about our peasants with such admiration, affection, and humanity.

It was at that very moment that *Pearl of China* was conceived.

In setting out to tell Pearl Buck's story I faced a number of challenges. I wanted to convey the full sweep of Pearl's life and also tell her story from a Chinese perspective. There are, of course, many sources in English about Pearl's life, but I wanted to see her as my fellow Chinese saw her. In order to do this, I proposed to tell Pearl's story through her relationships with her actual Chinese friends. As a novelist, I knew that the story of a single friendship, over many years, would be best. It is even my sense that such a friendship really existed. And yet, as far as I know, though Pearl had many Chinese friends, there was no one lifelong friend that made it into the historical record.

Using my license as a writer of fiction, I combined a number of Pearl's actual friends from different phases of her life to create the character of Willow. To respect the privacy of the living families of these individuals, and to protect their ongoing reputations in China, where my books are still banned, I withhold their names here. The other two major instances in which I have altered the historical record are the date at which Pearl Buck's father, Absalom Sydenstricker, dies (1931); and the date of the Nanking Incident, which occurred years earlier than it does in the novel. Both liberties were taken for the sake of the story.

I would also like to clarify that Pearl and Lossing Buck were married for eighteen years, from 1917 to 1935, and the reason for their divorce is not publicly known. Lossing Buck was a missionary agriculturalist who worked in China from 1915 to 1944, and produced the country's first land utilization study, which is still highly valued in China.

Anchee Min lived in China for twenty-seven years. Born in Shanghai in 1957, she grew up during Mao's Cultural Revolution (1964–1976). As a teenager, she was taught to denounce Pearl S. Buck as an American cultural imperialist. At the age of seventeen, Min was sent to a labour collective, where a talent scout for Madame Mao recruited her to work in propaganda films as an actress because of her proletarian look.

Min arrived in Chicago in 1984. She first learned English through American public radio, children's television programmes, and talk shows. To earn a living, she worked as a part-time maid, a waitress, a fabric painter and in construction and plumbing, while going to school at night. Her memoir, *Red Azalea*, was published in 1994 and was chosen as a *New York Times* Notable Book. Min is also the author of bestselling historical fiction, including *Becoming Madame Mao, Empress Orchid* (nominated for the British Book Awards Best Read of the Year 2006), and *The Last Empress*. Min's books have been translated into thirty-two languages.

The legacy of Pearl S. Buck continues at her charity, Pearl S. Buck International: www.pearlsbuck.org.